Doreen Rainey

Will to Love

ARABESQUE®

WILL TO LOVE

An Arabesque novel

ISBN-13: 978-0-373-83004-6
ISBN-10:   0-373-83004-1

www.kimanipress.com

Printed in U.S.A.

This book is dedicated to the faithful readers who
continue to give me their support!
Thank you!

Chapter 1

Here we go again.

The words rang silently in Dr. William Proctor's ears as he sat stoically across the dinner table, maintaining an unreadable expression on his face. He'd mastered the look many years ago for this very type of situation. He was able to call on it at a moment's notice, putting it in place in a matter of seconds. With only the tiniest of movements, his eyes narrowed ever so slightly. His jaw, though tightening inwardly, appeared outwardly relaxed. His lips, usually in a broad grin, barely curved upward—not quite a smile, but not a frown.

This evening had started out like many others over the past couple of months. A beautiful Wednesday night in May, he'd picked her up thirty minutes ago from her town house in northern Virginia. They talked about the ups and downs of their day while the smooth sounds of jazz played through the car speakers.

Seated at a small table near the window, they prepared for their meal at La Famille, a new French restaurant that received fabulous reviews in the *Washington Post* newspaper and the *Washingtonian* magazine. Ordering one of his favorite Merlots from the extensive wine list, Will settled into his seat, and nodded as his date talked about an upcoming movie she'd like to see.

"The critics have been raving about it."

"Sounds interesting."

"People are already throwing around the words *Oscar* and *blockbuster*. We should consider seeing it this weekend."

"Perhaps," Will said, not wanting to commit to any plans. It was Wednesday night, and while he did not have firm plans for Saturday yet, he was hesitant to commit.

"Maybe we should consider a few other things, as well."

Something in her tone told Will that their discussion was about to turn in a brand-new direction, and it didn't strike him as a place he wanted to go.

He didn't answer and felt the shift in the air. The mood for the evening had gone from congenial to guarded.

Squared shoulders. A slight forward lean. Hands clasped together in front of her. Her gestures suggested that whatever she was about to say, she'd been preparing for a while. But it wasn't until she took two full, deep breaths that the sirens started wailing in his head.

His reaction was immediate.

No! No! Don't do it. Please, don't do it!

As if she heard him, she hesitated a moment, taking a sip of water. The delay made it appear as if she was second-guessing her decision to say whatever she was thinking.

That's it. Think twice—no, think three times.

Her expression softened and confidence appeared restored as she placed her glass back on the table. Opening her mouth, she began her monologue.

I can't believe this is happening again.

Her initial sentences were like all the rest before her—using many of the same words, phrases, explanations and justifications.

No originality.

The inflection of her voice, strong and confident, in no way indicated that she had any qualms about moving forward with this discussion. Expertly presenting her case, she spoke as an attorney making a closing argument in a trial where her client's life was on the line. Big, brown eyes, enhanced by false eyelashes, focused intently on his. Clearly she was filled with a steadfast belief in all that she was saying, her posture reflecting certainty that she would be able to win him over to her way of thinking.

As she spoke, her voice remained even yet passionate, and Will gave her credit for the zeal with which she spoke. There was only one problem. The outcome of this was predetermined. The well-thought-out, exquisitely delivered presentation was doomed to fail the minute she uttered the first words. Anytime a woman chose to venture down this path—the path that she had chosen tonight—it always proved to be a mistake.

"I stopped dating other people a month ago," she

said affectionately. "I've come to realize I don't want to spend time with any other man. These last couple of months with you has made me fully aware of the spark between us. There's an attraction that pulls us closer and closer. I'm sure you'll agree that a strong connection has developed between you and me."

Spoken with such high expectations, it would be expected by many that her speech demanded that he reply in kind. Proper etiquette dictated that he should respond positively. One could argue that it was the polite thing to do. It was one of the unwritten rules that people adhered to all the time.

One person starts with, *"You're so special."*

The other reciprocates the same sentiment.

A person declares, *"I only want to be with you."*

The other quickly agrees they feel the same way.

A woman says, *"I love you."*

The man utters those same words from his mouth.

This was the protocol most people followed—regardless of whether their feelings were true. But Dr. William Proctor wasn't most people.

When it came to affairs of the heart, Will wasn't always polite. He rarely felt compelled to be politically correct and he wasn't always nice. He *never* felt obligated to reply to any declaration of affection. If his date hadn't figured that out yet, she was in for a rude awakening.

Alaina Vays entered Will's life four months ago at a fund-raiser for the United Negro College Fund. Seated at the same table, they'd flirted shamelessly with each other during dinner, and then spent that evening dancing until the band called it a night just after 2:00 a.m. Since that meeting, they'd continually gone out once or twice a week.

He was impressed with her intellect. Their conversations were varied and stimulating. A professor of economics at Georgetown University, she was well versed in world events, history and politics. The only rival to her brains was her beauty.

Six feet tall in flat shoes, she was a couple of inches shorter than Will. Her skin was the color of creamy beige, with hazel eyes, pronounced cheekbones and small lips. Able to kick back and relax, they enjoyed several leisurely dinners and discussed all sorts of topics that ran the gamut, including the greatest boxer of all time and who would likely be *America's Next Top Model.*

Alaina had become someone that he took pleasure in spending time with—but at thirty-four, she showed subtle signs that indicated where she wanted the relationship to go. She'd been dropping hints for the last month, but Will chose to ignore them.

First, there were the comments about her younger sister celebrating four years of marriage with the birth of their first child. The information came complete with a picture of the happy couple, a request to go to North Carolina with her to attend the baby shower and a suggestion that "they" get a gift from the registry for the new parents.

Two weeks ago, they were dining at a favorite Italian restaurant when Will had to endure Alaina's oohs and aahs at a couple with a set of twins. The little boy and his sister couldn't have been more than three months old. Alaina spent at least ten minutes at the young couple's table, talking to them about their new role as parents. Every now and then, she would turn to Will and smile, encouraging him to come over and take a look. Her smile faltered momentarily when she realized he had no interest in taking part.

If that wasn't a dead giveaway that Alaina was angling for marriage and a family, the comments she began to pepper their conversations with were:

"Our friends say we're the cutest couple, Will."

"My mom would love to have us over for Sunday dinner."

"I got an invitation to my good friend's wedding. Shall I put us down as a couple?"

When she began her conversations like that, Will was an active listener but never a responder. Why should he be? He gave her—as with every other woman he'd ever dated—no reason to believe that any of those things were of interest to him. Marriage? Commitment? Family? None of that had ever been a high priority for him. Will carefully and clearly outlined where he stood on the subject within the first five minutes of the first date. He called it "The Speech."

The ten-minute lecture—almost a sermon—had been perfected over the years. He'd begun crafting it in medical school, and though it had gone through several versions, the core of the message had always remained the same.

Easy to follow, he outlined five rules for dating him. Each one emphatically declared what a woman could expect, and not expect, from him. Reducing the language to the simplest terms, he often wondered how women could suddenly forget about them after they'd been seeing each other for any period of time.

Rule number one: A woman could expect companionship, good conversation and someone to enjoy great restaurants and the wonderful cultural events that were available in the Washington, D.C. area—and even around the world. But she was never to assume that they would date exclusively.

Rule number two: He cherished his freedom and respected the woman's freedom. There was rarely a need to know each other's every move and whereabouts. Daily conversations were never necessary and check-in calls were completely out of the question.

Rule number three: His medical practice was his top priority, and in that area he would never compromise. His three partners, Drs. Derrick Carrington, Sherisse Copeland and Jeff Cain, depended on him to continually improve patient care and the bottom line. No one came before that.

Rule number four: Commitment was not an option. If the woman wanted anything beyond dating, she was spending her time with the wrong person. Will wasn't the "marrying" kind, the "cohabitation" kind and rarely the "spending the night" kind.

Finally, there was rule number five: He usually repeated this one at least three times, making sure that there was no room for misunderstanding. If a woman broke rules one through four, termination of that relationship was not only necessary—but immediate.

This speech had garnered him varied reactions over the years. Some women kept their responses neutral, while others insisted on telling him exactly what they thought of his list. He'd seen all kinds of reactions. Appalled. Insulted. Disgusted. Amused. Angry. Some women simply stared at him, unable to respond at all. Others gathered their belongings and left on the spot. There were those who laughed, thinking it had to be some kind of sick, stupid joke. What kind of man could actually say those words with a straight face? When they realized there was no punch line, they bolted.

There were some who took a different approach to his rules. He'd been congratulated and admired for his honesty, and over the years women had shrugged off his rules, appearing not to be bothered. But those women had an ulterior motive. They secretly saw him as a challenge.

Time and time again, these women made it their mission to be the one person to change him. Each woman believed they would be the one to make him rip up those rules and toss them out the window. Their approaches varied, but they all had the same objective.

Some gave him too much room, hoping that he would miss them terribly and want an exclusive relationship. Others took him up on his offer to see other people, with the idea that if he saw them with someone else, he would become jealous and realize that he only wanted to be with them. Still others tried to smother him with attention, to create a level of comfort that would make him always want them around.

But persistence soon gave way to frustration. When it came to the rules, Will remained inflexible. Most women eventually faded away from his life. Then there were women like Alaina Vays—his date for this evening.

Educated. Professional. Accomplished. Established. Independent. On their initial date, she played down his speech, having no problem with his rules. As a matter of fact, she found his rules to be refreshing. Focused on a research study and writing a book on the impact of globalization on the U.S. economy, Alaina thought it the perfect arrangement. It would allow the two of them to enjoy their relationship without the constant pressure of getting bogged down in dealing with where the relationship was headed. Evidently, somewhere along the line, her "relief" at having the rules had deserted her, for here she sat, trying to change the rules and change him.

"I remember our conversation on our first date. We hadn't ordered drinks and you launched into your speech about dating and rules and understanding what type of man you were."

Her words were filled with empathy as she continued, "Those words are easy to speak when you haven't had a chance to get to know the other person. Before you spend time with that person and realize that there could be a future."

Will watched her eyes brim with expectation and anticipation. Unfortunately, no matter how full of affection and sincerity her words were, they wouldn't do much to help her cause. The good laughs they shared. The heated debates that had them on opposite sides. Orchestra seats at the latest plays and concerts. All of that would come to a screeching halt if she dared to break the rules. It was a decision he'd settled in his soul long ago—the rules were nonnegotiable. Always had been. Always would be.

When the wine arrived, Alaina stopped talking. She'd been rambling on for at least five minutes and Will had yet to interject one word.

Silence ensued as Will approved the selection and watched the waiter uncork the bottle. After a visual inspection and a quick sip, Will nodded again and the glasses were filled.

When the waiter departed, Will's relaxed body and placid expression gave no outward acknowledgment of anything she had said. Sure that she expected him to speak, he opted to remain quiet. She hadn't asked him a direct question and he felt no obligation to contribute to this conversation.

Watching her movements, she shifted in her seat and placed her hands in her lap. The first sign of discomfort. Not breaking eye contact with her, he took another sip of his wine. If she was waiting for a response, she was in for a long stretch of silence. There was nothing to say. The rules spoke for themselves.

Alaina readjusted her position and offered a small, shy smile. Reaching across the table to cover his hand with hers, she gently stroked his palm. When he didn't pull away, she took it as a sign of encouragement. "I know it's been hard for you to commit in the past."

It hasn't been hard at all.

"I'd bet money that it's because you haven't found someone that understands you like I do."

You'd lose the shirt off your back with that bet.

Offering a wider and more seductive smile, she scooted her chair closer to him and leaned forward, allowing a better view of the black satin-and-lace fitted camisole she wore. Accentuating her ample cleavage, she succeeded in being enticing. Had this been any other evening, Will would have allowed himself to indulge in what she was offering. Her well-toned body garnered admiration from other men each time they were together, but not this night.

Will didn't find it the least bit difficult to keep his focus off her body and on the conversation. The direction she'd decided to take this evening changed everything. He didn't have the luxury of getting distracted—no matter how tempting the offer.

"We enjoy the same things, we come from similar backgrounds, we're a match professionally in that we are both driven and have a desire to succeed. Each time we're together, I sense the power of our feelings for each other growing deeper."

You have no idea what I'm feeling for you—and deep ain't it.

"When we first started seeing each other, we talked about your expectations," she said, remembering the conversation where Will outlined what he was willing to give, and not give, to the relationship.

Yet you didn't take heed.

"You weren't looking for anything serious…commitment and marriage weren't in your future…companionship and living for the moment was all you could offer me."

Yep, that about sums it up.

She paused as if she expected him to jump in. When nothing was forthcomimg, she forged ahead. "But I understand that that speech served as a temporary barrier that we all tend to set up when we start out in a new relationship. It protects us from the unknown."

Wrong again.

"To be completely honest with you, I couldn't have agreed with you more when you so eloquently laid out your list of dating rules," she said, recalling that she, too, was in agreement. "I've had so many dead-end relationships, I could barely keep track."

Here comes the sob story.

"Men who couldn't handle my success," she said, her eyes growing sad at the memories of relationships over the years. "Men who couldn't deal with my beauty. Men who thought I would allow them to treat me any kind of way. Men who didn't see the value in nurturing a relationship.

"I've been hurt so much in the past, it was hard to believe that I could find someone. Then you came along, and you showed me that there were men out there who knew how to treat a lady."

Will maintained his silence. If she was waiting for a sign of encouragement, she wasn't going to get it.

Alaina paused and waited for something—anything that would let her know that she was on track with what was happening between them. Convinced that it wasn't a one-way street, she wanted confirmation from him. However, it became evident that Will had no intention of speaking until she had said all that she wanted to say.

Hesitating for only a moment, she filled the empty space. "Now that we've gotten to know each other… gotten to spend time with each other, all that has changed for me…as I'm sure it has for you."

Now for the big finish.

"So, how about it?" she said, relieved that she had come to the final part of her speech. Everything she'd talked about thus far was leading up to this moment. For the past couple of days, she'd rehearsed this scene in her mind over and over again. She'd hoped to have gotten a better indication of what he was thinking, but he stayed neutral with his body language.

She continued in spite of the ambiguity on his part. "How about giving 'us' a serious try? We could be the ones that we have been searching for our whole lives."

Chapter 2

Exactly one hour later, Will stepped into his tenth-floor loft in northwest D.C., locking the door behind him. With the shades pulled up along the large windows that spanned the two far walls, he kept the lights off and let the moon and the city lights guide him. A few seconds later, he heard the pattering of big feet as Apollo, his German shepherd, came barreling from the back of the house to land at his heels.

"Hey, buddy," he said, giving him a quick pat on the head. "I know I'm back early. Give me a minute to change my clothes and we'll go for a walk."

The thumping of the dog's tail on the hardwood floor indicated his approval of the plan.

As he walked through the main living area, he admired the open design that allowed him to entertain large groups of friends. The space flowed into the formal dining area, where the dark mahogany table had seating for ten. The kitchen, with its stainless-steel appliances and professional-chef's cookware, had become his favorite place. When he graduated from medical school, he promised himself he would learn to cook so he wouldn't have to endure cafeteria food and takeout during his residency.

Will trotted up the spiral steps to the second level. A small second bedroom was off to the left, but the remainder of the floor, almost as large as the first level, was the master suite. Flipping the light switch, he sat on the edge of his king-size bed untying his shoelaces. Instead of enjoying six courses of finely prepared cuisine and taking in a play at the Warner Theatre, his stomach was growling and he called his partner Jeff and offered him the tickets.

"I guess when I take you out, I need to grab me something to eat," he said to Apollo, who'd followed him up the stairs and sat at his feet.

Apollo barked once before lying down and resting his head on his paws.

Not quite eight o'clock, Will was home much sooner that he'd planned. Alaina left him no choice. All that talk about getting to know each other better, about growing feelings and committing to one another, phrases like "going to the next level" and "looking at our future" were grounds for ending the relationship. When she finished, he did what he had to do. Invoke rule five—immediately.

A lesson Will learned early in his dating life was that many of the women thought they could change him.

Choosing to play by his rules had only been a cover. They believed that somehow, someway, when it was all said and done, his rules would not apply to them.

Their plan was quite simple. Once he got a taste of their smile, their compassion, their niceness, their friendship, their body—it would be nearly impossible for him to maintain his distance. No way could he continue to see other people. No way could he go days without seeing them or talking with them. No way would he want them to date others. Each woman thought that she would be "the one." The one woman who would break through the emotional wall around his heart.

What these women failed to understand was that he wasn't a wounded soul in need of the love of a woman. There was nothing blocking his heart. No stack of bricks. No concrete cinder blocks. No unscalable wall. There wasn't an old girlfriend who treated him like dirt. Why woman found that so hard to believe he would never know.

The simple truth was that Will wasn't interested in all the relationship traps that so many people get caught in. When two people meet and feel attraction, passion, fun and pleasure, why would they choose to move beyond that? Once you move into the realm of commitment, love and marriage, it pushes all of the things you love about the relationship out of the way and replaces it with mortgages, meddling in-laws, boredom and drudgery. He preferred to always stay in the initial stage of the relationship—which was the place he was enjoying with Alaina. Until tonight.

When the waiter finally arrived to take their order,

Alaina stopped talking. Will's expression softened, as he gave her a genuine, caring smile. Taking that as a sign of agreement, Alaina's shoulders relaxed and she ordered her food before Will could get a word out. He asked the waiter to give him a few more minutes, and then broke the news to her.

He explained to Alaina that while he had grown to care about her, that did not change his position. He stated that what he'd said at the beginning of their relationship remained true. Commitment. Connection. Exclusive dating. Those were elements of a relationship he was not willing to explore—not just with her, but with anybody.

At least this time there were no tears, no yelling and no throwing of sharp objects. Will recalled several times when the breakup didn't go so well. Women who were mature, professional, controlled, rational people suddenly became irate, emotional, uncontrollable and loud. It was the most amazing transformation.

One minute he was enjoying dinner, a movie or an art exhibit, and the next minute all hell was breaking loose. Women who would normally never act out in a way that would create an embarrassing scene became wild— crazy. Vivid memories of Tasha Scott came to mind.

Will and Tasha dated for almost three months when she unexpectedly announced that she was going to put her house in western Virginia on the market to move closer to him. A veterinarian with a thriving practice, Will didn't want her to uproot her life for him. Because she was moving close to D.C. didn't mean that would change their relationship.

He'd explained that being closer physically wouldn't

equal being closer emotionally. As a matter of fact, nothing would change in the way their relationship was going. Of course, he said, she was free to make her own choices in life. But if she was making this choice with him in mind, she would be well advised to reconsider.

Fifteen minutes later, she'd destroyed almost every dish in his house, throwing them across the room, smashing them on the floor and tossing a few that were aimed at his head. In the midst of broken dishes, yelling and the tears, Will didn't respond, which had frustrated Tasha even more. In the end, she'd cursed him and slammed the door on the way out.

After Tasha, there was Victoria.

They'd been seeing each other off and on for four months. An auditor with the federal government, she had an extremely professional demeanor and never appeared to lose her cool, get frustrated or get angry. But her positive characteristics were nowhere to be found on their last date.

Victoria Jackson had caused quite a scene when she'd forced his hand during the intermission of a play at the Lincoln Theatre.

Giving him a full kiss on the lips, she'd said, "Don't you care for me as much as I care for you?"

"I do care, Victoria," he replied. And it wasn't a lie. He was sure his caring wasn't in the way she hoped, but it was the most she was going to get.

Locking her arms with his, she asked, "Don't you want to build a life together?"

"I think we should focus on having a nice time this evening."

Not quite the emotional response she was looking

for, she'd playfully stomped her foot. "Haven't you grown to love me as much as I love you?"

Reminding her that the second act was about to start and they should probably return to their seats didn't alleviate the demands she was making of him. Finally, Will stopped responding to her comments. The quieter he got, the more she asked questions, demanding to know how he felt about her. He stood by and waited until she was ready to go back into the theater.

The response she'd hoped for was not forthcoming, and the sweet tone in which she'd teasingly asked him questions took on an edge. Soon her questions were in a voice laced with anger. He tried to avoid telling her that his feelings for her did not match her feelings for him until the end of the evening, but she insisted on knowing right away.

Finally, he calmly and quietly reminded her of the rules and her agreeing to them. If she wanted to discuss the status of their relationship, he suggested they do it at the end of the evening. None of what he said went over well with her.

The ensuing scene that played out in the middle of the lobby was, without doubt, better entertainment for the other patrons than the play they'd paid money to see. Yelling and screaming that he was heartless and cold, Victoria had to be escorted out of the theater by two very big gentlemen. Neither saw the second act. Yet no breakup could top the one with Gretchen.

Gretchen Potts had attended the same medical conference as Will almost five years ago in sunny Destin, Florida. Sitting in on lectures and sessions highlighting the latest discoveries about the human body by day, the two of them made their own discoveries about each other's bodies at night. Of course, Will made his position clear about relationships the first night they met for drinks. Waving off his rules with little concern, Gretchen happily agreed to them.

Gretchen, who lived in Baltimore, thought it was the perfect arrangement. With a busy practice, she viewed Will as someone to get together with for some much-needed rest and relaxation. Initially, it was the ideal match. Splitting their time between Baltimore and Washington, D.C., there was never a lack of things to do whenever they got together. Two months after they met, Gretchen's carefree attitude about their relationship began to change.

It started with greater demands on his free time. Why couldn't he come to Baltimore more often? Why didn't he invite her down to D.C. more than once a week? Next came the accounting-for-time issue. Where was he? Who was he with? What was he doing? Finally, there was the "Can I leave my stuff at your place?" question.

Their conversations had suddenly become filled with hints that she'd focused on her career so much that she was now starting to think of children and family. The last time they had dinner at his place, she'd finally pushed him over the edge.

"Did I tell you my brother was going to pop the question tonight?"

Will didn't look up from the paper he was reading. "No."

"They are such a cute couple. They've been dating for about six months, but my brother knew it was love at first sight. After two months of seeing each other almost every night, they were practically living together."

Turning the page of the paper, Will didn't look up. "That's nice."

"They plan on starting a family right away. I didn't think the idea of a baby would appeal to me, but the more I hear them talk about it, the more excited I get at the thought of becoming a mommy."

"Hhhmmm," he said, closing the paper and setting it aside.

"Maybe we could make it a double wedding?"

With those words, Will enforced rule number five. On the surface, it appeared to be a congenial breakup. Gretchen said she understood and agreed that it was best they stop seeing each other and go their separate ways. It had become painfully obvious that they were headed in two different directions. She wished him well and headed straight back to Baltimore. But Will later realized that it was just the calm before the storm.

She'd taken a lesson from Samantha on *Sex and the City,* as Will found out when he walked into his parking garage a week later and saw the bright pink flyers on everyone's car, including his. Snatching the paper off the windshield, he mumbled under his breath. About to ball it up for the trash, he stopped when he caught a glimpse of the photo the flyer contained. It was a picture of him!

Walking up and down the aisles, he didn't miss one parked car, pulling off the flyers. A few times, he set off alarms but kept on going. Judging by the number of empty spaces and the fact that it was almost ten o'clock in the morning, he could only assume that those people that have already left for the day had their own copy.

When he arrived at the office, he was determined to put this incident behind him. Until Barbara, the office manager, came into his office with a stack of the same flyers. She'd pulled them off the cars in the medical building parking lot.

He thanked Barbara and tossed them in the trash. Before she left, she offered him some unsolicited advice. "None of this would have happened if you found a nice woman and settled down."

Not wanting to be rude to someone who was old enough to be his mother, he nodded and thanked her again before shutting the door to his office to calm down. He glanced down at the trash can; his face stared back at him with the caption: First Rule of Dating? Never Date This Jerk.

For a split second he almost let his emotions get the best of him, picking up the phone to call her. But a cooler head prevailed and he replaced the receiver and pushed back in his chair. Calling her would be the exact reaction she was looking for. What would he say? What difference would it make? Nothing would change between them. If he talked to her, he would only be adding fuel to her fire.

Turning in his chair, he looked out the window. He had one of the few offices that faced a small park instead of a noisy street or another building. It took almost a half hour for his anger to subside. Gretchen knew the rules from day one and she chose to continue to date him. If this is how she wanted to handle the breakup then so be it. He would not dignify her behavior with a response.

It took him months to live that one down. His friends made jokes at his expense for days and there were snickers from other tenants in his building. Still, he stayed strong in his position. Neither Tasha, Victoria nor Gretchen could keep Will from sticking with his course of action when it came to women.

Out of all his breakups, Alaina's ranked up there with the most amicable. Gathering herself, she'd quickly said good-night, reaching in her purse and placing a large bill on the table to cover her dinner that she had ordered but that had not yet arrived. Will told her that wasn't necessary and offered to pay and take her home. As if his offer was absurd, a glare of annoyance crossed her face. Within minutes, she had hopped into a taxi and rode right out of his life.

"Why do women do this?" he mumbled to Apollo, who didn't bother to raise his head. Loosening his tie, he walked into the large dressing area and pulled it from around his neck, placing it on the tie rack with the other hundred or so. He unbuttoned his shirt and strode purposefully back into the bedroom.

"They say they can live with the rules. They say they aren't looking for anything serious. They say they want to focus on their careers. They say that having children is the last thing on their minds. But do they mean it? Nooooo. If anyone should be upset at how these relationships turn out, it should be me."

This time Apollo raised his head, as if to offer some support.

"They want a man who's up front. A man that is a hundred percent honest. Someone who will let them know where they stand at all times. Someone who wouldn't use them and lead them on just to get what he wants. That's what they get with me. Yet they try to make me out to be the bad guy."

Realizing he was venting to a dog, he went back to the closet to finish changing his clothes.

One day he's wining and dining a woman, laughing and enjoying her company. The next, the woman instigates a serious conversation to discuss where they are headed. The pattern had repeated itself in relationship after relationship.

First, they begin to talk about how much their feelings have grown. Next, they tell him that what he said in his rules, he didn't really mean it. Finally they suggest that they both toss the rules aside and focus on building a long-term commitment. When he reminds them that he's not looking for a serious relationship, or interested in tossing his rules away, they seem shocked, floored, appalled and stunned.

Undressing, he hung his jacket and pants in the closet, tossed his shirt in the hamper and put on a pair of sweats, a T-shirt and his running shoes. As Will picked up the leash from the nightstand, Apollo jumped up and headed down the stairs, tail wagging.

Almost at the front door, his phone rang and Will glanced at the caller ID. Alaina. His experience taught him there were only three choices for what this conversation would be. She would either backtrack and say that she wanted to continue seeing him, knowing that it wouldn't lead to marriage, or her anger would have gotten the best of her and she would curse him out for treating her the way he had. Or, she would pick up right where she'd left off at the restaurant, trying to convince him to commit to her and move forward with a relationship.

Regardless of which route Alaina planned to take, they all led to the same place—a dead end. One of the lessons he'd learned years ago? When it was over, it was over. He couldn't recall one time when he'd gone out with a woman after a breakup.

Hooking the leash on to Apollo's collar, he opened the front door, letting the call go to voice mail.

Alaina Vays had made the fatal mistake. She'd tried to change him. However, Dr. William Proctor could not be changed. Not by her. Not by any woman.

Chapter 3

Caryn Stewart collapsed on her bed, fully clothed. After twelve hours from hotel room to front door, complete exhaustion threatened to overtake her body. The flight from Europe on the private Gulfstream jet, the limousine ride from the airport and the chauffer that carried her bags to her front door did nothing to alleviate her traveling woes. The clock on her nightstand read 7:00 p.m., but it felt more like midnight.

Flying in the lap of luxury didn't prevent her body from craving rest. Working out of the country for most of the last four weeks, she had been in so many time zones, she'd worn three watches at one point to keep it all straight.

Six days in Bangkok. Four days in Mexico. Three days in Toronto and this past week in Madrid. The hectic pace threatened to break her down, but she held it together and persevered. All of her deals closed and she, and her firm, made a handsome profit in the process.

She'd picked up small mementos for her family and friends, usually something from the airport or hotel gift shop that represented a little bit of the country she was working in. They admired her for traveling to places that most of them would never see. Contrary to what her family believed, the last thing Caryn did when she traveled for work was find time to make it a vacation.

Daily excursions, sightseeing tours, soaking up the culture or enjoying some of the finer restaurants were never part of her days. Instead, she shuttled between airports, hotels and conference rooms. For eight, ten, sometimes twelve hours a day, she crunched numbers, ate quick meals and sacrificed sleep to complete the deal.

Brokering mergers and acquisitions between companies that were sometimes as far away as Tokyo, Caryn was in and out of town frequently. With voice mail, e-mail and fax machines, it would seem that most of this could be done that way. But with billions— sometimes more—on the line, only so much could be done electronically. When it was time to close the deal a face-to-face meeting was the only way.

At least she could take comfort in the fact that she wouldn't be hitting the road again for another four weeks.

Feeling sleep starting to take over her body, she forced herself to get off the bed. She needed to take a shower, grab a bite to eat and then get into her own bed. It was one of the things she missed when she was away from home. Nothing compared to sleeping in her own bed. She'd tried everything on the road to make her nights more restful. Down comforters, piles of pillows, soft music and a soothing eye mask. Still, she rarely got a good night's sleep away from home. Tonight, she planned to sleep like a well-fed baby.

Stripping off her clothes, she moved into the large dressing area and dumped her slacks and blouse in a large white bag for the dry cleaners and threw her other items in the hamper. To make life easier, she only washed undergarments, towels and sheets. Everything else was sent out.

Slipping on the silk kimono she brought home from Korea, Caryn walked into the bathroom and admired the impressive space. Marble countertops, travertine tile floors, custom light fixtures and a handmade mosaic sink. Paying extra for the glassed-in shower with multiple showerheads had been worth it; the spray pounding against her body always gave the tensed-up muscles in her neck and back a relaxing massage.

Her mouth curved into an unconscious smile when she recalled the heated argument she'd had with the builder over placing a window above the tub. The large window framed a magnificent view of the courtyard, and in the summer, the colorful flowers that bloomed were postcard perfect. Then, there was the tub, with its sunken, oversize dimensions and Jacuzzi jets with four different settings. Caryn had visions of spending hours in it with wine, candles and a good book. That dream had remained unfulfilled.

The Boston condo had been her pride and joy when she purchased it almost two years ago. A two-bedroom unit with an office and an amazing view of the harbor. Caryn could still conjure up the feeling of giddiness she experienced the day she closed on the sale. It had been a challenge to oversee the build out with all of her custom features because of her business travels. But with e-mail, digital photos and lots of phone calls at all hours of the day and night, it all came together.

Brimming with big plans for her new home, she stocked up on design magazines and contacted several interior designers to assist with custom window treatments, furnishings that would accent the space and reflect her style, and artwork that would pull it all together. But none of those things had yet to happen. Two days after moving in, she was off to Amsterdam. It seemed as if she hadn't been home for any length of time since.

The designer she selected offered to pick out fabrics, some furniture pieces and accents based on her understanding of what Caryn wanted. By doing so, Caryn's work wouldn't interfere with the time line she'd set to complete the project. After thinking about it for several days, she decided against it. She didn't want to miss out on the process and was determined to find a way to be hands-on.

As she looked around her bathroom, the bare counters taunted her, reminding her of the results of the choice she'd made by putting her career above everything else. Shaking off the uneasy feeling, she smiled when she saw the aromatherapy candles she bought about six months ago while in Italy. Turning away from her original plan, she ditched the shower and for the first time, Caryn decided to relax in her tub.

Getting the water temperature just right, she searched under her sink for oils or bubble bath. Finding some oils she'd gotten in Morocco, she added them to the water and lit her candles. Her kitchen wasn't even close to being stocked, but she did have wine. Retrieving the bottle, a glass and the corkscrew, she started to get into the spirit of a relaxing evening.

Just as she was about to slip into the water, she heard the ring of her cell phone. The BlackBerry was her double-edged sword. She couldn't live without it—but at times wanted to toss it in the water. Walking back into the bedroom, she checked the number. For a split second, she thought of the perfect water temperature in the tub and toyed with the idea of not answering it. But a smarter head prevailed and she pushed the Talk button.

"Hi, Jeremy."

"Caryn—glad I caught you. Didn't know if you'd still be in the air."

"I just got back. I was about to—"

"Do you have the updated proposal for the Canterfield deal?"

Jeremy Bishop was almost sixty years old and still worked around the clock. President of the firm, he was on top of every deal the investment bank had made, was making or would make. His work ethic challenged the most dedicated employees and he expected nothing less from those that reported to him.

Having joined the company almost thirty years ago, he'd made enough money to quit three times over, but the thought never crossed his mind. Still willing to get in the trenches, he'd been a great mentor to Caryn. She could count on him to be there when she needed him. She often wondered how he ever found the time to get married, have children and play with his grandchildren. Balancing family and career was the one thing he hadn't taught her to do.

Caryn walked into her office and booted up her laptop, and inserted her wireless headset. She'd worked on the proposal on the flight home and planned to shoot it off to him tomorrow. Obviously, tomorrow was too late. "I'll e-mail it to you in five."

"Great," he said. "I'll look it over tonight and give you a call first thing in the morning."

Had he forgotten? She'd brought it up to him several times over the past couple of months just so they could avoid a situation like this. "Jeremy, tomorrow is—"

"Also, did you review the merger documents on Endo and Pershing? I have a feeling there might be some last-minute maneuvering. Let's plan to finalize that tomorrow, as well."

"Jeremy?"

"Yes," he said, finally allowing her a word in.

Caryn let a few seconds of silence elapse. This was her chance to remind him that she was officially on vacation. That tomorrow morning, she was supposed to be catching a flight that would take her away from all things related to work.

This was the perfect opportunity to remind him that she would be unavailable, unreachable and unresponsive to e-mail and voice mail. This was the perfect time to remind him that starting tomorrow, he would have to handle things without her.

Instead, she said, "Talk to you in the a.m."

"Great," he said. "I know I can count on you. We've got some things happening with this organization and I see you being a major part of that."

After hanging up, she searched for the file, mumbling under her breath. She'd worked with Jeremy ever since she joined the firm, so she'd had plenty of time to adjust to his ways. Cutting people off. Barking orders. Making demands. Over time, she'd gotten used to it, but every now and then she wanted to cuss him out. This was one of those times.

Did he forget the road trip she'd been on? Did he forget that she would be bone tired from the flight home? Did he forget that she was off the clock?

Opening her e-mail, she sent the document and noticed fourteen new messages. She'd checked her BlackBerry less than two hours ago and cleared out her inbox. Now she'd have to take some time to go through these. Forgetting about her bath, she sat down in the chair and started typing.

An hour later, Caryn stood and stretched her arms. Shutting down the computer, she picked up her phone and went back to the bedroom. Standing over the tub, she dipped her hand in the water. Cold. Opening the drain, she watched half the water run out before adding hot water. She may have gotten sidetracked, but she was determined to finish what she'd started.

Once again, with the temperature just right, Caryn clipped up her hair, turned on some R&B music and eased her travel-weary body into the steaming water.

The jets had the water pulsating against her and she leaned back, resting her head on the pillow she'd ordered from one of those shopping magazines she always browsed through when she flew. Taking a few deep breaths, she took a couple of sips of wine and tried to clear her mind of all things related to work.

As executive vice president for mergers and acquisitions for Carlton Barnes Investment firm, letting her guard down was a luxury she couldn't afford. Her mind had to be sharp every day—without exception. The world had become smaller economically. Companies were joining forces and needed intricate financial deals more than ever. Caryn completed one deal after another where hundreds of millions of dollars could be on the line at any given moment. It was not a job where she could be caught sleeping.

With a double major in economics and finance, she went on to get her MBA with an international business concentration. Add to that almost ten years of solid experience, she had been well prepared for her current position. What her formal education didn't prepare her for was dealing with varied cultures and customs.

Caryn had to be tough-minded and tough-skinned. There were times when she was the only female in the room, and many more times when she was the only African-American. In some places around the world, they didn't always recognize her power and authority. Some found it challenging to work with a woman, while others found it next to impossible.

She'd been in several meetings, both in the U.S. and abroad, where unexpected delays had occurred. Under the guise of "unresolved issues" about some financial matters, Caryn always had her suspicions that some of those delays happened because they tried to get someone else to broker the deal. Once they realized they had to work with her or risk losing the deal, they usually came around. They might not have liked it, but they couldn't argue with her competence or confidence. Caryn Stewart was damn good at what she did.

As an adviser to corporations and institutions around the world, she loved the challenge of her work. Starting as an intern her freshman year of college, she'd given Carlton Barnes twelve years of her life, practically living and breathing her job as she climbed her way to the top. Now, at thirty, she was sitting pretty.

Money in the bank, a fabulous home, the respect of her peers and the ability to give strategic input to the direction her firm would take, she garnered admiration from many, envy from some and jealousy from others. Profiled in *Ebony, Essence,* and *Newsweek,* her professional life was a dream. The only problem she had was carving out time to spend some of her money, decorate her home and mentor others to help them accomplish all that she had.

"Oh, well," she whispered to the empty room, taking another sip of her wine. "Can't have everything."

Between the wine, the music, the candles and her exhaustion, her lids slowly started to close and thoughts of contracts, mergers, loans, foreign businessmen and wire transfers faded into darkness.

His fingers slid sensuously down her arm and around her naked body, causing a stir of inner passion. The touch of his moist, firm mouth on hers caused heat rays to shoot from the top of her head to the tips of her toes.

"You are so beautiful," he whispered, nuzzling her neck.

Soft moans escaped from her lips as the sweet torture of his touch tested her resolve.

Moving his lips from her mouth, he went exploring. He nipped and tucked at her ears, neck and shoulders, tasting the sweetness of her skin. She arched her back, her body calling out for the warmth of his tongue.

"Oh, yes," she cried out, feeling the throbbing sensation in the core of her body.

She tried to contain herself as unfulfilled cravings coursed through her—seeking. Seeking to be pleased. Seeking to be satisfied. Seeking unbridled passion. Seeking unchecked sexual fervor.

Getting his fill from her swollen orbs, he moved lower, being sure to leave a mark on each place his luscious lips touched. When he reached her most private spot, she willingly spread her legs a little wider, positioning herself to receive all that he was offering her. When she felt his tongue touch that erotic spot, she screamed out in excruciating pleasure.

Caryn's eyes popped open and she jumped straight up, causing water to splatter over the top and onto the floor. Glancing around the empty room, it took several seconds to get her bearings. Feeling the tingling in her breasts and the yearning between her legs, the line between dream and reality had definitely been blurred. *It's been too long!*

Deciding she'd had enough relaxation, Caryn blew out the candles and recorked the wine. Wrapping her body in a towel, she headed back to the bedroom, glad that she'd found some time in her schedule to furnish this room.

The queen-size sleigh bed with the cedar chest at its foot centered the room. The comfortable chaise in the corner with the small table and lamp created the perfect place to catch up on her reading. The dresser was an antique she found one Saturday when she was out and about enjoying the city. She sighed audibly at the memory. She hadn't been antiquing since.

Opening her drawer, she stared at all the lingerie she'd collected over the years. The sexy silk tops, the lacy thongs and the skimpy teddies were designed to entice, beguile and charm the man in her life. Unfortunately, since her schedule barely left her enough time to meet a man, it definitely didn't afford her the luxury of seducing one. Trying not to slip into a funk over her personal life, or lack of one, she pulled out a pair of silk pants and a matching button-down top and decided to grab something to eat.

Walking into the kitchen, she took in the stainless-steel appliances, granite countertops, Italian-tiled floor and custom cabinets that lined the walls. Exquisite. Beautiful. Bare. The white walls and empty shelves reminded her that she hadn't used this room in quite a while.

Because of her schedule, Caryn knew her only choices for food were soup or a frozen dinner. A grocery store was a rare visit for her. Opening a can of chicken and vegetable soup, she poured it into a pan and waited for it to warm. Pouring the soup into a bowl, she headed back to her room just as her cell phone rang.

Passing by the empty living room and dining room, she hurried to check the number. Ronald Green.

Talking to him ranked at the bottom of the things she wanted to do. The man must have had a sixth sense to know when she was back in town.

They'd met the day she moved in. He'd been in the building about six months and offered to show her around the neighborhood. That one afternoon turned into several dates over the past year. Each time she'd come home, he'd be right there, ready to take her out. He couldn't understand her need to unwind. To spend some time alone. Each time she tried to explain that to him, he could never relate. His response was that she should stop working so hard and let someone else take care of her.

That attitude gave a clear indication that she could never be more than friends with him. Caryn didn't need anyone to take care of her. Being a kept woman had never appealed to any part of her. If that's what he was offering, she would have to pass.

After eating, she felt her body begin to completely break down and she crawled into bed. Picking up the remote, she debated turning on the television but decided against it. Her lids were heavy and she pulled the covers tight over her body.

When the phone rang again, she ignored it. Then, thinking it could be Jeremy with a question about her e-mail, she turned over and checked the number. Recognizing the number, she got a boost of energy. "Hey, girl."

"Please tell me your plans have not changed."

Caryn laughed at the hint of doubt in the voice, but couldn't blame her. "Don't worry. I am officially on a break. For the next month, I won't look at a chart, read a report or check the financial papers."

At the silence on the other end, Caryn acknowledged the little white lie. "Okay, maybe I'll check a few newspapers."

"That's more like it," Sherisse said, glad to hear her friend was safe and sound in Boston. "What time is your flight?"

Originally, she planned to get an early start, catching the shuttle around eight or nine so that she could be home in time to have lunch with her parents. But now that she had a call with Jeremy in the morning, some things would need to get switched around. He would probably have questions, revisions and a need to have it all done before noon. So much for getting an early start. "I'll probably get in around three."

"I don't blame you for sleeping in," Sherisse said, completely understanding that traveling was tough. "I know how much you love sleeping in your bed. I'm sure you've turned off the alarm clock and will sleep until you wake up."

Caryn let Sherisse think that was the reason for the afternoon flight. Everyone, including Sherisse, already thought she worked too much. She would only lecture Caryn about changing her plans, again, to accommodate Jeremy.

"I can't believe you're finally coming home."

"You or I," Caryn said. She had canceled her last three trips to Washington, D.C. "My parents have threatened to disown me. It's been over a year."

"Nineteen months," Sherisse said. "But who's counting?"

Caryn leaned back on the bed and laughed. Sherisse had been her best friend since they met in high school,

Caryn a freshman and Sherisse a senior. Caryn helped Sherisse pass economics and Sherisse dissected Caryn's frog for her.

They made big plans during high school. They were going to have good jobs, wear expensive clothes and have a ton of money. They promised each other they would travel the world together, be each other's maid of honor and raise their children together. The good news was that they were on track with their professional goals. It was the personal stuff that needed lots of work.

The thought of her personal goals saddened Caryn for a moment, but she quickly recovered. "I can't wait to see you and I'm really looking forward to meeting Barry. You two have been kickin' it for quite a while. I'm glad things are going good for you in the relationship category."

"Barry?" Sherisse asked, rolling her eyes at the mention of his name.

"Yes," Caryn said, a little confused by her tone. "The high school principal. The romantic guy that always sent flowers or candy. The man that wanted you to meet his family. The man—"

"The man I broke up with two months ago," Sherisse said, cutting her off in midsentence.

"Two months ago?"

"Yep."

Caryn tried to think back to their last conversation. "How did this happen? Why didn't you tell me? Where have I been?"

"That's easy," Sherisse said. "Europe…Asia… Africa…"

"Okay, okay," Caryn said as she was reminded of where she'd been. "What happened to you two? Last time we talked, you thought he was the one."

"Yeah, right," Sherisse said, thinking back to her time with him. "He was the one—until he decided he didn't want his doctor girlfriend to be more successful than him. The night I received an award from the American Medical Association was the night that man started tripping."

"What did he do?"

"Snide remarks," Sherisse said, her anger rising in her chest at the thought of him. "We'd go out to dinner and he'd say, 'I guess we'll let the big-time doctor take care of the bill.'"

"No, he didn't," Caryn said.

"Check this one out," Sherisse continued. "We're at a cocktail party with other teachers and administrators. He says, 'Can you believe I got the good doctor to go slumming with me this evening?'"

"What?" Caryn said. "I can't believe I missed all of that!"

"What do you expect when you spend your time gallivanting around the globe closing multipatrilliondollar deals? It's good if I talk to you every quarter. If it wasn't for e-mail, we'd have lost touch long ago."

The humor in her voice was evident, but Caryn felt a twinge of guilt. "I should have been there for you."

Caryn thought about all that she had missed with her family and friends because of her career. Her parent's thirty-fifth anniversary. Her cousin's engagement party. Another cousin's wedding. Her uncle's bypass surgery. Her high-school reunion. And too many birthday celebrations for friends to count.

"I can cry on your shoulder when you get here tomorrow." The last thing Sherisse wanted to do was bring Caryn down and make her feel guilty.

"About Barry?"

"Nope, Kevin."

Now Caryn was completely confused. "Who's Kevin?"

"I'll tell you all about him—tomorrow."

"That's why I'm looking forward to the next month," Caryn said. "Coming to D.C. and catching up with my friends and family is the best way to spend my downtime."

Sherisse couldn't agree more. "You have been working nonstop. I hope you really are going to take it easy."

The apprehension in her friend's voice couldn't be ignored—nor was it new. It was the same tone of voice she'd heard from her parents, a couple of her co-workers and a man or two that tried to develop a relationship with her. But Caryn couldn't give in to their concerns. She had a plan. A plan that would give her everything she needed—and wanted.

A successful career. Money in the bank that would set her up for the rest of her life. A paid-for home. And providing for her parents. It was a plan that was at least three years away from completion. Until then, she wouldn't rest. "Don't worry about me."

Sherisse heard the flippant comment and let it go. She had four weeks with her best friend to try to get her to slow down. "I'll see you tomorrow."

"Can't wait."

Caryn tossed the phone aside and stared at the

ceiling. Before Sherisse's call, she was five seconds away from falling asleep. Now her energy level had elevated. Picking up the remote, she aimed it at the television but put it back down without pushing the power button. No need to turn it on—she didn't have cable. Her iPod had been attached to her ear during the entire plane ride and she wasn't interested in listening to any more music. She thought of calling her mom, but she would see her tomorrow.

After several minutes, Caryn got up and walked to her office. Booting up her computer, she waited for it to come to life. If there was one thing that never failed her—it was work.

Chapter 4

"Dr. Proctor, you have a patient waiting in room three."

"Thanks, Barbara," Will said. "I'll be there in a few minutes."

Nodding, Barbara left the office, shutting the door behind her.

Will, dressed in a pair of dark blue slacks and a dress shirt, stood inside the office of Dr. Derrick Carrington, his business partner and best friend. He'd arrived almost thirty minutes ago and launched into the details of last night. The recap was almost complete when Barbara interrupted.

Once she was gone, Will continued, "Obviously, she backed me into a corner. I had no choice but to end it right there on the spot."

Derrick leaned back in his high-back leather chair and gave him a blank stare for almost a full minute.

"What?" Will said, wondering about the strange reaction.

Finally, Derrick threw his head back and roared with laughter.

The response was unexpected and Will didn't appreciate the lack of compassion that Derrick exhibited. "I'm glad you find me amusing."

"It's just that…" He was unable to finish through the tears that were starting to gather in his eyes.

Will clamped his jaw tight and waited for the bout of laughter to subside. "I don't see what the joke is."

"Oh, come on, Will," Derrick said, thinking of all he'd said from the moment he walked in the door. "You come into my office every couple of months playing the victim with these outrageous breakup stories. 'I had no choice. She forced my hand. I was cornered. No other option remained.' To top it off—you expect me to have sympathy for you?"

"You should," Will reasoned, agitated that this situation was being taken so lightly. "Breakups are tough."

Those words caused Derrick's grin to broaden and fall into another round of laughs. "Do you hear yourself?"

Taking a seat in one of the chairs in front of Derrick's desk, Will shook his head in disbelief. "I should have known better than to expect you to understand what I'm going through."

"Going through?" Derrick questioned. "You make it sound as if you've just lost your best friend…your one and only…your soul mate."

"Well…" Will said.

"Give me a break, Will. You wouldn't know a soul mate if it walked up to you and slapped you in the face."

"I'm offended," Will said. "I spent months with this woman."

Derrick knew there was a difference between dating a woman and truly knowing a woman. He wasn't so sure Will had that same understanding. "What was her favorite color?"

Will thought about it, but came up empty. "She wore red a lot, so maybe…"

"What's her favorite book…song…place to vacation? What's her favorite childhood memory?"

Will didn't like the direction of this conversation.

Derrick realized that he wouldn't get an answer because there wasn't one. It was the same pattern each time they had this discussion. "How can you be broken up about breaking up with someone you hardly knew?"

"Do you have a point?"

"Yeah," Derrick said, noticing there was nothing in Will's tone or body language that indicated that he was sad, sorry or miserable about the fact that he would no longer be seeing Alaina. "Breakups are tough—for people in real relationships. You, on the other hand, can't have a tough breakup when you say things like 'you had no choice' and 'guess it's time to move on.'"

"She forced my hand. I had to take swift, immediate action," Will said defensively.

"This isn't war, Will."

Derrick was trying to make him the bad guy and that wasn't the case. "Why continue in a relationship that's doomed?"

"I feel like a broken record when it comes to talking about your love life. However, I don't mind repeating myself if it will help me understand."

"What don't you understand? Everything I'm telling you makes perfect sense."

Derrick pushed his back off the chair and leaned forward, resting his elbows on the desk. "You meet a phenomenal woman, you find her attractive and she returns the sentiment. You spend several months getting to know each other—rarely having a heated argument. She tells you she thinks that you should explore a deeper relationship and you interpret all of this to mean that the relationship is doomed?"

Nodding, Will readily agreed with the assessment. "You know the deal, Derrick, just as she did. It's not my fault she couldn't abide by the rules."

Derrick threw his hands up in defeat at the mention of the rules. He had the distinct honor of being around when those rules first came to light. The fact that they were still in effect never ceased to amaze him.

Their first year of medical school, the pressure was enormous. Between the caseload, the homework and the reading, there was barely enough time in a day to eat and shower. Different as they were, Will and Derrick handled the pressure in two different manners. Derrick gave his undivided attention to his studies. Everything and everyone came in a distant second—including women. Will opted to take another approach.

Determined to graduate at the top of his class, Will believed that social interaction was important to maintaining his sanity. So he made time for dating—with the understanding that he could only offer a woman occasional dates with no strings attached during this stress-ful time in his life.

Over the years, that way of dating brought about his rules. After graduating, completing their residency and building a practice, Derrick thought that Will would have let go of all those rules by now. Instead, he held on to them tighter than ever.

What shocked Derrick most was not that Will had these rules. It was that he found women who would date him in spite of the rules. To go out with a man who made it very clear that marriage was out of the question always left Derrick confused. Still, Will managed to do it—over and over again.

Derrick watched his friend's nonchalant demeanor and wondered how any person could be that emotion-ally detached. The situation with Alaina had been repeated more times than he could remember in the past year, but Will continued to roll with the punches. "How can you look in the mirror after dates like last night? Don't you get tired of going through the same old exercise? You'll probably be better off if you retire those well-worn rules."

Ignoring the sarcasm in Derrick's voice, Will stood his ground. "They are not tired rules—they are the way I operate. It's the woman that says she can handle them and then ultimately wants something else—something more."

Will's words were spoken with such passion, they almost sounded reasonable. Almost. "How would you feel if you met a woman that was more attractive to you than any other woman you've met? This woman is beau-tiful, successful, smart, funny, strong and independent."

A mental picture of this perfect woman flashed in his mind and he nodded in approval. "Keep going."

"And she had a set of rules that mirrored yours."

Will thought about it for several seconds before raising his hands to the heavens. "Oh, if I could only be so lucky. Please, please, please, Lord, send me a woman who thinks as I think, lives like I live and has her own set of rules."

"You are one sick man," Derrick said, standing and walking around his desk. Slipping on his white jacket, he picked up his stethoscope and opened the door.

Will dropped his hands, and folded them in front of him. "What I'm sick of is women who say they can deal with 'no strings attached' and then can't. Who say they understand 'when we're together, we're together and when we're not, we're not,' but then demand an exclusive relationship. What I'm sick of is women who look me in the eye and lie by saying that they can deal with the rules."

"Maybe they think they can deal—in the beginning," Derrick offered. "But people change. Feelings grow."

"Mine don't."

Derrick couldn't believe he was being completely honest. "Are you saying that not once have you been tempted to throw away your rules? That there hasn't been one woman that you've encountered that got you thinking about the future?"

"No," he answered without hesitation. "I've never changed my mind about the rules."

"Well," Derrick said, "you know that women have the right to change their mind."

"I, one hundred percent, support the woman's right

to change her mind. What I don't support is her attempt to change mine."

"You say that," Derrick said thoughtfully, "but someone like Natalie could make you change your mind about all of those rules in a heartbeat."

Will playfully groaned and covered his ears at the mention of Natalie Carrington. He couldn't be in the same room with Derrick for more that five minutes without him finding a way to mention his wife of six months. No matter what conversation they were having, he always found a way to work her in.

During their courtship and wedding plans, Will heard almost on a daily basis how much he loved that woman, how much he cared for her, how happy they were going to be when they finally tied the knot.

Will recalled some of the ups and downs the two of them had gone through. While they were definitely in love with each other, Natalie wasn't ready to get married. "If I remember correctly, Natalie and I are a lot alike. You wanted to marry her and she wasn't ready for that next step."

"Yes," Derrick said, remembering that painful time in his life when the two of them wanted very different things. "But I loved her right through that—and look at us now. Happy. Wondering how we ever survived without each other. That's what will happen to you, Will. You'll meet someone that will love you right through all those barriers you keep up."

"I will give you partial credit for that answer," Will said. "You helped Natalie work through her stuff with her family, but where you veer off is talking about a woman changing me. Besides, you were always the marrying kind. I, on the other hand, define the term 'confirmed bachelor.' I wear the label proudly."

"I don't know, man," Derrick said, skepticism in his voice. "It all sounds good, but I saw you at the wedding. There was a moment when the ceremony got to you."

Will reluctantly remembered the day he stood by Derrick's side as his best man. The first to admit that he found the institution of marriage hard to endorse, he would readily agree that Derrick and Natalie were made for each other. Held in the evening, the candle-light ceremony was witnessed by about seventy-five of their closest friends and family members.

The service was moving along, just as they'd rehearsed, when they got to the vows. It was the first time they recited the special words they had created for each other.

Derrick,

The definition of a man means many things to many people. But for me, it's someone with integrity, honesty, the heart to serve and a heart to love. You have shown me what it means to care about someone. What it means to be there for someone. What it means to love someone. I pledge my life to you because you are truly the man of my dreams.

Natalie,

The moment I met you, I knew you were special. Not because of your outward beauty, but because of the light that shines from your heart and your soul. I promise to nurture that light. To protect that light. To love that light. It is what makes you special and I want to spend the rest of my life shining with you.

Feeling the power of the heartfelt confessions, Will

quietly cleared his throat as he felt a ball welling up inside him. Never had he been one to get caught up in moments like this. Words of love, commitment, devotion and fidelity rarely moved him. For a split second, he pictured himself standing at the altar, sliding a ring onto a woman's finger. This overwhelming sense of emotion shocked him and it took him several seconds to recover. Obviously, he didn't recover fast enough if Derrick noticed his moment of weakness.

Then the pastor proclaimed them husband and wife. The guests broke into applause and any feelings that were stirred inside Will were abruptly and completely pushed back down to wherever they came from.

Standing, Will followed him. "That's my cue that this conversation is over."

"You treat commitment like the plague," Derrick said, stepping into the hallway. "I've noticed that every time I start a conversation about Natalie and me, you suddenly have to go. Could it be you refuse to deal with the idea of a creating a home, having a family or planning a future—because you're afraid you might discover that those things aren't so bad after all?"

"Getting as far away from you as possible when you start to talk about Natalie has nothing to do with commitment," Will said with a slight smirk on his face. "It has to do with the twenty-minute monologue you normally launch into about how wonderful married life is. Between your honeymoon stories, your candlelight dinners at home, your evening walks under the stars and sharing breakfast together every morning, you would make the most romantic person want to vomit."

"Well," Derrick said, stopping in front of exam room

three, "you better get used to it, because I find it hard to talk about anything else these days."

Will shook his head from side to side, scrunching up his nose as if he smelled a skunk. "Marriage? I *never* want to get used to that."

Derrick heard the words and wondered if he would ever change that attitude. "One day, a woman is going to put you in your place."

This time, it was Will's turn to throw his head back in laughter. "Maybe you should take your own temperature, Doctor—because obviously you're delirious."

"You never know," Derrick countered.

"Oh, I know," Will said confidently. "The day I fall in love and commit to a woman is the day I sit down and look at all two hundred of those honeymoon pictures you've tried to shove in front of me."

Chapter 5

Caryn opened the double glass doors and stepped into the medical office Tuesday evening. Her flight had landed about two o'clock and she couldn't contain her excitement when she walked out of baggage claim and saw her parents waiting at the curb. The reunion was a long time coming.

Bonnie and Lloyd Stewart held their arms wide open. After a round of long-overdue hugs and kisses, Caryn threw her small travel bag in the trunk and settled into the back seat of the late-model Mercedes—a gift to her parents two years ago.

Arriving at her parent's home in Alexandria, Virginia, she was glad to see that her mother had prepared a late lunch and the perfect opportunity to play catch-up and find out what had been happening in her family's lives. Munching on turkey wraps and fruit salad, Caryn listened as Bonnie and Lloyd spilled all the beans about her relatives.

She was glad to hear that Aunt Gladys had retired and was thinking of moving to Arizona. After thirty years with the Internal Revenue Service, she was finally free to do with her days as she wished. The only problem was that Uncle Roy wasn't interested in going across the country. How would he see his grandchildren? It was an ongoing battle, and according to her mother, things were getting ugly.

Next, Bonnie caught her up on the latest with her cousin Veronica. About the same age, she had been married for four years and was about to have her second child. Growing up, they would have sleepovers at each other's houses. Crammed into their single beds, they would stay up late and talk about meeting their mate, having big weddings and little babies. The fact that that had only happened for one of them threw Caryn for an expected loop.

Unfortunately, Caryn missed the wedding and had only seen Veronica's daughter, Lauryn, twice—and she was three years old. She'd always planned to stay in touch more, but time kept slipping away.

Her somber feelings at hearing about Veronica turned to laughter when Bonnie told her that her other cousin Pamela was getting divorced—for the third time. For some reason, no one in the family was shocked to find out the marriage didn't last. The couple met while she was on vacation in Las Vegas. They married three days later.

Their lunchtime chat was interrupted several times

by Caryn's BlackBerry. The first time, she didn't bother to answer. It took all of her willpower, but she wanted to at least enjoy one day without dealing with her office. However, by the third time, she figured someone desperately needed her attention. When she picked up the call, her parents gave her a disapproving stare but didn't say anything. She took the call in the other room.

Based on the call, she spent another hour in her room reviewing some documents for an upcoming closing. If her mother hadn't reminded her of the time, she would have worked right through her evening plans. Making a quick change of clothes, she said good-night to her parents and left to meet Sherisse.

Caryn started to give her name to the receptionist when Sherisse came bursting through the side door with her arms wide open. With no regard for anything, or anyone, around them, they embraced each other and giggled like high school friends.

"You look fantastic!" Sherisse said.

"You cut your hair," Caryn exclaimed, touching the dark brown hair with highlights. "It's so becoming."

"You've lost weight," Sherisse said, a little alarm in her voice. With her small frame, Caryn couldn't afford to drop another pound. "What size are those jeans—a four?"

Choosing casual and comfortable clothes, Caryn wore a pair of blue jeans, a scoop-neck peasant top and cute stiletto shoes. "Oh, please, girl. I squeezed into this six. What about you? Looks like somebody has been hitting the gym."

Sherisse did a quick turn, taking off her white lab coat to reveal a casual black pencil skirt and a button-down dark green shirt.

"Work it, girl!"

"You know I am!"

Before Caryn could respond, the side door swung open again and three very handsome men walked out.

"What is going on out here?" Derrick said. "We thought a group of cheerleaders landed in our office."

Sherisse turned to her business partners, grinning from ear to ear. "Derrick…Will…Jeff, I'd like you to meet my dear friend, Caryn Stewart."

Caryn's eyes quickly perused all three gentlemen and all she could think was "wow." Standing side by side, they looked as if they had stepped out of the pages of a fashion magazine. Not only because of their designer clothes, but because they were all distinctly handsome.

Derrick, around six feet tall, sported a genuine smile that reached his eyes. His relaxed manner was inviting and authentic and she wondered if that platinum wedding band had anything to do with the happy and satisfied look on his face.

Jeff, a little shorter than Derrick, had an athletic build and a boyish face. The corners of his mouth lifted into a broad smile.

Finally, she turned her attention to the last man standing. Her travels had given her a broad view of the world and of its people. Brazilians, Spaniards, the French. She was no stranger to fine, beautiful men. But there was nothing like the sultry, sophisticated look of a good ol' fashioned African-American male. Will fit that description to a tee.

With him at six foot two, her four-inch heels just took her to his chin. His dark eyes, pronounced jaw and full lips sent her thoughts straight to her dream from last night. Now, *this* was a man that could caress, cuddle, embrace and stroke her—anytime. He would give playing doctor a whole new meaning.

Stretching her hand out to each of them, an easy smile played at the corners of her mouth. "It's a pleasure to meet all of you."

Derrick took her hand first. "We've heard quite a bit about you over the years. It's nice to put a name with a face."

Caryn nodded and replied in kind before turning to Jeff.

"Glad to meet you," he said.

"Thanks," Caryn said before turning her attention to Will.

Will waited patiently while she focused her attention on his other two business partners. He'd watched her from the moment he walked out and couldn't take his eyes off her. He was glad to see her acknowledge Derrick and Jeff first, because it gave him time to figure out what caused him to be so intrigued. The beauty was a given. The light brown hair, the well-cared-for body and the magnetic smile. No, it was something else.

When he'd heard the commotion in the back office, he, too, thought that a group of teenagers had invaded the office. How pleasantly surprised he was to find that the laughter belonged to someone so lovely.

Accepting her hand, he enclosed his fingers around hers. When his skin connected with hers, a vague sense of electricity crackled between them. An experience like no other, Will lost his train of thought for a second. But quickly, he regained control. "Derrick is only half-right. We have heard about you, but what Sherisse failed to share with us was how striking you are."

Will raised her hand to his lips and gently kissed the back of it. "You must leave a trail of broken hearts around the world."

Letting his lips linger before removing her hand, the few extra seconds gave her just enough time to make a quick assessment. Player. Charmer. Charismatic. Magnetic. Alluring. Compelling. She'd met his kind many times over the years and never had a problem handling his type. "I'm sure if I took a tour of this city, I'd find your trail, as well."

Will hesitated before he released a soft laugh. She was quick—and stunning. Her eyes moved from his and that's when it hit him. The uniqueness that caught him when he first laid eyes on her. The fact that she never wavered her stare told him she had confidence and boldness to go along with that sexy body and gorgeous face. Instead of responding immediately, he took a full minute to inventory her features from top to bottom.

The pair of dark blue jeans hugged her hips and made her legs never-ending. The black fitted top wrapped around her waist with a short sash hanging on the side. Moving the focus off her body and on to her face, he couldn't help but admire her natural loveliness. Makeup complemented and highlighted her brown eyes, soft cheeks and thin, kissable lips. "Touché."

Will went into the archives of his memory bank to recall all the things Sherisse may have said about Caryn over the years. Something about her job keeping her on the road. He thought he recalled Sherisse meeting her in Morocco and a mention about her family being from the area. But for the life of him, he couldn't remember anything about her personal life. There was no ring on her left hand, but that didn't mean there wasn't a man in the picture.

Peering intently at one another, neither spoke. Something undefined permeated the air. A mixture of curiosity, attraction and sincere interest surrounded them like a cyclone.

The others stood by, watching this exchange between the two, but Will paid attention to none of them.

Derrick shook his head in disbelief. Was Will really coming on to his partner's best friend?

Jeff, on the other hand, gave credit to Will. The brother didn't waste any time recovering from his latest breakup.

Sherisse, on the other hand, saw nothing amusing or interesting about it. Dr. William Proctor's reputation was well earned. She had watched him work his way through more women than she would ever try to count. Could she recall a time when he'd dated someone more than a couple of months? Was there one occasion when he spoke of anything beyond a quick fling? The answer to both those questions was a resounding no.

That's exactly why she wanted to smack that look he had in his eyes off his face. It was as if he was the lion and Caryn had become his prey. Sherisse wouldn't let Will loose on her worst enemy; she definitely wouldn't let him near anyone she truly cared about.

Stepping between the two of them, Sherisse gave Caryn a quick grin before turning her body to fully face

Will. Barely reaching his neck in heels, the difference in size didn't affect the power of her body language. Piercing eyes, a tight jaw and pursed lips, her disapproving posture left nothing to the imagination. Without raising her voice above a low whisper, she hissed, "Back off, Proctor."

Suddenly, without missing a beat, she relaxed her shoulders and turned her attention toward the group. "We're on our way to dinner to have some long-overdue girl talk. Caryn's only in town for a couple of weeks so we don't have time to waste."

"Then we won't keep you," Jeff said, heading back toward his office. "Have a great evening."

"Nice meeting you, Caryn," Derrick said. "If you're not busy Saturday night, I'm throwing a birthday party for my wife. We'd love to have you."

"Thanks," Caryn said, watching him disappear behind the door.

Sherisse waved goodbye and turned to Will, waiting for him to follow suit. When he didn't make a move, Sherisse rolled her eyes heavenward. *This woman is off-limits!* She hoped her thoughts could telepathically jump out of her mind and into his. "Ah, Will?"

Hearing Sherisse, he didn't respond right away. Instead, he took a step toward Caryn and casually put his hands in his pockets. "Sherisse tells me that you travel quite a bit and that it's been years since you've been home for any length of time."

Caryn refused to give in to the overwhelming power of his presence. She'd always lived with an unwritten rule that you allowed people at least three feet of personal space. Obviously, not everyone adhered to that rule, because he was so near. She could reach out and touch him. An unfamiliar feeling had her wanting to do just that. Instead, she forced her hands to remain at her sides.

Focusing on his words, she refused to allow him the slightest indication that she was off balance by his intense attention. She'd gone toe to toe with billionaire corporations and chauvinistic businessmen. Surely she could handle one very handsome doctor with an over-inflated ego. "It has."

"A lot has changed in this place," he said, refusing to acknowledge the darts flying from Sherisse's eyes. "There are quite a few places to see and enjoy."

Caryn nodded but remained silent, waiting to see where this conversation would lead.

He watched her watch him and couldn't get a read on what she was thinking. The situation had him feeling a little out of control. Her eyes stayed with his without giving anything away. "If you need someone to help you get reacquainted with the area, feel free to call on me. I'm an excellent tour guide."

"Why do you think I'm here?" Sherisse said, nudging him aside with extra force. Was he out of his mind? Did he actually believe that Sherisse would allow him to make a move on her best friend?

"Of course," Will said, refusing to take his eyes off Caryn. "But Sherisse has been such a homebody lately, I'm not sure she's the one I'd put in charge of showing me all the hot spots."

"I'm sure she'll do just fine," Caryn said, allowing the tingling in her stomach to spur on her flirtatious behavior. "But if not, I'll be sure to call on you.

Wouldn't want to miss out on all those hot spots you seem so familiar with."

Her flirtatious tone grabbed Will's attention and he started to respond. But Sherisse cut him off.

"Actually, Will is absolutely right," Sherisse said, putting on a sugary smile.

Will glanced at Sherisse with widened eyes, taken completely off guard by her sudden support. Based on her earlier words, he thought she would be working against him. Evidently he was wrong.

"While I've been sticking close to home," Sherisse continued, "Will has been hitting all the hot spots—with a different woman every night. Let's see if I can get them all straight. There was Beverly, Fiona and Amy—and that's just the list from this month. Of course, last night, there was Alaina.

"With his social calendar, it's tough to get in time to have coffee with Will, but I'm sure he could find a way to squeeze you in. And when I say squeeze, I mean it."

Turning to Will, she continued, "You usually go out on a date…what…um…every night?"

Facing Caryn once again, Sherisse finished up. "You'll probably need to book some time with Will days, if not weeks, in advance. With the number of women he juggles, it's hard to make last-minute plans."

"Ouch!" Will said, realizing he was way off track if he thought Sherisse was going to make this easier for him. He'd ignored all of Sherisse's subtle gestures to leave Caryn alone, and she'd obviously decided to retaliate by putting his business on blast. But Will recovered quickly, giving Caryn a quick wink. "Don't believe everything you hear, Caryn. I'm sure I could find time for you."

Caryn heard the playfulness in his voice and didn't have a problem playing along. "I'll keep that in mind, heartbreaker."

"You do that."

For a split second, his stare held her and he searched her eyes. Her good-humored expression was wide and inviting, but as the seconds ticked away, the center changed and they were more curious and intriguing. Finally, he caught a glimmer of stress and a moment of sadness. And then it was gone.

Caryn's body reacted to the intensity of his eyes. A warming sensation traveled from the top of her head to the bottom of her feet that soon turned to discomfort. Shifting her weight from foot to foot, she tried to maintain control of the situation. But Will didn't waver. She cut her eyes away.

With a slight nod, Will turned and walked back through the door.

Caryn watched his back disappear from sight. Without warning, her breath had become slightly ragged.

"Are you okay?" Sherisse asked, splitting her attention between Caryn and the closed door.

Pushing aside the feelings, she focused on her friend. "Sure…what's on the agenda for tonight?"

The exchange between Caryn and Will rubbed Sherisse the wrong way. He chased anything in a skirt and usually ended up hurting the person. That wasn't the road she wanted to send Caryn down.

She started to voice her opinion, but decided against

it. Caryn was too smart and savvy to get caught up with a man like Will. His tired game could be spotted a mile away. "There's a great restaurant that just opened up right around the corner. We can start with a few drinks and take it from there. I'm going to grab my purse, and we'll be on our way."

"Great," Caryn said, pulling out her BlackBerry. "I'll wait here and check a few e-mails."

Walking into her office, Sherisse moved behind her desk to shut down her computer. As the screen saved her information, she began to make a few notes in the file of the last patient she'd tended to.

Picking up her purse from inside the desk drawer, she walked to the door and hung her white jacket on the back of it. When she pulled the door back open, Will stood on the other side, leaning casually against the jamb with his hands in his pockets.

"You scared me!" she said, jumping back at seeing someone standing less than a foot away.

"Didn't mean to," he said. "I wanted to catch you before you headed out."

Will didn't say anything further and Sherisse took in his cavalier stance and his questioning eyes. She didn't need any words to figure out what he wanted. "Forget it, Proctor."

"Come on, Sherisse," he asked nonchalantly. "Why not?"

The words were said with such naiveté that she couldn't hold back a snicker. "Are you seriously asking me that?"

"You don't think I'm good enough for your friend?" He tried to play it as if his feelings were hurt, but

Sherisse wasn't falling for that. He knew what he was, just as she did. "No, you're not."

"I'm offended," he said, pushing off the door and raising his hands to dramatically cover his heart.

"You should be," she answered without the least bit of guilt. "You treat women like objects—to be used and discarded at your convenience. Why would I subject my best friend to that?"

"Because maybe this time—just maybe," he said solemnly, "it would be different—*she* would be different."

She watched him lower his head and soften his voice. The man should have been an actor instead of a doctor.

"And maybe—just maybe," she said, mocking his tone, "I'll hit the lottery."

Will frowned at hearing his own voice. Not into playing games, he wondered where those words had come from. He'd never spoken those words about another woman. "You make me sound like a monster when it comes to women."

"Then my work here is done."

Pushing him to the side, she left him standing there without a backward glance.

Chapter 6

Caryn tasted flavorful, authentic foods from around the world and she'd come to realize that very few restaurants in America had been able to capture the true essence of India, France or China. That's why Caryn was glad to see they were eating at a regular American restaurant.

The steak house would satisfy her appetite for a juicy piece of meat, a thick pile of mashed potatoes and a slice of warm apple pie with cinnamon ice cream. Sherisse must have sensed that she had a strong craving for all things American and she couldn't wait to dig in.

At that thought, a picture of Will popped into her head. Now, *that* was something else all-American that she would like to dig into. Of course, based on Sherisse's reaction to their harmless flirting, she had to think about the best approach. "I want to hear everything that's been going on with you, girl. Your work. Barry. Kevin. This revelation of you being a homebody."

After ordering a round of drinks, Sherisse decided on her dinner and set her menu aside. "We'll get to that, but I want to hear all about you. India, Spain, Amsterdam. You know you are the envy of all our friends. Traveling the world. Wheeling and dealing. Big title. Company perks. Not to mention that you do it all while styling in your St. John, Gucci and Jimmy Choos."

"You're one to talk," Caryn answered, turning the tables. "Dr. Sherisse Copeland. Top doctor. Successful practice. Philanthropist. I've read every article you've sent me about your work—both in medicine and the community. I won't get started on that convertible Lexus we rode in tonight. You got it going on, girlfriend."

Sherisse held her expression in place as she listened to all the accolades. Digesting Caryn's compliments, she was quiet for almost a full minute. Unexpectedly, she broke out into a broad grin and pumped her hands in the air. "Yeah, that's right. I am all that and a bag of chips!"

They both laughed as they relished in their successes. They'd made it through SATs, the freshman fifteen, grad school, medical school, internships, residencies, the doubts, the fears and the school loans.

"I always admired the dedication you have to your work, Sherisse," Caryn said. "You don't see a successful black female doctor every day. I'm proud of you."

"Look who's talking," Sherisse said. "Corporate jets,

limousines and six-figure bonuses is hardly a horrible way of life."

Caryn had to admit that when you heard her life described that way, it did sound fabulous. She'd been around the world twice, and though most of that time she barely got to be a tourist, she'd managed to sneak in a few things. But those moments couldn't make up for some of the sacrifices she was making for her career. "Remember, to get all of that, I'm away from family and friends. I can't get a dog. I have a P.O. box and no cable. There's no furniture in my house, no paint on my walls and I have to look up my building entry code every time I go home."

Sherisse had heard all of this before. Each time Caryn came home she would break out into this same song. Complaints about what she thought she was missing out on because of her job. It usually lasted for a week or two, and then she would hear about an upcoming deal she would be working on and excitedly head off to conquer the world. "You say that now, but I'm sure when it's time to head to Tokyo or Bangkok to close a multimillion-dollar deal, you'll jump into a private jet and happily settle into that plush leather seat, counting down the minutes until takeoff. Very soon, you'll be president."

Caryn recalled all the times that she had done just that. Regardless of her complaints and feelings that she was missing out on something, when it was time to wheel and deal, all of her juices got flowing and she would forget all about her bare apartment, the time away from her family and the lack of a man in her life.

"Face it, Caryn," Sherisse said, watching the waiter

place their drinks in front of them. "You're a classic overachiever. If you had to spend your days getting on the subway, going downtown to spend eight hours in an office, and then jump back on the subway to head home, that life would drive you insane. Monotony. Same old, same old. Routine. Those words are nowhere in your vocabulary. Globetrotting, secret meetings with government officials, sitting in rooms with some of the most influential businessmen in the world? Those are the very things that give you life."

"I hear you, Sherisse," Caryn said thoughtfully. "The question is—what do you do when the deals, cities and players all start looking alike?"

Sherisse paused. It was hometown vacations like this that allowed Caryn to regroup and head back to her hectic lifestyle. She always followed that same pattern. This time, there was a sense of longing that hadn't been there before. "This vacation is exactly what you need to rejuvenate. You'll get some rest, spend time with your family and catch up with friends. You'll get connected to your world again so that you can go back to work fully refreshed."

"What I'd like to do is get connected to a man," Caryn said, breaking into a broad smile and releasing some of the tension that had built up in her shoulders and neck as she thought about her career.

"Girl, you and me both," Sherisse said.

Since she was no longer with Barry, Caryn figured her dry spell could be just as long as hers. "How long has it been since you've been *connected?*"

Sherisse glanced around as if she was about to reveal a well-kept secret. Leaning forward, she barely spoke above a whisper. "Let's just say I haven't been plugged in for over a year."

"You're doing better than me," Caryn said, thinking of her lack of time to foster any type of relationship with a man—physical or emotional. "The closest I've come is this guy in my building—Ronald Green. Our paths have crossed a few times and we've done a couple of dinners. He's successful, single and travels just as much as I do."

"Sounds like there could be some potential. The two of you have some things in common."

"I know," Caryn said, thinking about the similarities in their lifestyles. They both had hectic schedules and made their career a top priority. "But the truth is, nothing about him excites me."

"But he sounds wonderful."

"Don't get me wrong," Caryn said. "He's a great catch, I'm just not sure I want him on my hook."

"Maybe you could hook him long enough to get *connected!*" Sherisse said, a mischievous grin on her face.

"You are so bad," Caryn said. "What I'd really like to do is get connected with that fine doctor."

Buttering bread, Sherisse's hand froze. "Doctor who?" The sinking feeling in her stomach indicated she already knew the answer.

"I'm not talking about the one with the wedding ring or the boyish face," Caryn said, though both were easy on the eyes. "I'm talking about the one with that killer smile and sexy body."

Leaning back in her chair, Sherisse took a big bite of her bread and chewed slowly. When her mouth was empty, she took another bite, rolling her eyes in the process.

"What?" Caryn asked when she got no response.

Narrowing her eyes, Sherisse swallowed the last of her bread and took a sip from her glass. Taking her time, she set the glass back down and crossed her arms at her chest. "You know what."

"Okay, Okay," Caryn said, remembering her brief encounter with Will. "I will admit that he had playa written all over him."

"And?" Sherisse prompted.

"The comment you made about him seeing lots of women says that he's probably a serial dater."

"And?"

It wasn't hard to figure out what Sherisse was trying to do and Caryn didn't find it that difficult to get an idea of the type of guy she was talking about. His flirty comments, easy, confident demeanor and that kiss on the hand were dead giveaways. "He's probably more interested in the body than the mind and the soul."

Satisfied that Caryn had an accurate picture of her business partner, Sherisse relaxed in her chair and resumed eating her bread. "Trust me when I tell you, Dr. William Proctor is the last person you would *ever* want to get involved with. His long-term relationship record is nonexistent."

Caryn appreciated the heads-up and the warning she heard in Sherisse's voice. There was just one thing she didn't think Sherisse understood. Her life didn't allow for relationships—long-term or short-term. "Who said anything about a relationship—I'm talking about getting *connected*."

The waiter set salads in front of each of them and neither wasted any time digging in.

"Be serious," Sherisse said between bites. "The idea of you dealing with him makes my skin crawl. I could tell you stories that would make your eyes pop and your mouth drop open."

Caryn didn't doubt that for one minute. He'd never denied being a heartbreaker. "I am serious."

Pulling her BlackBerry out of her purse, she opened her calendar for the next several months. "Things are tough for me in the dating world. Look at this."

Sherisse didn't need a close-up view to know what it looked like. Full of meetings, travel plans and conference calls, it was tough on Caryn.

"I have zero time for relationships."

Sherisse sympathized with her situation but couldn't subject her to the crazy dating world of William Proctor. Softening her voice, she put her fork down. "I hear you, Caryn. I really do. But you have to trust me on this one. Will is nowhere near the answer to your dating dilemma. He has this thing called 'The Speech.'"

"The what?" Caryn asked, intrigued.

"Oh, you're gonna love this," she said, hoping that after Caryn heard the details, the subject of Will would be dropped once and for all.

Caryn sat back and watched her friend physically transform. Sherisse cleared her throat, sat ramrod straight in her chair, lowered her voice and drew her eyes in so tight they almost closed. Pointing her finger at Caryn, her voice came out deep and harsh.

"Now, you listen to me, little lady. I'm very attracted to you, Caryn. You're pretty, intelligent, full of grace and style. Any man would be proud to have you in his life. A man would jump at the privilege of being your husband. Unfortunately, that man won't be me.

"I'm a successful doctor. I'm good looking. I will treat you like a queen. *But,* I'm not looking for a serious relationship. As a matter of fact, I'm not interested in any type of relationship. All I want to do enjoy each other's company. Share some memorable dates. Anything beyond that isn't possible. If you dare to try to make it something more, this relationship will be terminated immediately. Any questions?"

Caryn laughed at her friend's attempt at the manly words and gestures. "Sounds like he's arrogant, egotistical, overconfident and big-headed."

"Oh, he's all that and more," Sherisse said, relieved that her friend was starting to see what a grave mistake it would be to get involved with Will. "It's a good thing he's a gifted doctor, otherwise, he'd be a definite lost cause."

"Does he have the goods to back it up?"

Sherisse recalled a few conversations with Will and some of the women he'd dated. He had the wooing stage down pat. "Oh, yes. He's flowers, gifts, candy and romantic dates 24/7. Just don't get used to it, because the minute you start to have real feelings for him, he'll drop you like a hot potato."

"Sounds good to me," Caryn said, trying to remember the last time she'd been treated so well by a man.

"What sounds good?" Sherisse said, wondering if Caryn had heard anything she'd just said in the last five minutes.

"Flowers. Candy. Romantic dates. It sounds good to deal with someone who understands the art of dating."

"Maybe I wasn't clear," Sherisse said, not sure why Caryn was only focusing on the latter part of her description of Will.

"You were," Caryn said, "but I don't think that speech sounds too bad."

"Okay," Sherisse said, slowly trying to find any reason to agree with her. She came up empty. "I'm revoking your membership in the sistas' club."

"Hear me out," Caryn said

"Now *this* I got to hear."

Caryn wasn't naive enough to believe that her point of view would make sense to most of the female population, but many women were not in her situation. For them, jobs were stationary or travel was limited. They had the chance to become entrenched in their community. They could join churches, keep in touch with sorority sisters and have some consistency in their dating life. "I've been on a whirlwind for years, wearing three watches set to different time zones to stay on top of my meetings, conference calls and travel arrangements.

"I spend my days poring over numbers and hard-line negotiating with people I sometimes can't understand—working with one, two and sometimes three translators. I've attempted to form relationships with men, and I have failed miserably. Every time I meet someone, we're both so busy trying to figure out how we can make our relationship work that we spend all our time *discussing* it instead of *having* one."

Sherisse would offer no argument with her. Between

her medical training, her residency and working her butt off to build a successful practice, her time for developing relationships was limited, as well. Still, did that dictate they had to resort to desperate measures—because dealing with Will had desperation written all over it. "I'm waiting for you to come to the part where that speech didn't sound too bad."

"I'm only going to be in town for a month. After that, I'm off to Japan and Paris," she said, feeling the slight muscle pull in her neck at the thought of her upcoming schedule. "I can pretty much cancel out meeting my Prince Charming, falling in love and figuring out a way to make it work between now and the time I leave."

"So you'd rather get involved with someone like Will?" Sherisse asked. "There are a million guys in this city. Why him?"

"I just want to have some fun," Caryn said, getting excited just thinking about it. "Go on a couple of dates. Indulge in fine restaurants. Catch up on some sights—new museum exhibits, a couple of shows. All without the cloud of a relationship hanging over my head. I've accepted the fact that this is my life for right now. All career. It's a choice I've made and I'm prepared to live with it. But for the next four weeks, I'm free of that part of my life."

"Okay," Sherisse said, relenting to her situation. "Let me introduce you to David. He's a pediatric surgeon who—"

"Oh, no," Caryn said, interrupting her before she got too far into the details. "The last thing I want is a blind date. I've been down that disastrous road before."

"Then what about Leon Graves?" Sherisse offered,

trying to hide the desperation in her voice. "You met him a couple of years ago at happy hour. I ran into him a couple of weeks ago. You could call him and—"

Caryn laughed at her attempt to steer her to any man besides Will. "Forget it, Sherisse."

"You're determined to date Will?" Sherisse said, holding on to one more ray of hope that this situation would magically go away.

"Is he seeing someone?"

"He's *always* seeing someone."

"You know what I mean…is he seeing anyone serious?"

"Haven't you been listening to me? There is no 'serious' with Will."

"Then the door is wide open."

"Are you sure?"

"I've met him, he's cute and I'm intrigued."

"Intrigued?"

Caryn remembered the hold his eyes had on her. His confidence had never wavered, even when Sherisse slammed him with a list of the women he'd been dating. Something about him drew her closer. "I know he's a player, Sherisse. A blind person could see that. That move of kissing my hand? Classic player move."

"So you understand what kind of jerk he is," Sherisse said, hoping to knock some common sense into that head.

"What I understand is that he's probably cocky and arrogant enough to deliver on everything he promises in that whacked speech of his."

"You're losing me."

"You said it yourself, he's a master at wining and

dining. Flowers, romance, the whole nine yards. Sherisse, I want," she said, stopping and leaning forward for emphasis. "No, I *need*—to be wined and dined."

As the food arrived, neither said a word. Finally, Sherisse spoke. "I'm still not convinced, Caryn."

Caryn appreciated that looking out for her best interests was at the heart of Sherisse's objections. If the roles were reversed, she'd no doubt do the same thing. But there comes a point where friendship ends and each person has to choose their own path. "I appreciate your concern, but I don't need your permission—or your approval."

Not offended by her statement, Sherisse nodded in understanding. "Don't say I didn't warn you."

Chapter 7

Wednesday morning, Will sat in Derrick's office sipping a cup of coffee. The strong flavor boosted his energy level after a fitful night of sleep. He'd gone out with Juanita Cooke last night, an attorney he met appearing in traffic court to fight a speeding ticket over six months ago. Meeting for lunch two days later, he'd presented her with his rules before the food was ordered. Somewhat taken aback and a little offended, she'd elected to have him finish his meal alone.

However, three days ago, she left him a message at work asking if he'd like to get together sometime. Initially, he had no intention of going out with her. He'd been content with his relationship with Alaina. But after they broke up, he decided to give Juanita a call.

They met at her favorite restaurant in Georgetown.

After ordering drinks, she told him that she may have been hasty in her decision not to continue to see him and that she wanted to get to know him better. Agreeing that he would like that as well, they placed their dinner orders.

Fifteen minutes later, Will wondered what had he gotten himself into. Their conversation was strained and awkward and the long windows of silence were only interrupted by bouts of small talk about the weather and the latest news item. Normally, Will could converse with anyone, and Juanita should not have been an exception. Seemingly charming and easy-going, she still couldn't hold his attention.

He'd walked her to her car, and neither had wanted to continue the night with a walk around the historic area, an after-dinner coffee or a dance at a nearby jazz club. They said good-night with a chaste kiss and neither mentioned getting together again.

When he arrived home, Apollo met him at the door, surprised that his master was home early again. Following his previous routine, Will changed his clothes and took the dog for a walk. Around eleven, Will climbed into bed and waited for sleep to come. An hour later, he was still awake.

He'd never had a problem sleeping and tried to decide what he could attribute this bout of insomnia to. There wasn't a major issue going on with a patient. He and Juanita had agreed that it was best if they didn't see each other again. There was only one reason that kept popping into his mind, but each time he fought to keep it at bay. Caryn Stewart.

The woman who boldly stood strong and stared him

directly in the eye, not waffling under his intense scrutiny. The woman who flirted and played along with him, all the while giving him an endearing smile. The woman who, according to his business partner, was off limits. Tossing and turning, he refused to link his sudden bout of insomnia to Caryn.

"What time do you think Sherisse will be in today?"

Derrick stopped writing at hearing the question. With four doctors, six nurses, two insurance coordinators and two receptionists, their practice was growing and extremely busy. It was all they could do to keep up with their own patients and appointments. Tracking another doctor's schedule was next to impossible.

"I think her first patient was scheduled for eleven," Derrick said, trying to recall what he saw at the front desk.

"Do you think she'll come in any earlier?" Will asked.

"Since when did you become so concerned with Sherisse's comings and goings?"

Shrugging nonchalantly, Will took another sip from his cup. "Just curious."

Derrick watched Will's foot tap on the floor and his eyes glance back toward the door, as if he was willing someone to walk through it. Derrick dropped his pen and closed the file. This display of nervous energy peaked Derrick's curiosity. Will was calm, cool and always collected; there weren't too many things that could knock him out of sorts.

Running through a mental list in his mind of the last few days, Derrick tried to pinpoint where this could be coming from. Could it be a patient? Every now and then, there could be a diagnosis that affected a doctor more than usual. But Will hadn't mentioned anyone in the last week or so. Next, he thought of Alaina. He'd broken up with her, but nothing seemed out of the ordinary when they'd talked yesterday. Then he remembered last night and everything clicked. He remembered Caryn. Now this conversation made perfect sense. "Yeah, right."

"I can't ask about the person I'm in business with?" he asked matter-of-factly.

"Not when you have ulterior motives."

Will stood and walked around the chair, staring at the picture of a mountain scene that hung on the wall. The idea that Derrick may have figured out what he had been trying to deny surprised him, and by having his back to his friend, he tried not to give it away by his expression. "I have no idea what you're talking about."

His face split into a wide grin and Derrick wondered who Will thought he was fooling. "Two words for you—Caryn Stewart."

The mention of her name put her picture in his head and sent an unwelcome surge of excitement through him and his heart thumped erratically. The strong reaction caught him by surprise and he quickly recovered. The effect of her name and face was a unique experience and Will wasn't sure he wanted to explore the implications. At least a half-dozen times since he'd met her she'd caused an internal stirring in him.

When he hooked his cuff links onto his sleeve as he'd dressed for his date last night, her sparkling eyes made an encore appearance. Feasting on succulent lobster with Juanita sitting directly across from him,

Caryn's full body came into view, including the way her hips filled out those jeans. As he turned out the light and lay in bed, there she was again. Smiling. Enticing. Beautiful.

Will remembered his fitful night's sleep and his attempts to blame it on incompatibility with Juanita. But the more he thought about it, the more he allowed himself to admit that there was something about Caryn that caused him to want to know her. "Well, since you bought her up, I probably will ask Sherisse about her."

Derrick heard the hesitation in his voice and quickly went into prevent mode. "You might as well give up on any plans you have that involve Caryn. You've lost your mind if you think Sherisse is going to let you get anywhere near her."

Turning to face him, Will shrugged. "Why not?"

The innocence with which he asked that question shocked Derrick and he tried to hold his sarcasm in check. Will spoke as if he really didn't have a clue as to what the answer might be. The look of innocence and confusion etched on Will's face wasn't fooling anyone—especially him. They had known each other too long. "Maybe the acoustics in this office are bad and you didn't hear what you said."

"I heard it, and still want to know why you think Sherisse would have a problem with this."

"You want your friend and business partner to set you up with her best friend—knowing that absolutely nothing will come out of the relationship?"

His approach to dating had never bothered Will before, but listening to Derrick, it was the first time the rules didn't totally sit right with him. Pushing the feeling aside, he remembered the value in dating by those rules. Things stayed simple. They didn't get complicated. It was a straightforward, effortless and easy way to approach dating. Confident, he turned to Derrick. "I would be completely up front with Caryn—it would be her choice."

Derrick pushed back in his chair and stood. Picking up a file from his desk, he strode around the desk and stopped in front of Will. Playfully, he hit his friend upside the head with the file. "This is the best friend of your business partner! We've all heard Sherisse's dating horror stories. Men who can't handle her success. Men that cheat. Men that lie. We've witnessed her funky attitude when a relationship she was in goes south. She's made it quite clear that she's looking for Mr. Right. I would bet money that her friend wants the same thing. Can you think of one good reason why she would set her up with someone who is certifiably Mr. Wrong?"

"You think I'm Mr. Wrong?" Will said.

"I do…Sherisse does…Jeff does…Alaina does…the woman who cried after you turned down her marriage proposal does…and how could we forget the woman who came busting up in your office about a year ago, cursing, screaming and yelling after she declared her love for you in front of her family and friends and you didn't return the sentiment."

Will physically cringed at the memory of that last incident. "I can't argue with any of that, but there are two sides to every story."

Derrick, much to his dismay, knew what words were going to be spoken next.

"It's the woman who chooses not to believe me

when I say I'm not interested in getting married and starting a family. It's the woman who gets the idea in her mind that she can change me. It's the woman that starts talking about this friend or that friend that's getting married and asking me to come to the weddings. It's the woman…not me."

"What's going on, fellas?"

Derrick turned to Jeff, who entered the office dressed in a pair of tan Dockers and a dark green shirt. "You'll love this. Will is trying to convince me that Sherisse should set him up with Caryn."

Instead of giving a response, Jeff's eyes widened in disbelief before the small smile turned into a big laugh. "That was the best joke I've heard in a long time."

"I'm glad to see I could provide your morning entertainment," Will said, wondering if he should be offended that no one supported him on this.

"Come on, man," Jeff said. "We're not talking about any woman—we're talking about Caryn. I know you just broke up with Alaina, but I'm sure there're at least three other women you could call right now. Let them put up with your BS and leave Caryn alone."

"BS?" Will said. "If anything, I should be applauded."

"Here we go," Jeff said, cutting his eyes to Derrick. The knowing exchange that passed between the two of them indicated that this wasn't the first time they were hearing this.

"How many men dog their woman out? How many men juggle two, three or more girlfriends at one time, yet tell each one of them that they are their one and only? How many men do you know sweet-talk a woman, filling their heads with the idea that they found their Mr. Right and want to make it official—only to sleep with the woman and never call her back?"

Jeff and Derrick couldn't argue with that. Each could name at least half a dozen guys without thinking too hard. That was the problem with Will's twisted philosophy. At times, it made perfect sense.

"I'm not like that," Will said proudly. "I let a woman know straight up what the deal is as soon as we start dating. I don't whisper and I don't stutter. I tell it to them loud and clear."

For that, both men had to give him credit. It could never be said that Will lied to or led a woman on.

"You know the problem with women?"

"Please, oh wise one," Jeff said with amusement. "Enlighten us."

"Yea," Derrick said, taking out his notepad and pretending to write.

"I believe I heard Maya Angelou say it best."

"We're listening," Jeff said, wondering how Will was going to take his dating theory and tie it into the renowned poet.

"When a person tells you who they are…believe them."

That afternoon, Sherisse waited outside Will's office as he finished talking with a patient. She'd tried a thousand different ways to discourage Caryn from getting involved with Will, but her friend wasn't interested in heeding any sisterly advice. Once Caryn got Sherisse to admit that Will had a knack for making a woman feel special, she became more convinced that she could take pleasure in spending time with him.

When Caryn asked for his phone number, Sherisse volunteered to give Will Caryn's number. She told Caryn that even though she didn't think he would mind, she wanted to get his permission first. However, the truth was that Sherisse wanted a chance to talk to him before the two of them got together.

"Your HDL count is looking much better, Mr. Bearson. Keep watching that diet and exercising. Your cholesterol levels will keep declining."

"Thanks, Dr. Proctor."

Will motioned the man toward the receptionist area before he noticed Sherisse. Motioning for her to enter his office, he gave her a pensive look. "Just the person I've been waiting for."

Sherisse didn't like the sound of that. Over the years, she'd come to know her partners pretty well. Their likes, dislikes, moods and attitudes. She could usually tell when something was about a patient, a business matter, whether something was going on in their personal life or if they wanted a favor. This tone had favor written all over it. It was a signal to put her guard up.

Standing behind his desk, Will noticed that she didn't follow him. Turning up the charm, he pointed to a chair. "Come on in, Sherisse. Have a seat. This won't take long."

Shutting the door behind her, she chose to stand. She was dressed in a brown skirt and a short-sleeve cashmere sweater; her hair had been pulled back into a loose ponytail. With her large eyes, curvy body and friendly bedside manner, her sweetness appealed to the staff and patients. Except for today. Today, there was nothing congenial about her. She was all business. "You wanted to see me…here I am."

"How has your day been so far?"

Sherisse wasn't in the mood to pretend that this was a run-of-the-mill conversation. Rarely did he call her into his office to shoot the breeze. Instead of playing along, she waved off his question and rolled her eyes heavenward. "Cut the crap, Will, and get to the point of this conversation…Caryn."

He appreciated her directness because he'd never been one to play coy when it came to women. Obliging her request, he took a seat and shrugged. "It's simple. I want to get to know more about her."

She may not be able to tell Caryn who she can or cannot date, but Sherisse was determined to get her opinion heard. "By that, I take it you mean whether she would be interested in going out with you—and more specifically, someone *like* you."

Over the years, Sherisse had met some of his girl-friends and didn't have an opinion either way. What went on in his personal life was his business. But that was before his personal business involved her best friend. The disapproval in her voice came through loud and clear. "I'm a direct guy—but you already know that. I'm not into playing games or beating around the bush. When I meet a woman, I have no problem assert-ing my interest. I don't need a middleman. In this situa-tion, I wanted to let you know my intentions."

"Which are?" she asked hopefully. Not that she thought a zebra could change his stripes overnight, but if he was willing to open himself up to the possibility of developing a real relationship, then hooking the two of them up might not be such a bad idea.

"The same as always."

"So, in other words, you're going to treat her like crap."

"Sherisse, you're overreacting," Will said. "I know how to treat a lady. I would never treat Caryn—or any woman—like that. All I'm going to do is see if she wants to go out."

Will was right and she knew it. Believing her actions were justified didn't change the situation. If both of them were determined to hook up, all that was left to do was hand over Caryn's number and step out of it. They were both adults and didn't need a babysitter for their relationship.

Fingering the business card in her pocket, she was out of stall tactics. She'd talked to Caryn and now Will. Pulling out the piece of paper, she tossed it on his desk. "She's in town for four weeks and staying at her parents' house. You can reach her on her cell."

Will picked up the card and stared at it for several seconds. Lifting his eyes to hers, it took a moment to figure out what had just happened. "You weren't just passing by my office, you were waiting for me. You were waiting to give me this. Why?"

"For someone unknown reason, Caryn expressed an interest in you."

"Really?" The idea that Caryn had shared this with Sherisse and passed on her number told Will something else about her. She wasn't afraid to go after something she wanted—and that impressed him. From the little he knew about her work, he would guess that she had to be aggressive and insistent when needed. He liked a woman who wasn't afraid to make a move. Turning the card over and over in his hand, there was a flutter inside his stomach and for a second, he felt nervous about calling her.

Sherisse watched Will's face and for a quick moment, she thought she saw a hint of anxiety. The look of victory she expected to get didn't show up. Instead, there was surprise, followed by confidence, then ultimately apprehension. In a flash, it was gone and Sherisse wondered if her eyes were playing tricks on her. "Believe me. I did everything I could to convince my friend to stay as far away from you as possible."

"Should I be insulted?" he said, committing the ten digits to memory.

"Yes…but I know you aren't."

Will stared at his partner for a moment and took some time to think about the situation from her perspective. Placing the card on the desk, he softened his voice and exhaled. "She doesn't have to play by my rules if she doesn't want to."

She threw her hands up in resignation. This was the one part about Caryn she didn't understand. "That's just it. I told her all about 'The Speech' and your stupid rules."

Will thought of all the times he'd said the words to women. They flowed from his lips with ease. However, instead of feeling elated that she'd given Caryn a heads-up, a strange feeling appeared—disappointment. As with his earlier bout of unexplained feelings, he pushed this aside, as well. "Then there shouldn't be any problem."

Standing, she decided this conversation was over. "No, there shouldn't. But here's fair warning. If there is a problem...and my friend gets hurt, you'll be the one needing medical attention."

Chapter 8

Caryn lazily stretched her arms above her head and yawned loudly. Turning over, she glanced at the clock and blinked twice. The time was three minutes after seven in the morning. She and Sherisse closed down the restaurant and Caryn didn't crawl into bed until almost 2:00 a.m. Sleeping had been at the top of her list when she planned this time off, but it appeared as if her body wasn't going to participate. Her regular workdays had her up before six, in the gym soon after and ready for her first meeting around eight-thirty.

Instead of jumping up right away, she decided to lie around and do nothing. It was such a rarity in her life, she relished the simple pleasure. She lived by her calendar and felt rushed just about every day. If it wasn't a meeting, it was a conference call. If she wasn't on a plane, she was heading to the airport. Even her so-called vacations seemed to mirror her work life.

Technology made it easy to have a mobile office. With a laptop, BlackBerry, e-mail and fax machines, working vacations had become her norm. She could recall lying on the beach and taking calls, or shopping with her mother and checking voice mail. There were a few times when she would lie back and watch a good movie, only to pull out files and crunch some numbers. This vacation, she finally put her foot down.

Jeremy wasn't that happy about his superstar taking a month off. That was considered high treason. How dare someone take time for themselves when the company needed them so much? She held firm in her request to limit her e-mail and calls. Only after she told him how much she needed this time off and that she would come back refreshed and reenergized did he finally relent. The last thing either of them wanted was for her to burn out.

From the moment she came on board, everyone in the company knew that she was something special. Smart. Intuitive. Savvy. Shrewd. Insightful. She had a special gift for seeing the details and the big picture of any negotiation and found a way to pull it all together. Handpicked early in her career, she got the mentoring, opportunities and advances that propelled her to the top of the company. On the fast track, Caryn lived, breathed and slept one goal: Career success.

Everything else fell by the wayside. The friendships. The husband. The children. They were all put on hold so that she could establish herself professionally. Over the years, she'd heard all the hoopla over women having

in luxury cars wearing the latest designer fashions. When Bernard decided that he wanted more, that's when Caryn had to put on the brakes. The complaints about her travel. The comments about her late nights at the office. The complaining that he wasn't a priority in her life. The night he put an ultimatum on the table was the night she called it quits. How dare he ask her to choose between her job and him? Didn't he know enough about her that he would be on the losing end of that deal?

That's why she decided to stop searching for her Prince Charming. No matter how much they admire your drive, cheer for your success or root for you to attain all your goals, they eventually want you to give something up for them. That was a deal Caryn was unwilling to make. But it wasn't always easy to maintain that position, so she constantly gave herself pep talks.

Stop fretting over dates for Valentine's Day. Stop feeling guilty for missed birthdays. Stop worrying about the length of time between calls with friends. It was the only way she could continue at the pace she'd set for herself. In terms of her love life, the most she could hope for was a decent night out with a colleague who didn't expect anything from her because he understood her lifestyle. When her plan was completed, only then would she focus on her personal life.

But every now and then she allowed herself a moment to think about how nice it would be to have a man around. A companion. A good conversationalist. A good listener. And definitely good in bed.

Girl, don't you go down that road!

Overheating in the bath the other night, she didn't

want to deal with those cravings again. Especially if there was no man in sight to remedy the situation. That's when she thought of Will.

Seductive eyes. Playful smile. Powerful stance. Undeniable charm. She'd been in his presence for only a few short moments, but his impact was indisputable. Not so much because of his overwhelming physical presence, but because of that air of confidence that surrounded him that bordered on arrogance.

He'd commanded attention from her, overshadowing the other two men. Looking her directly in the eye and invading her personal space was bold and audacious. For many women, that may not be an attractive feature. But for Caryn, it was a must-have.

To reach any level of success, a person not only had to have the knowledge but also the guts to apply that knowledge to rise above those comfortable with mediocrity. Over her career, she had met many women who had the smarts, the know-how and the formal education to take their career by the horns and make it anything they wanted. But most of them didn't. Most of them got to a level of midmanagement or director and stalled. Not because they lacked the skills to move to the top, but because they lacked the nerve.

It takes guts not to worry about what people think or say about you. It takes guts to sit in a meeting and stand your ground when no one else is on your side. It takes guts to take on a new program and let the success or failure of that program rest firmly on your shoulders. It takes guts to sit in a roomful of men and demand what is rightfully deserved. It takes guts to be extraordinary. That's the vibe she got from Will. She would bet money that Will had the nerve and the guts to go after—and probably get—anything he wanted, because he was that good.

Turning over, Caryn let her mind run a little free in thinking about Will and the one area she would bet money that he was excellent at. Just the thought of it had her body tingling and her temperature rising. Lying in bed, she could only imagine the things that he could do to her with those strong hands, that athletic body and that smart mouth. Pushing the covers back, she decided to get up. No use getting worked up when there was nothing she could do about it.

Caryn chuckled at the expression on Sherisse's face when she told her to pass her number to him. Undeterred by the revelation of the speech he gives to women and his attitude about commitment, Caryn thought it could be the perfect arrangement. Believing she was setting Caryn up with some monster that would chew her up and spit her out, Sherisse tried to change her mind for almost half an hour. But Caryn wasn't worried. She was tough, strong and handled herself in all types of situations. Dr. William Proctor wouldn't be a problem.

"Look who decided to finally join the rest of the world."

Caryn smiled at her mother as she entered the kitchen. Having showered and dressed hours ago, Caryn had spent time on her laptop. Close to two-thirty in the afternoon, she decided to finally shut it down and come out of her room. "I'm on vacation. I make my own schedule."

Bonnie Stewart folded the newspaper she'd been reading and set it aside. Standing, she walked over to the refrigerator, glad to see her only child looking vibrant and refreshed. It was a definite improvement from yesterday.

When they met her at the airport, she almost didn't recognize Caryn. The circles around the eyes, her frame at least two sizes smaller than the last time they saw each other and the small carry-on was explained by the fact the she was too tired to pack. She thought it easier to buy whatever she needed.

Bonnie and Lloyd shared many late-night talks about their only child. How could someone survive happily working around the clock? Surrounded by associates and clients all day, when could she ever do anything for herself? Periodically, they would corner Caryn and work to convince her to slow things down. To smell the roses. Each time, they were met with the same answer.

I'll slow down—I promise. After I reach my goals.

Bonnie couldn't understand why Caryn was so driven, determined to focus at least another three to five years on her career. She only hoped that it wouldn't cost her the truly important things. "Your father and I have already eaten, but I'd be glad to fix you something."

Caryn waved off the offer and guided her mother back to her seat. At fifty-nine, Bonnie had done her share of cooking over the years. Her mother prepared all their meals growing up. Bonnie was a mother that believed in family dinners. Caryn recalled a childhood where everyone gathered around the table in the evening.

The food was nothing fancy, but it was homemade and full of love. Around six-thirty each evening, they all sat down and talked about their day. It was where her father, a city maintenance worker, complained about his boss not listening to his ideas. It was where her mother, a legal secretary, talked about the interesting cases her boss was working on. It was also the place where Caryn got rewarded for her good grades, grounded for breaking curfew as a teenager and it was where she told them she was moving to Boston to go to college.

She'd never forget the look on her parents' faces when she made the decision to take the scholarship from Boston University. Neither liked the idea of her being away from home, and Caryn made all kinds of promises to get them to say yes—including a promise to come home on all holidays and summer breaks. They didn't believe she would keep those promises, but Bonnie and Lloyd put on a brave front and sent their little girl out into the world.

After graduation, her parents didn't expect her to move back home, but neither did they expect her to disappear from their lives. With her career on the fast track, she was working most weekends and she hadn't seen a real vacation in years. Visits home were few and far between and the longer she stayed away, the less her parents asked her to come home. Bonnie stopped asking her to come home because she didn't want to make her daughter feel guilty.

The next month would be the most time she'd spent at home in eight years. The last thing Caryn would have her mother do was wait on her. "Don't worry about me. I'll fix myself something."

Bonnie sat back down and watched her daughter open the refrigerator and chuckled at the sight. "Since when do you know how to fix anything?"

It was one of the traits that Caryn did not pick up over the years. Living in the dorm all four years of college, she usually ate in the food court or cafeteria. When she entered grad school, she was on an accelerated program, barely finding enough time to eat, so she definitely didn't carve out any time to cook. But now that she was home and taking things slow, she decided to give the kitchen a little attention. "I cook!"

"Pouring milk over a bowl of cereal and pushing more than two buttons on the microwave is not cooking," Bonnie said, thinking of the limited time her daughter told her she had to spend in the kitchen. Enjoying cooking and the concept of eating dinner as a family, Bonnie tried to pass that on to Caryn. But her efforts were in vain.

As a little girl, she helped Caryn bake cookies from scratch, and they came out flat and dry. When Caryn was a teenager, she tried at least five times to fry chicken. If the outside was a crispy brown, the inside was bloody red. If the inside was juicy and tender, the outside was burnt to a crisp. Finally, before she left for Boston, Caryn decided to make the final family meal.

Bonnie and Lloyd had tried to keep a straight face as they chewed through the tough Cornish hens. They both cut their eyes at each other as they forced their forks through the lumps in the mashed potatoes, and Caryn's dad didn't attempt one forkful of the green stuff. He couldn't tell whether it was peas, broccoli or string beans. Ten minutes into the meal, Caryn was the first to break. Declaring the meal a disaster, she accepted her marginal culinary skills and all three went out to eat.

"You would think by now I'd be able to at least bake chicken or make spaghetti," Caryn said, pulling lettuce, tomatoes and leftover grilled chicken out of the refrigerator. "At least I can't mess up a sandwich."

"No, you can't." Laughing along with her daughter, Bonnie got up to help her. She could never sit by idly while someone else was in her kitchen. Opening the cabinet, she got a glass to fill it with iced tea and then went to the pantry to retrieve some chips. "Hopefully, we'll find some time to work on your culinary proficiency before you leave. How are you ever going to get a husband if you don't learn your way around a kitchen?"

The last question stopped Caryn in her tracks. Bonnie Stewart had the cunning ability to take any conversation and reduce it to the fact that she didn't have a husband. Caryn could mention that she was putting her car in the shop and her mother would respond that a husband could take care of those things for her. In the winter, they would be talking about how much snow they thought would fall and Bonnie would suggest that a husband could help shovel the walkway and driveway. Bonnie huffed and puffed when Caryn reminded her she lived in a condo. "First of all, Mother…"

"Uh-oh, here we go," Bonnie said, grabbing fruit salad and putting some in a bowl. "You called me Mother instead of Mom."

Caryn ignored her mockery. "The reason I am husbandless has nothing to do with the fact that I'm lacking in the cooking department."

"That may be the case, but when you meet someone, how do you expect to hold on to him if you're feeding him microwave popcorn all the time?"

Her mother was definitely a product of old-school thinking. *The women's job was to cook for her man. The way to a man's heart is through his stomach. Knowing how to take care of a home was the most important thing a woman could learn.* She'd heard words and phrases like that her entire life. But Caryn didn't buy into that train of thought. As a matter of fact, she was hoping to find a man who could do all these things for her. Suddenly, a picture of Will popped into her head and he was wearing nothing but an apron. Maybe they could cook something up that had nothing to do with food.

Snapping back to reality, Caryn added a little mustard to her bread. "Married or not, the last place I'm going to spend most of my time is in the kitchen. If the man in my life wants a good meal, he'll have two choices. Fix it himself or dial our favorite restaurant to deliver."

There was nothing surprising about her response. Bonnie had heard it all before. "How will you know whether he cooks or orders out? You'll be gallivanting around the globe closing one deal after another. Is he going to be comfortable with you gone for weeks at a time? And don't get me started on your poor children. Will they know their mother? Will they rebel against you always being on the road? Can they adjust to spending most of their time with their father? Unless, of course, he has a similar career. Maybe he won't be around, either. What if the children—"

"Please, mom," Caryn said, hoping to snap her out of her frenzy. It was the same thing each time they got together. Caryn remaining blasé about her future and her mother practically giving herself a heart attack with all the worrying and concerns she had about her daughter's personal life. "I can only defend myself against one imaginary person at a time. Why don't we stick to my invisible husband before moving on to the yet-to-be-born children?"

Hearing the playfulness in her daughter's voice took the tension out of the conversation, but it didn't change the point that Bonnie wanted to make. "I managed to have a career, a husband and you—but making it work had to be a priority."

"That's because us mere mortals didn't have your superpowers," Caryn said, biting into her bread.

Bonnie had a reply on her lips, but they were interrupted.

"Well, if it isn't my two favorite ladies."

"Your timing couldn't be better," Caryn said, giving her mother a wink as she walked across the kitchen floor to give her father a hug. "I'm fixing me something to eat. Do you want anything?"

Lloyd Stewart cut his eyes at his wife before politely declining. "I'm not in the mood for anything cold or microwaved."

Giving her father a lighthearted punch in the arm, Caryn defended her position. "You guys can tease me all you want, but one day I'm going to prove all of you wrong and cook the best meal you've ever had."

"Sure you will, sweetie," Lloyd said, turning to his wife and scrunching up his face.

"I saw that," Caryn said, popping a few chips into her mouth.

Lloyd pulled a glass out of the cabinet. "I'd be honored to have you cook for us. Just let me know which night so I can be sure to make reservations at a nice restaurant."

Caryn watched him fill his glass with water and noticed the pills in his hand. Placing both tablets in his mouth, he swallowed them quickly.

"Is everything okay, Dad?"

"Oh, sure, honey," he said, putting the empty glass in the sink. "A little arthritis. Nothing these two pain pills can't take care of."

Caryn's eyes narrowed in skepticism. As with many girls, her father was her hero. Tall with broad shoulders, he was strong, hardworking, and Caryn could never recall a time when he was sick. Now, since he was almost sixty, Caryn could understand if there were a few aches and pains here and there. But could it be something more serious? She hated to admit it, but for the past ten years, she'd only been a blur to her parents. In and out of their lives a few weekends and short holidays, she had no idea what could be going on with them. "Are you sure?"

Giving her a comforting kiss on the cheek, her father reassured her with a quick hug. "I'm fine."

Turning to Bonnie, he said, "I'm going to make a run to Home Depot to replace the front lights."

After he left, Caryn turned to her mother looking for confirmation of her father's words. Was it just arthritis? Should she be worried?

Bonnie could read the unasked questions in her eyes,

along with the distress and fear. "He *says* it's nothing to worry about."

Caryn didn't like the sound of that. Lloyd was a hard worker and full of pride. He'd worked for the city in their maintenance department for thirty years. Physical labor had always been a part of his life. The idea that he was slowing down was natural, but for Caryn it caught her off guard.

"What do you say?"

"I say he needs to get that chip off his shoulder."

Bonnie didn't have to explain to Caryn what that meant. Lloyd was a man full of pride—sometimes foolish. Wouldn't read the instructions that came with any electronics. Would never admit to being lost. Had a tendency to try to figure things out instead of asking for help. "What does the doctor say?"

"That's the million-dollar question."

"Meaning?"

"Meaning that man has been self-diagnosing himself for years."

With a slight roll in her eyes and an exasperated sigh, her mother's frustration was clear. Caryn could tell this wasn't the first time this conversation had come up. "Go on."

"I've tried to tell him that he knows how to build things and fix things. Everything except his body. I've reminded him many times that he didn't graduate from medical school," Bonnie said, thinking of the numerous occasions over the past few years she'd nudged him to make a doctor's appointment. "Unfortunately, to get him to a doctor is like trying to put a square peg in a circle. Impossible."

Caryn read reports over the years about men's discomfort with going to the doctor, often putting off appointments until the condition worsens. "Do you think it's something serious?"

"He calls it old-age aches and pains," Bonnie said, her voice laced with worry. "But at his age, I don't want him to take anything for granted. I was hoping you could talk to him."

"If he won't listen to you, what makes you think he'll listen to me?" Caryn said, thinking her father wouldn't give her concern the time of day.

Bonnie stood and started to clear the dishes. "He calls it arthritis, but he's moving slower and slower and getting more and more stubborn. Each time I bring up the subject, he digs his heels in deeper, telling me I worry too much and like to make mountains out of molehills. Maybe you could talk to Sherisse?"

Helping with the cleanup, Caryn thought about her mother's request. How could she say no? "I'll see what I can do."

Chapter 9

William shut the door and hung up his white coat. Nonstop since his first patient at eight-thirty, it was now close to five o'clock. Plopping into his chair, he relished one of the few quiet moments of the day. He always took this time of day to regroup and recharge for whatever plans he had for the evening. Tonight was no different.

His social calendar rarely found an empty spot. Filled with events surrounding his professional associations, his work with the community, his involvement with his fraternity and all the general happenings in and around the nation's capital, he usually had his choice of when and where to go.

An invitation to a medical-society fund-raiser for Children's Hospital sat on the corner of his desk. An invite sat in his e-mail in-box offering free drinks at the opening of a new restaurant. He'd retrieved a voice mail from Leanna about an hour ago asking if he was available to escort her to a birthday party. Will contemplated what to do, but for the first time in a long time none of his options were appealing. He thought of the reason why. Caryn Stewart.

On three separate occasions, he came to his office with the intention of calling Caryn. Every single time, he headed back out to his patients having punched in no more than three numbers. The last time he tried the call, he slammed the headset into the receiver in frustration. Since when had he become so gun-shy when it came to going after a woman?

From the first number he pulled from Patricia Cords in the eighth grade, up until he met Sylvia Warner two weeks ago, he never had a problem making the first move. Caryn Stewart came along and challenged that record. What was it about her that had him twisted?

Maybe it was all the warnings from Derrick, Jeff and especially Sherisse. All three provided an abundance of reasons not to start anything with her. They outlined all the possible consequences of getting involved, including upsetting the partnership. Or maybe it was the fact that Caryn and Sherisse were good friends.

Every move that the two of them would make would, no doubt, be communicated to Sherisse. That's what a typical girlfriend relationship included—dating gossip. Could he survive being under a microscope? Everyday living would be scrutinized, analyzed and maybe criticized by Sherisse. And speaking of Sherisse. Will didn't know her to make idle threats. If he messed things up with Caryn in any way, he believed Sherisse would do exactly as she said. Would it really be worth it to go out with Caryn?

Taking a seat, he noticed the flashing light and punched in his password for voice mail. The first two were business related, but the third took him by surprise.

"Will, it's Nicole. We met about four months ago at the gym. I was wondering if we could get together sometime. Call me."

Grabbing a pen, he wrote down the number on his day planner and discarded the message. He'd noticed Nicole a couple of times when he worked out. After exchanging numbers, they met one evening for drinks. Of course, he gave her The Speech and she immediately thought he had lost his mind. He hadn't heard from her since—until this message. This could be the answer he was looking for. It would be just as easy to give Nicole a call back and leave Caryn alone. Picking up the phone, he dialed Nicole. Before the phone could ring, he hung up.

What is wrong with you?

Picking up the phone again, he stared at Caryn's number. Hesitating, he ran a few greetings in his mind before he stopped himself. "I'm acting like I've never done this before."

The empty office didn't answer and the quietness gave him more time to think. Should he ask her out for dinner? Offer to let her choose an activity? Would she prefer crowds or something off the beaten path? The questions swirled in his head and he closed his eyes, wondering why the teenager in him had made a sudden appearance.

The knock at the door saved him from having to explore the answer to that question.

"Come in."

"Natalie's working late and Jeff and I are headed out to grab some dinner," Derrick said. "You in?"

"Ah, yeah—I mean no," he said, replacing the receiver.

"Everything okay?" Derrick said, noticing the look of bewilderment. "You look as if you got some bad news."

"Shut the door."

Derrick stepped inside and frowned at the seriousness of his tone. "Is it a patient?"

"I was about to call Caryn and wondered if…"

Derrick raised his brow at the revelation and pondered Will's sanity. "Caryn—Sherisse's Caryn?"

"Yes," Will answered, his voice harsh and edgy.

Over the years, Derrick had questioned Will's choices in how he handled his relationships. The ability to break if off with a woman without a backward glance could be cold and unfeeling. Could he treat Caryn the same way? "Let it go, Will."

"What is that supposed to mean?" Will said, staring down at the number again. At this point, he could close his eyes and recite it by heart. "Since when have you ever cared about who I call?"

"Let me break it down for you," Derrick said, counting off his points with his fingers. "You are in business with Sherisse. Caryn and Sherisse are friends. Your relationships never last. You can stand here and tell me you don't see a problem with this?"

"Caryn is a grown woman. She can make her own

decisions. I'm sure she doesn't need approval from Sherisse, just as I don't need approval from you." The statement was made with an even tone.

"Why do this, Will?" Derrick said, thinking about the list of women Will could call at any given moment. "What happens to this partnership when this relationship goes bad? Sherisse will blame you. You'll blame Caryn. I don't think Jeff and I could take dealing with two partners on the warpath. Why start something that's doomed to fail?"

Will heard the words but refused to acknowledge that they were true. "What makes you think it will go bad?"

This time, all the frustration and worry left Derrick's voice and was replaced with relaxed shoulders and an easy smile. "You, me, hell, everybody we know can attest that your relationships *always* go bad."

"I don't think *bad* is the proper word," Will said. "Women break the rules. That's what happens to my relationships."

Regardless of the woman or the circumstances, Will was always able to detach himself from the failed relationships. In his mind, when a relationship fell apart, it wasn't because of anything he had done. "Explain it however you want, but it all equals the same thing. You and Caryn will eventually not be seeing each other."

"How can you be so sure?" Will asked.

"Because you won't commit to a woman," Derrick said, feeling as if he was stating the obvious. "Every woman you become involved with, sooner or later, will be looking for that commitment. Caryn will be no different."

Will sat forward and crossed his hands on the desk. For a moment, he didn't say a word. What Derrick explained was one hundred percent correct. When a woman could no longer abide by the rules, Will said "bye-bye." But things with Caryn could be different. "Don't worry, my man, the medical practice of Proctor, Cain, Copeland and Carrington will remain intact."

"The business isn't the only thing I'm concerned about. The four of us have a good vibe. Don't mess that up," Derrick said. "Pursuing the best friend of a business partner could get messy."

Derrick's last statement reminded Will of an important piece of information he had yet to share with him. "For your information, I'm not doing the pursuing."

"Excuse me?"

"That's right," Will said, feeling his confidence slide back in place. "Sherisse came to see me. Evidently, the attraction wasn't just on my part. Caryn asked her to pass me her contact info."

Narrowing his eyes and cocking his head to the side, Derrick stared at his friend suspiciously, wondering if he was telling the truth. "I don't believe you."

"Believe it, man," Will said, recalling his earlier conversation. "Sherisse sat in that same chair and handed over this."

Derrick took the business card, but still wanted to question Will's version of events. Sherisse made no secret that the last thing she wanted was Will to start something with Caryn. Why would she hand over her friend's phone number? Something wasn't quite adding up and he said so.

"I'm serious, Derrick. Evidently, I wasn't the only one who felt a connection."

Hearing those words, Derrick walked around the desk to his friend. Placing his hand on Will's forehead, he acknowledged that he didn't have a temperature. Next, he put his stethoscope on and attempted to press it against Will's chest.

Will slapped his hand away. "What is wrong with you, man?"

"Me?" Derrick said, taking a seat and hoping to talk some sense into that thick head. "The better question is, 'What's wrong with you?'"

When Will stood silent, Derrick continued, "Are you listening to yourself? Do you hear the words coming out of your mouth?"

"Get to the point, Derrick, because I'm getting tired of this conversation."

"I'm checking you out because you must be coming down with something," Derrick said. "Did you just say that you felt a *connection?*"

The final word was said with such astonishment and suspicion that Will raised his chin and frowned, obviously offended. If anyone listened to Derrick, they would get the impression that Will was unfeeling, cold and detached. That wasn't the case. If anything, he had a great ability to live in the moment. What he didn't have was the desire to create a relationship beyond those moments. "Is that so unbelievable?"

"Yes!" Derrick said. "To hear you say you felt attraction—yes. Lust—yes. But connection? That involves more than I've ever known you were willing to give. The closest connection you've ever had with a woman is deciding what to pick out for her from Victoria's Secret."

"I'm still waiting for your point."

"Fine, here it is. If this is going to end just like all of the rest, why start anything at all?"

"She's only in town for a few weeks. Her expectations can't be any different than mine."

Standing, Derrick gave up. They were talking in circles and this is where he got off. "I'm outta here. I'll see you tomorrow."

Alone again, Will ran his conversation with Derrick back through his mind. Maybe he was right. Too much was at stake to go on a date with Caryn. But Will realized it was a risk he was willing to take. With a burst of confidence, he picked up the phone and dialed. Voice mail.

"Hi, Caryn, it's Will. It was a pleasure meeting you the other day. I'd like to make good on my word to show you around the city. Give me a call."

"I thought you weren't going to work for the next few weeks?" Sherisse said.

Caryn sat in her parents' living room Thursday afternoon pecking away on her keyboard. She'd only been on vacation a couple of days and it appeared as if her team, and one of her deals, was falling apart.

Initially, she'd promised herself that she would leave her laptop and BlackBerry in Boston. But that was unrealistic for someone in her position. There were too many projects in various stages to cut herself off completely from the business world. As a compromise, she agreed with herself to only check in once a day, in the morning, for no longer than an hour. Unfortunately, it was after two o'clock in the afternoon and she'd been glued to the Internet for the last five hours. "I'm responding to this last e-mail and then I'm shutting down."

Sherisse wondered how many times she'd said those words today. Walking around the table, she pulled up a chair and sat beside her, not more than an inch between them.

Caryn stopped typing and turned to her. "What are you doing?"

"Making sure that this is really the last work thing you do today."

"I don't need a babysitter," Caryn said, already allowing the feeling of guilt to creep up in her. They should have left the house an hour ago.

"No, you don't," Sherisse confirmed. "What you need is a vacation—which I thought you were on."

Caryn hated to admit that her friend was right. The point of taking this time off was to keep her from burnout. She'd made a special point of updating her team, yet she spent her entire morning in communication with them. Her e-mail was on "out of office," providing another person to contact if the problem couldn't wait until she got back, but she responded anyway. Caryn suddenly stopped typing in midsentence. She closed out of Outlook and shut down her computer.

"Good choice," Sherisse said as she stood and reached for her purse. "I cleared my appointments this afternoon, so let's go eat. I'm starving."

Settled at their table in the small café, Sherisse waited until their orders were placed to pick up the conversation where they left off at her parents' house. "The first night you arrived, you checked your BlackBerry before we went to dinner. Last night, you were waiting on a fax and today, I arrive and you've got your laptop, BlackBerry and have files spread across the table. That doesn't sound like a vacation to me."

Caryn quickly averted her eyes and studied the different breads in the basket. The truth stared her in the face and she found it hard to face the music. She'd been working the past couple of days, and not only was Sherisse annoyed by it, her parents had given her several lectures. They had plans to spend time with her, to have the family over, but every time they tried to plan something, they were interrupted by a phone call or an e-mail.

The look of guilt encompassed her face and Sherisse sucked her teeth. "I knew it."

"What?"

"Don't try that innocent tone with me," she said. "You told me you were going to spend time shopping for your house and visiting new exhibits at the Smithsonian."

Breaking off a piece of corn bread, Caryn refused to look her friend in the eye.

"Something tells me you didn't do any of those things."

Shrugging, Caryn bit into the bread. "I have plenty of time to check those things off my list."

"Please tell me you haven't been glued to your computer since you've been here?" Sherisse said. "You can say what you want about having plenty of time, but one week of your vacation is quickly coming to an end. This time will be over before you know it and all you'll have to show for it is a roomful of upset family and friends."

"Oh, all right, all right. You caught me," Caryn said, waving her napkin in defeat. "Are you happy now? I admit it. I have been working more than I'd planned to. But I had no choice."

"No choice?" Sherisse asked. "Who is it that decides whether to answer the phone? Who is it that determines whether they are going to go into their e-mail? Who is it that has the power to say no?"

"I'm scheduled to go to Italy soon after I return to work. There are at least twenty things that must be done and—"

"And you passed on everything before you came," Sherisse reminded her. "You said it yourself, you need a break. My question is—why aren't you taking it?"

"I am," Caryn said. "I'm sitting her with you, aren't I?"

"Don't take credit for this. I forced you."

Her BlackBerry rang and Caryn didn't make a move to answer it.

When it stopped, Sherisse smiled. "It probably almost killed you to let that go to voice mail."

"I'll survive," she said, hoping it wasn't an emergency.

"What you need to do is turn it off and leave it at home."

"Not carry my BlackBerry?" The idea of being that completely disconnected from her office sounded good in theory, but now Sherisse wanted her to actually carry it out.

"I'll move in with your parents if I have to and make sure you're following these orders," she threatened.

"Not necessary," Caryn said, believing every word of that threat. "I promise. Very minimal work."

That was more than likely the best commitment Sherisse was going to get. "Now that you're really off the clock, what will you do tomorrow?"

"My mom's been after me to go shopping. I didn't bring nearly enough clothes."

"Be sure to go to Danielle's. A great boutique and the owner is a good friend of Natalie and Derrick's."

"I will," she said, getting excited at the thought of a long-overdue shopping spree. "Maybe we'll go into Georgetown. It's been ages since I've been there."

"That sounds like a plan."

"I'll also give Will a call," she said, thinking of the tall, chocolate man she'd pushed aside the last couple of days. "He left me two messages and I haven't gotten back to him yet."

A small smile curved at the tip of Sherisse's lips. "I heard."

The reaction was surprising considering Sherisse's opinion of him. "You sound amused. I thought you would launch into all the reasons why I should save my soul and stay far, far away from him."

"I'm torn," Sherisse admitted. "I'm not fond of him dating anyone I know, but it's been fun watching him around the office the last couple of days. The fact that you haven't called him back has him out of sorts."

Everyone around the office was whispering about the foul mood Will had been in the past few days. He played dumb whenever anyone asked him about it, but

Sherisse, Derrick and Jeff knew the real deal. He'd contacted Caryn and had yet to hear from her. First dates came easy for him and he never had to worry about getting a return phone call from a woman he just met. This was new territory for him and Sherisse was enjoying every minute of it.

Caryn laughed at the thought. "Oh, please. I'm sure the last thing that man is thinking about is getting a return call from me. His little black book is probably filled with women who keep him very occupied."

"You're right about that," Sherisse said, remembering the parade of women that had been out with him over the years.

Caryn took a sip of her iced tea to cover up her frown. She'd been so caught up with work, she hadn't had a chance to call him back, but each time his face appeared in her mind or his name came up, a powerful surge of intimate energy embraced her. Outside of the meeting at the office, she hadn't spent one moment with him. Where would this reaction be coming from?

"Caryn?"

Snapping back to the present, Caryn tried to remember what her friend was saying.

"I was talking about Natalie's party. Derrick's throwing her a birthday bash Saturday night."

Caryn remembered the invitation that had been extended to her. "Do you think she'll mind?"

"Of course not," Sherisse said with confidence. "Not to mention there'll be lots of single guys there."

"And Will—can I expect to see him?"

"I don't know why you're a glutton for punishment, but yes, Mr. Rules himself should be making an appearance."

"Then count me in."

Chapter 10

The stately home of Dr. Derrick Carrington and his wife, Natalie, was ablaze with lights when Sherisse pulled into the circular driveway. Handing her keys to the valet, it was clear by the sheer number of cars that the party was in full swing.

"I can't remember the last time I've been to a party that wasn't work related," Caryn said, pulling the shawl around her shoulders. She'd stayed true to her promise and checked in with her office only a couple of times. Instead, she'd spent yesterday with her parents. They'd gone into D.C. and pretended to be tourists instead of lifelong residents. After visiting the National Air and Space Museum and enjoying lunch at B. Smith's, they took a stroll around the Mall, walking from the reflecting pool to the Lincoln Memorial.

It was one of the most relaxing days she'd had in years. She found out that her father had become quite skilled at bowling, that her mother was thinking of volunteering at the elementary school a few blocks from their home and both of her parents brought up the conversation of her personal life—or lack of one. When she told them she was coming to this party this evening, they both were thrilled at the idea of Caryn meeting someone.

Today, she'd spent the afternoon at Danielle's with her mom. The wide variety of fashions and styles appealed to her and she tried on a stack of casual wear, business attire and cocktail outfits. When it came time to decide what she would wear tonight, she confused her mother with the amount of effort she was putting into the selection.

First there was the strapless black dress that accentuated her small chest and slim waist. Next, there was the dark green pantsuit with flare ankles and a cropped jacket with one button in the middle. Double-sided tape would be a necessity with this ensemble. Finally, there was a lavender silk dress with the wraparound halter-top bodice and flared skirt. The color blended with her complexion perfectly and once she added the earrings, shoes and bag, she felt like a million bucks.

Caryn hated to admit that she was doing something she hadn't done since her college days. Dressed with a man in mind. Each time she twirled in front of the mirror at the store, she wondered if Will would like it.

Sherisse hadn't done so badly herself in the dressing category, either. With her statuesque posture and curvy but slim body, the shimmering gold after-five dress made her look as if she'd stepped out of the pages of *InStyle* magazine.

Leading the way, Caryn followed Sherisse up the stairs that led to the front door. "I know we'll have a good time tonight. Natalie and Derrick are great people and you'll love their family and friends."

Caryn was only interested in meeting up with one of their friends—Will. She'd called him back yesterday, but he was with a patient. The funny thing about it was that she hadn't called him back for two days, but once she did, she couldn't wait to talk to him. The level of disappointment she felt was only slightly alleviated when she got home from shopping and had a message from him that said he couldn't wait to see her. "Then come on, girl…let's get this party started."

"What—or who—are you waiting for?" Derrick said, walking into the foyer. Almost eight o'clock, half of the one hundred guests had already arrived for the party. He'd lost track of Natalie fifteen minutes ago and was searching for her when he came across Will. "Have you been standing in this same spot since you arrived?"

"You're trippin'," Will said, glancing at the door one last time before turning his back to it. "I've been standing here…what…maybe five minutes?"

"Okay, fine, it's been five minutes," Derrick said, not believing him. "I'm about to head out to the patio and look for Natalie. Why don't you come with me."

Will shook his head. "You go ahead. I'm going to hang out here."

"Who is she?"

"Who is who?"

"The woman you're waiting for—because I know you're not standing here for your health."

"For your information, Caryn said she was coming and—"

Derrick raised a curious brow at that bit of information. "Caryn? I thought you were going to cool your heels with her."

Not in the mood to defend his position tonight, Will simply stated, "No, *you* suggested I cool my heels. I, on the other hand, see nothing wrong with two people getting to know each other."

Before Derrick could respond, the door opened again and in stepped the topic of their conversation.

Derrick watched Will straighten his back and break into a slow smile. The slight crinkles around his eyes added an extra sparkle to them and he took a slight step toward her. "Well, I'll be damned," Derrick said under his breath. This was the first time he'd seen such a complete and immediate reaction to a woman from Will. Maybe there was something to this after all.

Will watched with interest as Sherisse and Caryn greeted Natalie. Handing Natalie a small silver gift bag, Sherisse made the introductions. After Natalie and Caryn embraced, Caryn gave her a card-size envelope.

When Caryn came to the office, her casual clothing of jeans and a shirt was in contrast to her stiff shoulders and rigid stance. She was a woman with a lot on her mind. But tonight, she seemed to have shed whatever had her tied up in knots.

Wanting to celebrate the special occasion in style, there were going to be close to one hundred people milling around the grand foyer, the family room and the outdoor patio where there were floating candles in the pool, cocktail tables scattered about the lawn and a dance floor with several couples already getting their groove on. But all of them faded into the background when she walked into the room.

The dress. The hair. The smile. The walk. The body. All of it came together to form the closest thing to perfection he'd ever come across. In a word, she was breathtaking.

Caryn felt the eyes of someone on her the moment she stepped across the threshold. The large entryway was filled with several guests and Natalie had made an immediate appearance. Through the introductions and the pleasantries, Caryn tried to shake the feeling, but it remained. When Sherisse and Natalie started talking, Caryn took the time to make a quick scan of the room. That's when she saw him—staring at her.

The first thing she noticed was the suit. Not its rich gray color, or the amazing smoky-colored tie, but rather the fit. Letting her eyes peruse his body, she slowly moved them from top to bottom. There was no doubt that it was custom—no one could get a fit like that off the rack. The perfectly covered broad shoulders. The four buttons down the front. The cuff on the pants that just grazed the bottom of his shoe. Raising her eyes, she focused on his face. His smooth skin, dark eyes and slight grin drew her in and she had to remind herself to breathe.

"Caryn?"

"Oh, I'm sorry, what did you say?"

Both women glanced in the direction of her stare. Natalie smiled and Sherisse exhaled loudly.

"Why don't we head over there," Natalie said. "Derrick is supposed to dance with me."

The men watched all three women make their way over to them and Will took a quick sip of his drink. His mouth had suddenly gone dry.

Derrick saw the gesture and chuckled. "Since when do you get nervous?"

"Since never," he said, trying to regain the upper hand. He thought he'd gotten rid of those teenage tendencies after he had left her the first message, but the boyhood insecurities were determined to make their presence known.

Derrick cut his eyes to Will's hand and they both noticed the slight shaking.

Appalled at the effect this woman was having on him, he set the glass on the tray of a passing waiter and squared his shoulders. *Get it together, Will.*

"How's my beautiful birthday baby?" Derrick said, taking his wife's hand in his and giving her a loving kiss on the lips.

"Ready to get down on the dance floor," she said, dragging him in the direction of the outdoor deck.

All three remaining partygoers laughed at the look on Derrick's face. It was obvious that he was only doing this because it was her birthday.

"How about it, Caryn?"

The request caught her off guard, but Will held out his hand to her and before she could think it through, she placed hers in his.

Sherisse watched them walk off and decided to let her worries go. If Caryn wasn't concerned about the effects of dating a man like Will, there was no need to occupy her mind with the situation. The only thing she could do was be there for her friend if she needed her.

"Sherisse?"

The voice sounded familiar and she smiled at the handsome face of Dr. Lawrence Garrett. "Hi, Larry."

"I'm headed over to get some food. Would you like to join me?"

Sherisse locked arms with him and strolled toward the buffet. All thoughts of Caryn and her love life went flying out the window as she began to focus on her own.

Caryn followed Will through double French doors that led out to the yard. The music, the latest in the hip-hop craze, had people moving, shaking and spinning around. But to her surprise, when he led her to a spot near the rear of the floor, he scooped her into his arms and swayed back and forth.

She opened her mouth to speak, but when her body aligned with his, all words were lost. His left arm wrapped around her waist and held her at the small of her back. His right hand intertwined with her fingers. The scent of his cologne wafted through the air and tickled her nose. The unique scent added to the sensual feel of the moment. As the crowd cheered at the playing of another hip-hop song, Caryn finally found her voice. "I don't think this is a slow-dance song."

"You didn't strike me as someone who would go with the crowd," he whispered in her ear.

The cool breath caressed her lobe and goose bumps made a rare appearance on her arms and legs. "You didn't strike me as someone who would be willing to dance this close," she said.

Will defied that statement by pulling her closer. Her

chest and thighs rocked, molding to the contours of his. The crowd became irrelevant as he treated her like the only person in the room. "Because?"

Caryn recalled all that Sherisse had said about Will. Judging from his actions so far, he had the "make the woman feel like a queen" down pat. From the moment she walked in the room, he zeroed in on her, making her believe she was the only one that mattered to him. Were those the actions of someone who was known to be emotionally detached? "A man who walks around laying down rules for dating would tend to be less interested in activities that are intimate. Activities that would require you to be so close…so near. It defies who you say you are."

Staring down into her eyes, his seductive smile pierced her heart. "Believe me, Caryn, I have no problem getting close and near."

The double meaning in his words didn't go undetected. "I'm not talking about sex, Will. I'm talking about intimacy. Not the touching of bodies but the touching of souls."

Her statement hung in the air as he studied her face. Words such as those from a woman were red flags to him. It signaled that she was looking for something more than he would give. "Are you looking for someone to touch your soul?"

Caryn thought carefully before she answered. Every now and again, she had that longing—that need for someone to be with her on such a level. How would it be to share her life with someone? How would her life look if she made love a top priority? What would be different if she tossed her career plan out the window and let whatever happen—happen.

Those moments would sometimes last a minute, an hour, or sometimes a day. But they always came to an end. Having that kind of life at this point was impossible. Her career wouldn't allow her the luxury. When she had reached the top of her profession, then she would take the time and nurture a man, have a family and create a life outside of a computer and BlackBerry. "You and I are very alike, Will."

Will stopped moving at her statement. "How so?"

"Simple," she said. "You have your 'speech' and I have my career. Both of them keep us from anything more than this. Touching the soul is not an option."

The words were the truth and Will had preached them often. However, coming from her mouth left him with a profound sense of disappointment. Sliding his hand a little farther down her back, he pulled her another inch closer. "What about touching bodies?"

The soft timbre in his voice told Caryn exactly what he had in mind when it came to her body. "You can always keep hope alive."

The sparkle in her eyes and her playful smile amused him and he couldn't get enough of the tête-à-tête. Her flirting was only second to his. He never expected her to be so forward—or honest. "You've been warned that I'm the Big, Bad Wolf. Someone to stay as far away from as possible, yet you're here, dancing with me."

"Yes, I am," she said.

"My question is why? What do you want from me?"

All kinds of pictures flashed in Caryn's mind at that

question. The dream from her bath. Him naked in her kitchen. All the *connecting* she could possibly handle. Of course, those were her hormones talking and she always kept her hormones under control. "You strike me as someone who knows how to date a woman. Fine wine, good food and entertainment."

"I also like shooting pool, watching movies with a big tub of popcorn and relaxing out by my pool," he said, letting her see his relaxed side.

Caryn appreciated that lifestyle. He could be as comfortable at a black-tie affair as he would kicking back a few beers at the local pub. "Then you're perfect."

"For?"

"Making good on your offer."

Will thought back to their initial meeting. "You're in the market for a tour guide?"

"Not just any guide," she said, ignoring the gyrating bodies around them. "I need an expert. Someone who knows his way around."

"Oh," he said, taking a step back and giving her a solid once-over. "You can believe I know my way around."

"That, Dr. Proctor, I don't doubt," she said. "But be warned, I'm the one in charge of what you go around."

Will spun her and let his arm rest in the small of her back. For a couple that had never danced together, he found their movements came with ease. Two puzzle pieces that were a perfect match. While the music playing encouraged them to shake, twist and turn, they created their own music, with tenderness, affection and strong attraction. Caught up in the moment, he stepped out and dipped her to the side.

Leaning over her, he watched the concentrated rise and fall of her chest and knew that his breathing was as erratic as hers. A magnetic force beyond anything he'd ever experienced caused him to lean closer. Less than an inch from her lips, his insides screamed to take what he so desperately wanted. The urge was so strong that he had to remind himself to breathe. The dizzying current racing through him couldn't be throttled and he wasn't quite sure he'd ever had a moment like this. Just as unexpectedly, he raised her up.

Both stared, wondering what had just happened between them.

Caryn worked to recover from the trance that he put her in. One minute, they were dancing and flirting, the next, her heart hammered in her chest and she became completely enveloped by the strength and power of all of him. The combination of comfort, reassurance and calmness held her captive, and if he hadn't broken the spell she wasn't sure she would have been able to.

Another couple bumped into them, causing them to both break into a forced smile.

Reaching for her hand, he led her back toward the house. "Let's go."

"Excuse me?" she said, following behind him at a brisk pace.

"Your tour," he clarified, holding the door for her to enter through the sunroom. "I know the perfect place to begin."

The idea of the tour put Caryn at ease. That topic she was comfortable with. She could easily handle Will in the role of tour guide. It defined who they were to each other. Temporary. Short-term. Momentary.

It was the Will who'd embraced her on the dance floor that scared her. That was a person she'd rather not have to deal with. "What time should we get started tomorrow?"

"Uh-uh," Will answered. "I'm not talking about tomorrow."

Caryn didn't answer right away as the mischievous expression on his face made her wonder if he was talking about tonight.

Realizing that was exactly what he meant, she began to shake her head in the negative. "I just got here ten minutes ago. Most people haven't eaten, and based on the number of cars that were pulling up when we arrived, some of the guests hadn't arrived yet."

"Do you have a point?"

"Yes," she said, her mind working overtime to make sense of what was happening. She'd come with the thought of seeing him, and now she was contemplating leaving with him. "We can't leave, I just got here. They haven't made a toast, sung 'Happy Birthday' or cut the cake."

Will couldn't have cared less about the traditions of celebrating a birthday. He'd already given his best wishes to the guest of honor and was sure he wouldn't be missed if he snuck away early. "I'm sure it will be fine."

"I don't know."

Will allowed her a few minutes to think it over. It was never his intent to suggest going someplace else, but Caryn had him doing strange things the last couple of days. Sitting by the phone. Checking his messages more frequently. Now that he had a chance to spend some time with her, he preferred not to do it without a hundred other people. "What if I guarantee you champagne and a piece of cake?"

"Will you sing, too?" she teased, nudging him in the arm.

His heart skipped a beat. Before he could analyze or fight it, he face grew more serious and his voice lowered. "For you—anything."

There was something in those words that made Caryn pause. She'd never had a man say anything remotely related to that in her entire adult life. Most of her conversations with the men she saw on a personal level revolved around their needs and how her travel schedule didn't allow her to meet them. This was the first time someone offered to accommodate her. To make her needs the priority. "I don't know…I came with Sherisse."

Will gently turned her body around and pointed to the buffet area. Sherisse was sharing a plate and smiling with a guy who was almost as cute as Will. "I think she'll be all right."

"It's almost nine o'clock at night, where are we going?" Caryn was fairly confident that the monuments, museums and cultural centers had closed hours ago.

Will leaned in close to her ear. "I'm the tour guide, not you. Are you in or out?"

Caryn ran through her options quickly in her head. These four weeks were supposed to be about fun, relaxation and putting work out of her mind. He was offering the chance to do that. Caryn decided to throw caution to the wind. "Let me talk to Sherisse and I'll meet you at the door."

Chapter 11

The night was clear and a soft breeze moved through the air. Late May in Washington, D.C., could produce absolutely wonderful weather. Wrapping her shawl around her arms a little tighter, they stood at the top of the driveway, waiting for the valet to bring his car.

Opening the passenger side, Caryn slid into the front seat of a Jaguar, hooked her seat belt and sank back into the plush, leather seats, resting her head. Taking it easy had always been her objective for this time off, but between e-mails, voice mail and reports, she had yet to achieve that. Will was putting her on the right track.

Inhaling deeply, Caryn allowed her body to surrender to the atmosphere, the environment and the man. Releasing all the stresses that came with her job could be a job unto itself at times. But at this moment, she'd succeeded in achieving it. She wished there was a way to bottle this feeling and keep it with her.

As Will drove away, Caryn secretly observed his profile and wondered if this feeling of euphoria she'd begun to experience was the result of the weather, the car or the man in the driver's seat. However, reality set in. Regardless of which one it was—none of them were going back to Boston with her.

"This should be about a twenty-minute ride," he said, hitting the button on the sound system, filling the airwaves with the Temptations.

"I see you like your old-school tunes," Caryn said.

"It depends on my mood," Will said, turning the sound down a tad. "Some days I'm blasting my favorite jazz artist, other days I'm getting my fill of world events listening to NPR. Then there are days when I have to have a dose of the latest hip-hop jams. But those doses are few and far between."

"I'm on the road so much, I barely have time to keep up with the latest news. I'm rarely up to speed on the hottest song, biggest television show or latest celebrity gossip. Don't laugh," Caryn said, ready to make a confession.

"What?" he said, taking his eyes off the road for a second to look at her.

"I didn't recognize any of the songs the DJ played at the party."

"That's nothing to be ashamed of," Will said, leaving the state of Maryland and crossing into Washington, D.C. "In fact, that's something to be proud of. This country has become so celebrity driven, I can't pick up a *Newsweek* or a *Time* magazine without having to read about the latest celebrity-marriage breakup, baby news or fashion party. Why would I care what someone wears, where they live or who they may or may not be sleeping with?"

"I agree," Caryn said, thinking of all the magazine covers at the newsstands in airports. "I have enough going on in my own life to keep up with. Every day I'm looking for opportunities to gain new clients, while servicing the clients I have. I can't tell you how difficult it is to keep all the balls in the air."

Will watched her body tense up at the mention of her job. He hoped to be someone that could help relieve some of that stress and pressure. Turning left, he pulled up to the curb and waited for the valet.

Caryn paused at the entrance and narrowed her eyes at him in disappointment. Did he actually think she was going to get out of the car? "I'm not going in there with you. I don't know what your definition of *tour guide* may be, but obviously we're using two different dictionaries."

"Things aren't always what they seem, Caryn," he said, getting out of the car and handing his keys over. Opening her door, he motioned for her to get out. "Any man with half a brain would take one look at your body and want to make it his—I'm no exception. The difference is, I wouldn't insult you by assuming you would give it to me."

Caryn stepped out and appreciated his candor, and his underhanded compliment. "Then why are we here?"

A mysterious smile appeared on his lips. "To see the city."

His explanation didn't erase the skepticism in her eyes and he held out his hand for her. "Trust me."

The simple request was not a question but a statement made with confidence. The outstretched fingers beckoned her and she hesitated for only a moment. He was offering her exactly what she said she needed; she couldn't back out now. Nor did she want to.

There was a hint of mystery and excitement in this evening and Caryn believed it was just the beginning of something memorable. Something she could carry with her as she grinded out the next several years. Something—and someone—to give her an experience like no other. She decided to trust him to give her that. Sliding her hand into his, she felt warmth from him shoot up her arm and settle in her body.

Will raised his eyes from their intertwined hands to her face, sensing the surrender she was giving to him. She nodded "okay" and it became abundantly clear that she was trusting him with more than this one night. Absorbing that came with her unspoken request, warning bells sounding in his ears. *Too much. Back off. Too deep. Keep your distance.*

These feelings weren't jibing with who he was as it related to women. There were supposed to be rules, agreements and understandings. The arrangement was cut-and-dry. Fantastic dates and good times. Will never signed on for undeniable attraction, compelling desire, butterflies in the stomach, unspoken connection and anticipation of what could be. Still, he moved forward with the evening.

Without letting her hand go, they entered the building as the doorman held it open.

Caryn's steps slowed as they entered the lobby of the Hotel Washington. With its old-world style, the decor was from a period in time before glass buildings and modern structures. Moving through the lobby, she admired the antique flair of the furnishings and decoration. Bypassing the registration desk and lobby bar, he pushed the button for the elevator.

Once the doors closed and they began their ascent, Will flourished his arms and waved his hands. "Welcome to the Hotel Washington, the oldest continuously operating hotel in the city."

Caryn snickered at the booming voice that sounded like he was a game-show announcer. "It's a good thing we're alone."

Making a fist, he put the closed hand under his mouth and spoke into his makeshift microphone. "It's the official home of the Hillary Clinton Fan Club and also houses the national turkey the night before he joins the president on the lawn of the White House."

"You take this tour-guide seriously, huh?"

Dropping his hands, he lowered his head to hers. "I aim to deliver."

The doors opened on the eleventh floor and they walked into a fairly small, crowded hallway. Leading her to the front of the line, he patiently waited while the hostess spoke with a couple at the podium. After whispering a few words in her ears, she nodded in understanding.

"It will be just a few minutes before they'll have a table for us," he said, giving her a quick wink and a knowing smile.

Caryn decided to hold off her questions until after

they were seated—which mainly revolved around how he cut the wait line to get them in.

About ten minutes later, they were led into the Sky Terrace and seated at a small table at the railing. Sitting across from each other, he watched her reaction. It didn't take long. Her mouth opened into a small "o" and she scanned the cityscape before her.

Breaking into a small grin, she had to give him his props. "Magnificent."

The White House stood majestic with its bright lights, waving American flag and perfectly manicured lawn. The terrace overlooked the grounds and gardens and Caryn felt as if she could reach out and touch trees that were on the property. A feeling of patriotism swelled in Caryn and she couldn't believe that she'd grown up in this area and never experienced the city from this angle.

"Beautiful, isn't it?" he said, pleased to share this experience with her.

Caryn turned her attention to him and nodded, feeling her throat get tight. Not one for outward displays of emotion, she swallowed deliberately to hold back the tears.

"Are you okay?" Will asked, noticing the strong reaction.

Fanning her face, she willed her tears not to fall. "I don't know what has come over me. I guess I just realized that for someone from the city, I never took the time to get to know it. I've been too busy."

Will leaned across the table and gently wiped away the lone tear that fell down her cheek. "That's why ʸᵒᵘ have me—to show you all that you've been miss

Caryn closed her eyes as his fingertips brushed against her skin. She'd gotten used to the warming sensation that traveled through her body whenever they touched, but she wasn't prepared for the tenderness with which he stroked her. Uncomfortable with the feelings that his touch set off, she moved back, forcing him to break contact. Picking up her menu, she chose to ignore the scene that had played out a few seconds ago. "Since I didn't eat at the party, I'm starving. Do you have any recommendations?"

Will reluctantly pulled his hand away her just as the waitress arrived. "I promised you champagne."

Ordering a bottle of Cristal, he continued to order a pasta dish while Caryn chose a salad with grilled chicken.

Finally, he relaxed back in his chair. "So, tell me, Caryn Stewart, what makes you so driven that you can't find the smallest amount of time to date?"

"Oh, no," Caryn said, waving her finger at him. "We're not going to talk about me until we talk about you."

"Believe me," Will said, thinking of his medical practice, "my career is a top priority—but I *always* find time to date."

"So I hear," Caryn said, thinking of the warnings Sherisse set off when she'd tried to convince Caryn to leave this man alone. The comment was made flippantly, but the thought of him with other women gave her an unexpected tremor in her chest. She hardly knew the man, why would it matter who he dated?

The edge in her voice was unexpected, yet Will found that he was pleasantly surprised. It also made him wonder what Sherisse had told her. "Hearsay is never the best way to receive information. Whenever possible, you should get it straight from the horse's mouth."

"Hearsay tells me you're a serial dater with no designs on settling down," she said, remembering Sherisse's attempt at steering her clear of Will. "My instincts tell me my source is more than likely correct."

"Then please," Will said, taking off his jacket and loosening his tie. "Allow me to set the record straight."

"I'm all ears," Caryn said, trying to keep her eyes from staring. When she'd first laid eyes on him at the party, he was suave and well put together. Now that he'd laid his jacket aside and unbuttoned the top button on his shirt, he appeared more rugged—sexier.

"It's no secret that I've dated my fair share of women," he confessed. "However, I take any job I have extremely seriously. My job for the next several weeks is tour guide—and you're the only client I have in my books."

Caryn sat silent as the champagne arrived. As the glasses were filled, she assessed all that Sherisse had told her about Will and compared that to the man who was sitting in front of her. Foolish would be to discount her initial assessment of him and to abandon the opinions of Sherisse. Will Proctor did not, all of a sudden, become a different person. She'd wrapped her mind around who he was and how he related to the women he dated and that was the main thing Caryn needed to remember.

He raised his glass to propose a toast.

Caryn didn't follow suit, refusing to hono

request. This was the part of the date where he told her the rules. This part of the evening she couldn't skip.

In the short amount of time Caryn had spent with Will, they'd shared some extremely intense moments. The power of their handshake when they met, the intense connection that passed between them when they danced and his recent confession that he was all hers for the next three weeks. She didn't want to hear The Speech for his benefit, she needed it for herself.

The plan of a temporary relationship that had spearheaded this rendezvous kept easing to the back of her mind the more time she spent with him. Will Proctor was a distraction she couldn't afford. Three weeks. That's all she had. What better way to solidify that reality than to hear The Speech.

She shook her head from side to side, her glass remaining on the table. "From what I've heard, you always give your speech before the first drinks are served."

The Speech. How could he forget? He'd almost broken one of his cardinal rules. The Speech always happened on the first date. Always.

"Don't disappoint me," she said, leaning back and folding her arms across her lap.

Crossing her legs, the bottom of her dress raised a couple of inches to show off a smooth, chocolate thigh. The bare skin against the strappy heals created an aura of appeal that caused him to make a few adjustments in the way he sat. His eyes stayed there until her voice forced him to raise them. Will couldn't recall a time when a woman had come across so enthralling.

"Come on, now," Caryn said. "Out with it. I know you have this part of the date down pat. Let's hear it."

The moment she'd walked into the lobby of his office, his initial interest was driven by physical attraction. Now that he'd spend time with her, held her in his arms and caught a glimpse of her personality, there was an unchecked desire to get to know her.

Sherisse made no secret that her friend's time in town was limited and that his rules were the perfect solution to her stressed-out situation at work. Once this vacation was over, she was going to hit the ground running with her career, making room for nothing else. How ironic that the one thing about him that turned most women off had been the very thing that drew Caryn to him.

Will set his glass down and lowered his voice. "I'm sure you're quite well versed in the main points of my speech."

"Who knows, maybe I've gotten something wrong," she said, encouraging him to spit it out. "It's best if you just go ahead and give it to me."

Will opened his mouth—but no words came out. In his head, the sentences were flowing. *Caryn, I think you are a wonderful woman and I'm attracted to you and want to get to know you.* But for some reason, his vocal cords weren't cooperating. *I think it's only fair that you understand where I stand in terms of where this relationship will and will not go.*

"Will?" she said, wondering why he'd become unnaturally quiet.

He cleared his throat and tried again. *I'm not looking for a commitment, exclusive dating and marriage is definitely not in my future. I respect your putting your career ahead of us and I need you to respect me the same way.*

Nothing.

The next portion was key to maintaining control of the dating situation, but his mouth wasn't following the commands of his brain—it was listening to his heart and it remained silent. *If any of what I've said doesn't sit right with you and you can't agree to abide by it, we should end what we have before it begins. I'm not willing to negotiate.*

"Are you okay?" she asked as his eyes looked beyond her.

Snapping back, he shrugged his shoulders to shake off the unfamiliar feelings. "What's the use in giving The Speech? You're only in town for another three weeks. It's a given that the rules are in effect. What could possibly develop between us in that short period of time?"

The words were always spoken to remind himself of their status. Because a strong sense of attraction radiated between them, Will wondered just how much could happen in the time they had together.

Caryn exhaled a breath she didn't realize she held. Accepting his explanation, she let the topic drop. After all, it made perfect sense. The idea of anything more developing between them was impossible. Based on all she had learned about him, he didn't want it and her lifestyle didn't allow her to have it. Their reasons might differ, but the results were the same. All they could have would be temporary.

Raising her glass to him, she said, "What shall we toast to?"

Relief flooded through Will when she moved on. "To setting aside rules, speeches and demanding jobs. To completely living in the moment for the next three weeks."

"I'll drink to that."

Chapter 12

After sipping from the flute, Will thought it best to get off of the topic of his rules and returned to his original question. "Why are you so driven?"

The simple question came with an easy answer. "I want success, money, respect and the ability to do what I want when I want. It was something I didn't have growing up."

She paused to remember the times of her childhood when her parents gave reluctant no's to her request for some new thing. "We didn't have a lot. I overheard my parents talk a lot about their financial challenges. Overdue bills. Hand-me-downs. Going without. I refuse to let money be a hindrance to having what I deserve and want."

Will watched her and witnessed the confidence waver as she thought about her childhood. Painful memories could wreak havoc in an adult life, causing one to make decisions to erase the hurt. "From what Sherisse told me, you've probably met those goals. The rewards your job gives you must be great and well earned."

Making well into the six figures last year, Caryn thought about all that her position had afforded her. She'd bought her parents a house, two cars and sent them on vacations a couple of times a year.

Names like Chanel, Gucci, Marc Jacobs, Jimmy Choo, St. John, Versace and Halston filled her neat but bulging closet. There was a convertible Benz in one reserved parking space in her building and a Lexus SUV in the other. Charity donations had become a staple in her life as she gave much and often. She had surrounded herself with everything she'd ever wanted. "Yes, I am. It's afforded me the opportunity to accomplish things I only thought were a dream."

Will listened as she rolled off a list of things that she'd garnered from committing her full self to building an amazing career. As he listened, he waited for the passion, the enthusiasm, the excitement that comes with doing something that you love. Instead, he heard her speak about her work as if it were a to-do list. The means to an end.

When she finished, he drank from his glass, all the while studying her.

Caryn felt the power of his gaze and nervously took a sip, wondering why he remained quiet. Patience exuded from him as if he was waiting for something more. Setting her glass down, she readjusted her seat. "What about you—do you enjoy your work?"

The stammer in her words meant he made her uncomfortable. Her nervous motions of picking up her napkin, and then almost immediately placing it back in her lap, followed by her moving her glass around on the table, confirmed his suspicions. What was she hiding? "Before we move on to me, let me ask you this."

Caryn wasn't sure she wanted to hear what he had to say. When it came to her work, she was one hundred percent confident and assured, but in the process of singing the praises of all of her accomplishments, she'd started to ramble, seemingly talking a hundred miles an hour. Not sure if she was making sense as she talked of her projects and achievements, she'd simply decided to shut up. Hoping to take the focus off of her, she'd asked about his work. Apparently, he wasn't ready to let the subject of her work drop.

"Why do you do what you do?"

"What kind of question is that?" Caryn said. "I just spent the last ten minutes talking to you about my job."

"What you told me is what you've gotten for your work," Will said, thinking of the laundry lists of tasks and rewards she'd given to him. "I want to know *why* you work."

Not sure she understood his question, she said, "I do what I do because I'm good at it. I bring companies together so they can grow their business. I'm a part of a team that's moving business beyond a country's border."

"That's admirable."

"Thank you," she said, relishing his compliment. For some reason, she found herself seeking his approval. Wanting him to be proud of her.

"But it doesn't answer my question."

The waiter arrived to let them know their food would be out shortly and Caryn welcomed the distraction. She didn't identify with what Will was asking of her. She wasn't sure what he wanted her to say.

She'd attended enough networking functions, meet and greets, and training sessions to articulate, quite clearly, what she did and how she did it. Will's question had been posed to her on several occasions, including interviews, panel discussions and at conferences and workshops. No one ever had a problem understanding her answer. Until now.

"Becoming a doctor was a childhood dream of mine."

Glad to see that they'd moved off of her job, she exhaled her breath and relaxed back in her chair, finishing her glass of champagne.

"Many people told me I couldn't do it," he started. "Teachers. Friends. Guidance counselors. College professors. I was too dumb, too broke or too undisciplined to accomplish this career goal."

"But you proved them all wrong," she said proudly.

"I did," he said, thinking back to all the times he wondered if the naysayers were right. Struggling in one of his undergraduate classes, anxiously awaiting acceptance to medical school or standing in a hospital emergency room on the first day of his residency. "Caring for my patients is the most rewarding work I can imagine. People look to you for answers, hope and solutions. They literally place their lives in your hands. I become just as invested in their health—and life—as they are. I've been privileged to deliver life-changing good news, and held hands, and hearts, through some of the most devastating times in people's lives.

"It's challenging at times, dealing with patients who don't take care of themselves, insurance companies that haven't quite gotten on board with covering preventive measures and increasing costs that keep people from getting the care they need. But I wouldn't exchange it for anything. Being a doctor is not what I do—it's who I am. I found my true calling."

Caryn grew quiet as she listened to the passion in his voice. Words from a man who loved what he did. If she closed her eyes, she could see him in an examination room with one of his patients. Genuine joy in his work reflected in the zeal with which he spoke. His rewards reached far beyond the external, they were internal. *Purpose, true calling* and *commitment* flashed in her mind.

Will noticed her thoughtful expression. "Now it's your turn."

"My turn?" Caryn asked. "For what?"

"I want you to tell me what your career gives you."

Caryn's nervous laugh failed to cover up her discomfort. "I already did."

"No," he clarified. "What you told me involved all the financial rewards you are getting."

"Isn't that why millions of people get up and head out every day—for the financial rewards?"

"Is that the only reason you do what you do?"

"Is there another?" she said, her uneasiness turning to agitation. What did he want from her?

"Okay," Will said, deciding to approach this from a

different angle. "So you get all the things you didn't have as a child, but where's the fun?"

Caryn didn't like the direction of this conversation and felt her defenses rise. Who was he to question her work? "I have fun."

Her indignation told Will that she was losing patience with this, but he laughed at the harshness of her tone. "Yeah...right...fun."

"That's right," she said, raising her tone, challenging the fact that he evidently didn't believe her. "F-U-N."

"Several years ago, the Boston Red Sox broke the curse and won the World Series," he said, a hint of challenge in his voice. "There must have been all kinds of parties and celebrations. I heard companies were having parties to celebrate during working hours. Fun was all around you. How did you participate?"

"I don't like baseball," she said, huffing at the nerve of him.

"In other words, you were working."

His arrogance, which she once admired, was starting to grate on her nerves and she refused to answer.

"Sherisse had a huge birthday party last year. She'd planned it for months—yet you weren't here. Why not?"

"I don't have to answer that. It's none of your business."

Undeterred by her growing anger with him, he continued, "I left you two phone messages this week, yet you didn't call me back. What were you busy doing?"

"Aren't you full of yourself," she said. "Maybe I just didn't want to talk to you."

Will couldn't help but laugh at her indignant tone. "Or maybe you were working."

Caryn recalled the last couple of days and tried to wave off his question.

"I'd bet money you were working."

"So," she said in annoyance. "Is that so bad? I have three major deals coming up. I'm going to be halfway around the world next month and I've got a team to get in place."

The muscles in her neck and shoulders tightened and Caryn moved her head from side to side to try to offset the discomfort.

"I thought you were on vacation?" he asked casually.

"I am."

Her words were clipped and short, but he didn't mind. "Why?"

"What kind of question is that? Why does anyone go on vacation?"

"Look at you," he said, standing and walking around her chair.

Caryn had no idea what he was up to, but she refused to give in to him and continued to face forward.

Will stood behind her and placed his hands on her shoulders. "Each time your job comes up, stress overtakes you. Your smile disappears, your body stiffens and your breathing becomes short."

Caryn inhaled deeply at the touch of his skin against hers. His fingers pressed in and he slowly rubbed and massaged the tense muscles around her neck.

His voice softened. "You haven't been home in years. You've stayed away from your family and friends and now that you've made the choice to take time off—you can't. You won't allow yourself to completely let go."

Caryn allowed the sensuous stroke of his touch to melt away the knots that appeared when the subject of work came up. Closing her eyes, she had no regard for where they were. She didn't care if people stared. All she cared about was the soothing feeling of his healing hands.

"That's it," he said, leaning forward and whispering in her ear. "Let it go."

Their food arrived and the waiter's appearance broke the spell. Realizing where her emotions were going, she reached up and smacked his hand away. "I don't have a problem letting go."

"Yeah, right," he said, reclaiming his seat. "You're running so fast from letting go, but I sense you're getting tired of the race."

Will was supposed to be a distraction. Someone to show her a good time. What she didn't expect him to do was make her question and doubt her choices. The somber mood shook her and the only way to get out of it was to change the conversation, taking the focus off of her and putting it on him.

Picking up her fork, she took a bite of her salad. "What happened to the man that likes to keep it light— the player…the Mac daddy…the man who could wine and dine a woman better than anyone?"

Those were the same questions Will asked himself. He hadn't intended to give her an impromptu massage, but he could see the tension mounting and he couldn't stand by and do nothing. The moment he touched her, he knew he'd made a mistake. If he thought the power that was between them was a fluke, this proved otherwise. She'd leaned back into him and at that moment, he wanted to make all her troubles go away. That was a definite warning sign.

Why would he be concerned with the tension in her body when she spoke of her job? Why should he care about the flickers of sadness he'd caught in those striking brown eyes? What difference did it make to him whether she garnered true satisfaction from her job? Why did he feel compelled to uncover all that might not be right with her life and fix it?

Not ready to explore the answers, he decided to go with her flow. "So that's all I am to you—your three-week boy toy?"

"You said it, not me," Caryn said, feeling the earlier tension lifting.

"I'm offended," Will said melodramatically, biting into his pasta.

"You asked me where was the fun in my life?" she said. "Well, I'm looking at him. You talk about a job— let's see if you can handle this one."

Looking out over the spectacular view, he said, "I think I'm off to a good start."

Caryn had to admit that between the dancing, the view, the champagne and the impromptu massage, he'd already made good on his promise. "I'll give you credit for tonight. But I'm sure this isn't your best stuff."

Will stopped eating and leaned toward her. His eyes, brimming with seduction, matched the low tone of his voice. "Are you sure you can handle my best stuff?"

"Believe me, Dr. Proctor, I can take anything you

dish out," she said, not missing the sexual undertone. "And for the record, I'm talking about dates."

Will sat back and smiled at her sassy comment. He had a feeling this was going to be the best three weeks of his life.

Two hours later, Will pulled up to her parents' house. The porch light was on, but the rest of the house was dark. "It's been a long time since I brought a date home to her parents' house."

"It's been a long time since I've been brought home from a date—period."

Will heard the longing in her voice and began to understand what she'd given up for the sake of her career. Opening his door, he stepped out and trotted around to the other side to open hers. Sliding her hand into his, he helped her out of the car. Neither of them said anything about the fact that they continued to hold hands as they walked up to the door.

Standing under the porch light, Will pulled her close and wrapped his arms around her. "I could say things like 'I had a good time' or 'thanks for a great evening,' or one to beat around the

his statements demonstrated the that attracted her to him and she gave a coy smile. "Good, because I'm not one for small talk, either."

"I want to kiss you."

"I want to be kissed."

Will lowered his head and brushed his lips against hers. The initial contact was sweet, but soon changed when his lips fully covered hers and she opened her mouth to receive him. Pulling her closer, he felt her hands clasp around his neck, causing their bodies to mesh together.

With her pressed against him, Will's heart pounded in his chest and he couldn't stop every part of himself from reacting to the surge of exhilaration that touched every part of his body. Unable to recall any of his rules, speeches, conditions, guidelines, principles and strategies for dating, he only wanted to deepen the connection that had been created with this woman.

Caryn leaned back against the door as the power of the kiss took her by surprise. His expertise must have come from years of practice, but she didn't care. The lips. The tongue. The hands. They all moved in perfect unison to set her entire body on fire. For the second time that night, goose bumps appeared on her arms and she waited for the shock of the moment to subside. But it didn't. The more he explored, the more unsteady she became. Finally, he pulled away and she started to regain some control.

"You'll be ready at ten tomorrow morning?"

The request caught her off guard and she fought to keep her bearings. "For?"

He gave her a mysterious grin and a quick peck on the cheek before heading back to his car. "F-U-N."

Chapter 13

Caryn sat in her room putting the finishing touches on her face. Per his instructions, she'd dressed casually and comfortably, opting to forgo most of her makeup routine and settling on powder, mascara and gloss. With her hair pulled back in a small ponytail, she felt at ease in her tan capri pants and scoop-neck cotton top.

"For someone who has no idea where she's going or what she's going to do, I can sense your excitement."

Bonnie had entered her room a few minutes ago and sat on the bed to keep her daughter company as she finished getting dressed. The gesture bought back memories that Caryn had long ago forgotten. Times when her mother sat on the bed when she was growing up, helping her get ready by hanging out in her room.

The room she sat in now was a far cry from the room she had growing up.

The small row house in the lower-class section of the city had been her home her entire childhood. The living room, dining room, galley kitchen, two bedrooms and one bath could fit into the first floor of the house her parents lived in now. Her old room, the size of her walk-in closet in Boston, held a single bed, a small dresser and a table where she did her homework. Though small, her mother made the room nice, sewing curtains for the window that matched her bedspread.

There were many memories of her mother in her room. The day after her sixteenth birthday, her mother sat in the same spot helping Caryn dress for her first date. Michael Lewis had asked her to the spring dance. Caryn had been begging her parents since she was fourteen to go to the movies, to go roller-skating or swimming with a boy. Each time, she received the same answer. *No dating until you turn sixteen.*

Caryn wasted no time in implementing that rule the day after that magical birthday. Michael's mother was going to drop them off at the school gymnasium. It was the first time her mother was going to let her stay out past nine o'clock and Caryn thought she'd arrived.

The week before the big date, her mother took her to the mall to get shoes for her gym class, when Caryn spotted a yellow dress with spaghetti straps. Perfect for the dance, she begged her mother to buy it for her, but, as with many of these types of requests, it went unfulfilled. There wasn't enough money.

That left her to wear her blue skirt and white button-down top. At the time, she felt like the only person who wouldn't be wearing something new. Still, her mother made such a fuss over everything from her hair to her nails that she felt like a princess when her date arrived.

A couple of years later, Bonnie stood in that same room helping Caryn get ready for her senior high-school prom. Peter Duncan had been the finest boy in school. Not only did he play on the baseball team, but he was also class president. They had only gone out for a month before he asked her to the prom. Dressing up and going out with no curfew had been too exciting for Caryn. This time, when Caryn saw the perfect dress in the window, her mother bought it. It was weeks later when she overheard her parents talking. They'd put off a car repair so that she could have that dress.

Three months after the prom, Caryn headed off to college, never to live in her parents' house again. Today, while it was a new room, a new bed and a new boy, Caryn felt like that little girl of years gone by when she had her mother helping her get ready for a date.

"It took almost a week, but I'm finally starting to relax and actually take pleasure in my vacation," Caryn said. She still hadn't slept in, and she'd taken one call from Jeremy, but her laptop sat on the nightstand, untouched.

"I'm glad to hear that, because your father and I think you work way too hard and play way too little," Bonnie said. "At least once a month, we play this game called 'where in the world is our daughter?'"

"What?" Caryn said,

"Your calls are so sporadic. Your visits are nonexistent. We could never catch you at the office or at home. If it wasn't for e-mail, we'd have to send a search and rescue team out to find you—just to make sure you were still alive and kicking."

"Am I really that bad?"

"Every time your aunt Betty, uncle Chester or your cousin Veronica asks about you, we have no answers."

"I keep in touch," Caryn said, hoping to convince herself more than her mother.

"Last month, Robin, the woman who lives across the street… Her son moved back to the area and I thought the two of you would get along, but of course I didn't have a clue if you would actually make it home this time. Your plans change so often, your father and I are never sure if you're actually going to show up. You've canceled more visits than you've kept."

Caryn stopped applying the makeup and turned to her mother. "Is this about my not coming home—or is this your way of getting me to meet Robin's son?"

"He does look nice in the picture she showed me," she said, pulling out a photo from her pocket.

"Mom," Caryn said, refusing to take it out of her hands. "I'm going out with a guy today. Isn't that good enough?"

"Okay, okay," Bonnie said, not wanting to spoil what was turning out to be the first day in a long time that her daughter didn't focus on work. And she was right. She was going out with this guy—again. "Tell me about him."

Bonnie might have dropped the topic of her working too hard, but she couldn't cover up the undercurrent of hopefulness that was behind that question. Each time Caryn mentioned a man's name, Bonnie would launch into a million and one questions about him.

Where did you meet him?
Where does he live?
Have you met his family?
Where does he work?
Do you think he'd be a good husband...a good father?

Underneath those questions stirred all the dreams she had for her daughter. Wedding bells. Bridal showers. Baby carriages. Ultimately, Bonnie's inquiring mind only led to disappointment when she realized that none of those things were going to happen anytime soon.

Caryn didn't want to give her mother hope. The time she spent with Will last night had been delightful. Everything about him turned her on. His looks. His style. Even his questions about her career. But she wasn't fooled. He was who he was—and she would not allow herself to forget that.

Instead of giving her mother false hope—and herself—she told the truth. "Dr. William Proctor is a card-carrying, founding member of the Bachelor for Life club. Sherisse told me, and he confirmed, that he was not looking for a committed relationship. We plan to hang out over the next three weeks. No more. No less."

Bonnie listened to the words and couldn't believe that her daughter would actually date a man like that. "Hang out?"

"Yep," Caryn said, applying her lip liner and gloss.

"What does that mean?"

"Nothing...which is exactly what Will and I will be when I go back to Boston."

Bonnie crossed her arms across her lap and took a deep, unapproving breath. Is this the kind of daughter she'd raised? Valuing herself and having a desire to accomplish her own goals and achieve professional success had always been what Bonnie wanted for Caryn. What she didn't want to raise was a woman who would sacrifice love in the name of a job. "This arrangement—hanging out—that's fine with you?"

Squelching the little girl inside of her that wanted to please her mommy, Caryn didn't answer right away. When she was five hundred or five thousand miles away from home and having these conversations by phone or e-mail, it was much easier to make her point and stand her ground. But there was nothing standing between Bonnie and Caryn, and she had to maintain her position with her mother face-to-face. "I'm only in town for a short visit and my upcoming work schedule is crazy. Not to mention when I'm not traveling I'm putting in ten- or twelve-hour days. What good would it do to start something with someone when it would have to end? This way, I get to have some fun—even if the man I'm with is temporary."

"Are you listening to yourself?" Bonnie said.

"I know you don't understand, Mom," Caryn said, moving from the mirror to sit beside her. "You met Dad when you were eighteen years old and married him two years later. You had love, companionship and you treasured raising your family. What you didn't have was money. The way I'm doing it, I get to have it all."

"Money?" Bonnie asked. "Is that what this boils down to?"

Covering her mother's hands with her own, Caryn

thought of growing up. "I remember, Mom. No new clothes. Hand-me-down furniture. No extra money for piano lessons, school trips or a sweet-sixteen party."

Bonnie would never deny that there were times when they didn't have a penny to pinch. When there was more month than money. When ends were nowhere near meeting. There were lean years that included layoffs, late bills and turn-off notices. It was challenging, but they'd made it through. "Is that all you remember?"

The emotional question threw Caryn for a loop. The strong reaction was compounded by the small drops of water she watched form in her mother's eyes. Hugging her mother, Caryn whispered, "I remember family dinners. Belly laughs. Homemade ice cream. And lots of love."

Bonnie hadn't linked how deeply Caryn's childhood would have such a profound impact on her adult choices. It was no secret that the driving force behind Caryn's mad dash up the corporate ladder stemmed from the incredible financial rewards. What became clear at this time was that she wasn't working for her future, she was working to somehow make up for the past. Sitting back from her daughter's embrace, she offered an enlightened smile. "Because of your overseas travel, your father and I have been privy to your personal information."

Caryn nodded. The majority of the countries she went to were deemed safe and friendly to Americans and women. Yet, if something happened, she needed someone in the U.S. that had access to everything.

"Last year, your father and I visited your *empty* condo in Boston."

Caryn nodded in agreement. They came up for six days, and with her best effort, Caryn only managed to spend a few evenings with them.

"We've ridden in your two-year-old Mercedes—the one with less than three thousand miles on it."

Because Caryn traveled so much or used car service, she rarely drove her car.

"When you bought this house for us, you paid it off in three years."

Caryn remembered how proud and happy it made her to do something for her parents. Making that final mortgage payment gave them the freedom they'd never known.

"The clothes you bought when we went shopping?" Bonnie said. "Twenty-seven hundred dollars and you didn't blink when you charged them."

"It had been a while since I shopped," Caryn said, defending her position.

"We've gotten the e-mails with the photo attachments from some of the receptions that you attend on behalf of your company, standing next to political figures and Fortune 100 businessmen. We also hold copies of your insurance policies and investment portfolios."

Bonnie paused to make sure her daughter was listening. She was trying desperately to get through to her. Cupping her hands around Caryn's face, she leaned forward and kissed her daughter's cheek. "When is enough, enough?"

"Caryn, honey, there's a fancy vehicle pulling in the driveway."

Both women turned to the door when they heard Lloyd's booming voice.

Caryn jumped at the chance to get out of a conversation that out of the blue made her anxious. "Be right down."

Standing, Caryn checked herself in the mirror one last time before giving her mom a hug. "Don't worry, Mom. I got this."

Bonnie watched her daughter disappear into the hallway. "I hope so, honey."

Will sat in his car, staring at the house. Last night, he left her at the door. Today, he was more than likely going to meet her parents. Will could only recall a couple of times when he'd met the parents. Just once or twice in high school. Never in college, and maybe three times since then.

To him, it had become an exercise in futility. Why become intertwined with a girlfriend's family—as it would only make it that much more difficult for the rules to be followed. Mothers, fathers, siblings and other close friends could be a thorn in his side if they began to joke around or push for Will to move the relationship to another level. In all cases where he allowed himself to indulge in family birthday parties, holidays and other general family gatherings, sooner or later his girlfriend would take on the concerns of her family and friends and begin to push him for more than he was willing to give.

Will didn't worry himself when women asked about meeting his family. They lived in California and Will went West far more than any of them came East. Over the years, many thought that maybe his rules were a result of witnessing a bad marriage as a child, but that wasn't the case. Others thought that if he just found the right woman, she would change his mind and all the things he thought he didn't want would suddenly become attractive to him. What they didn't realize was that he had dated some women who would make a great life partner. They were kind, giving, great conversationalists and had a heart of gold. But that didn't matter to him. His rules weren't applicable based on the woman. It was who he was.

That's why the fact that he allowed himself to be sitting in front of Caryn's house, about to meet her parents had him wondering what he was doing. He could have easily asked to meet her somewhere—anywhere—yet, here he sat, already breaking one of his own personal rules—no more meeting the family.

Reminding himself that she would only be here several more weeks, he rationalized his behavior. What was the use in going through the exercise of putting so much emphasis on the rules when they'd be history soon? With renewed confidence, Will opened the car door and made his way up the walkway.

Caryn took the stairs two at a time. She had no idea what was in store for her today, but the thought of spending it with Will had her heart racing. Opening the door before he could knock, she stepped aside to let him enter. "Good morning."

Before he spoke, he pulled a small bouquet of flowers from behind his back. "Breathtaking flowers for a woman who can take a man's breath away."

The schoolgirl in Caryn came out and she had to stop herself from giggling as she accepted the colorful bunch. To some the gesture might be considered corny, but she had told him she was desperate to be courted and he was laying it on thick—and it suited her just fine. "Thank you, Will. You don't look so bad yourself."

The first time she met him, he had on his doctor's white coat. Last night, he was decked out in his evening best. Today, he was casually fine. The jeans were hugging him just right and the polo shirt hung loose around his strong arms and chest. For some unexplained reason she didn't stop to analyze, she leaned up and kissed him on the cheek.

The action took him by surprise and for a moment his eyes popped open like a deer caught in headlights. Caryn's smile faltered at his reaction until his face relaxed and he released a slow, approving smile.

"Ahem."

Caryn turned when she heard the throat-clearing and saw her parents standing behind her.

Bonnie watched her daughter's cheeks grow warm as she lowered her eyes in embarrassment. Although they were few and far between, she recalled the times she'd met other men that Caryn was dating. None of them had invoked a sense of playfulness in her. Caryn's entire body beamed.

"Mom, Dad, I'd like you to meet Dr. William Proctor.... Will, this is Bonnie and Lloyd Stewart."

Finally taking his eyes off Caryn, Will reached out his hand toward her father. "It's a pleasure to meet you, Mr. Stewart."

"Please, call me Lloyd," he said, giving him a firm shake and a good once-over from head to toe.

Nodding in appreciation, Will turned to Bonnie. "It would sound stale to say that I can see where Caryn gets her beauty from, but it would still be the truth."

Bonnie took his hand and her eyes never left his. What kind of man would be a serial dater? What kind of man would declare himself to be a bachelor for the rest of his life? Too polite to ask the questions now, she promised herself that she would stay on top of this. The last thing she wanted was for her daughter to get hurt— and the way she was staring up into his eyes, that was a very real possibility.

"Can I offer you something to drink?"

"No, thank you, Lloyd," Will said, checking his watch. "We need to get going."

"What are your plans for the day?" Bonnie asked. "Don't forget we have dinner plans for six o'clock."

Will glanced at Caryn and watched her eyes widen in expectation. He didn't want to be rude, but he didn't want to give it away. Gently grabbing her arms, he turned her toward her parents. Not able to see his face, he mouthed the words to them. The look of surprise was classic. It assured him that the activity was original and that Caryn would have a good time.

"That sounds like fun," Bonnie said. "I don't think we've ever done that."

Lloyd smiled in approval. "Good choice."

Caryn didn't like being in the dark. Anyone who spent more than three seconds in her presence quickly realized that she had to maintain some level of control. Being out of the loop was not her forte and she struggled to handle being placed in that role. "That's not fair."

Will reached around her waist and gently pulled her to him. Amused at her childish answer, his eyes mocked her. "I only promised to be fun. I didn't say anything about being fair."

Her parents exchanged knowing glances when Caryn punched him in the arm and stuck out her tongue. When Caryn entered college, it was as if she had left her silliness behind. She was all business, all the time. So uptight, so wound up, so inflexible. Instead of taking it easy when she came home, she usually managed to stress everyone else out.

No matter how long she stayed, she rarely took a break. She'd been joined at the hip to her laptop, and her earpiece had become a permanent extension of her ear. There'd be conference calls with clients, meetings with Jeremy and updates from her team. In between, she would try to squeeze in dinner with friends, time with family and personal time for herself. But this visit was turning out to be quite different and the only new variable in the picture was Will.

"I'll have her back in plenty of time for dinner."

Lloyd and Bonnie watched from the living-room window as Will helped Caryn settle into the passenger side of the SUV.

"What do you think?" Lloyd said, not taking his eyes off the couple.

Bonnie let an unhurried smile form. "I think this will be an interesting vacation."

Chapter 14

Settling into his Cadillac Escalade, Caryn surveyed the inside as he buckled up. Checking out the sound system, the wood-grain trimming, the navigation system and the plush leather seats, she completed her investigation by pulling down her visor and checking her makeup in the lighted mirror.

"Does it pass inspection?" he asked, pulling out onto the street.

"I figured you were a top-of-the-line kind of guy. Looks like I was right."

"You have a problem with that?"

"Not at all," she said, closing the mirror before facing him. "Of course, it's no Lexus GX 470, but still a good choice."

Will laughed at the comparison. "I see your competitive nature is not just in the boardroom."

"I just call it like I see it."

"You'll have to give me a ride in yours—so I can see for myself."

The idea that he would ever be in her truck sent her mind racing. Her Lexus was in Boston. That would mean that he would be in Boston. The thought threw her off balance and she immediately dismissed it. "Of course, the Jag you drove last night was cute. But my convertible SL Benz is better."

They merged onto Interstate 95 as the sounds of Kem played through the speakers. "I see you have a competitive streak in you…and also a petty streak."

"Excuse me?"

"You're still a little perturbed because you have no idea what this day will bring and it's driving you crazy," Will explained, already having picked up on her control tendencies. "So, you assert your control someplace—therefore, the conversation about our cars."

"I thought you were a medical doctor," Caryn said smartly. "Why don't you leave the psychoanalyzing to the experts?"

"I think I touched a nerve," he said lightly, reaching over to rub her thigh.

"Okay, Mr. Know It All," Caryn said, pushing his hand away. "Let's talk about you."

"What about me?" he said, wondering what she could possibly bring up.

"For someone who has his set of dating rules, you seem to have charming parents down to a science. The nervous stance. The anxious look on your face. The sappiest parent line ever— 'I see where Caryn gets her beauty from.' Please! Give me a break."

Will thought back to the introductions. Could his uneasiness really be that transparent? "How about this—for someone who is only interested in her career, you practically jumped in anticipation of spending the day with me."

"Let's just hope you live up to all your hype," Caryn said dryly.

"I feel no pressure," he said confidently. "If it's one thing I've mastered over the years, it's living up to my hype."

Rolling her eyes at his pompous statement, she said, "Were you born this arrogant or did it develop over the years?"

"The only reason I'm not offended is because I believe that's part of my charm and attraction for you."

"Charm!" she said. "Attraction! Spoken like someone truly arrogant. Why would I want someone like that?"

"Simple," he said. "You need someone who can go toe to toe with you. Challenge your mind and help you reach the next level. Not just in business but in life. You have to have someone just as strong, just as driven and just as passionate as you. You need someone to help you handle everything that you are and everything that you want to be. Not to mention you need someone who won't put up with any of your crap—otherwise you'll roll right over them. And if you're honest with yourself, you'll recognize that the very qualities you see in me— you have them in yourself."

"I told you before that we were a lot alike," she said, thinking of their conversation last night. "But arrogance—uh-uh—that's where the similarities end."

Will was well aware of the negative connotations that came with that word, but there were times when not only was arrogance necessary, it was critical to getting what you wanted out of life. "Arrogance is overconfidence, audaciousness, boldness, daring and having pride in what you do. I find it impossible to believe that you didn't have some of those traits to break through that glass ceiling. How many challenges you must have come up against during your career. A woman? A black woman? You must have had daggers coming at you from several angles.

"Haters. Chauvinists. Racists. You had to take on some of those people and demand respect, to insist on getting everything you deserved. To claim your rightful place in that boardroom. You had to exhibit some of that, not only to be the best, but to make them recognize it.

"Without a healthy dose of arrogance, you'd be stuck somewhere in middle management, trying to break into six figures and wondering when you were going to get a break. Now, I'm not saying you use all of that to put somebody else down or destroy others, but you do use it to pull yourself up."

When Caryn didn't respond, he took his eyes off the road for a moment to gauge her reaction. "Am I right?"

"I won't give your arrogant behind the satisfaction of answering that question." Her tone was superficial, but Caryn turned to look out the window as her heart beat erratically.

A strange inner joy pulsed in her, causing shivers. Someone finally got her. Someone finally understood her experiences. Someone finally related to all her ups and downs and the challenges that she faced every day.

Someone finally understood that she had to come with her "A" game each and every time she stepped into her office. Someone finally understood what it took to get where she was instead of questioning her decision to go after her goals. Relief flooded through her, bringing liberation with it.

"You okay?" Will asked, hearing her deep, short breaths.

Gone were the flippant responses and Caryn decided to come clean. "Working my way up hasn't been easy. You just summed up the last ten years of my life."

This time, when Will reached over and squeezed her thigh, she didn't pull away.

Riding in silence, they both seemed to be lost in their own thoughts. Then, Caryn saw a sign. "Welcome to West Virginia?"

"Yes."

"What could possibly be fun in West Virginia?"

"Be nice, Caryn," Will said, playfully scolding her. "I'm sure the residents of this state would take offense to that question."

Peering out the window more intently, she looked for anything that would give her a clue as to where they were headed.

Watching her examine every street sign, Will decided to distract her with stories about some of his more memorable patients.

"There was an elderly woman who would come in at least once a month to complain about something. Madelyn Harper was her name and she was a seventy-year-old former ballet dancer. One month, it would be pain in her knees. The following month, she'd fuss about her back. The next time, she pointed to her side, wondering if it could be her appendix. Finally, after running several tests and finding nothing wrong with her, I recommended she seek psychiatric help. I guess that referral forced her to finally fess up."

"To what?" Caryn said, confused as to why anyone would keep going to the doctor if nothing was wrong.

"Eloise Johnson."

"Who?"

"Eloise Johnson was her granddaughter. She thought I would be perfect for her and each time Madelyn came to see me, she tried to work up enough nerve to say something. Once she confessed, she couldn't stop talking about Eloise.

"She showed me a picture and recited her bio to me. MBA from Duke. Organizational development consultant. Independent. Successful. Available. Madelyn wanted me to give her a call right then and there."

The idea of Will dating someone else caused a shadow of annoyance to cross Caryn's face. Mixed feelings surged through her. Why did it matter to her? What did she care about Madelyn or her granddaughter? Frustrated that she was dealing with these feelings for a man that would be out of her life in three weeks, she lashed out at him. "I'm sure if you gave her a copy of your rules, she would change her mind and realize that you're not all that."

"Wow," Will said. "I pegged you as feisty, tough and someone that could challenge me. But I would have never thought you would be the jealous type."

"Me?" she asked, pushing his hand off her thigh for the second time. "Jealous? Don't be ridiculous. That's the arrogance coming out in you."

Will said nothing, but figured he'd hit the nail on the head. The thought of him with someone else troubled her. However, his excitement at the revelation soon died down as he realized that the thought of her with someone else made his skin crawl. "Sure it is. How about we change the subject?"

"Okay," Caryn said. Wanting to get Eloise off her mind—and his—she thought about her dad. "What about people that are afraid of going to the doctor. How do you think people should handle that?"

"Caryn," he asked teasingly, "are you scared to get a checkup?"

"Oh, no," Caryn said, thinking of the executive health plan her company provided. "I have to get a complete physical twice a year—company policy."

"That's too bad," he said, obviously disappointed.

"Why?"

"I would be more than happy to give you a complete physical," he said, giving her a quick once-over. "I'm the best at playing doctor."

"Oh, shoot me now," Caryn moaned. "How lame can a line get? How many times have you used that one?"

Laughing right along with her, Will had to admit that early in his medical career, he'd used that more times than he cared to remember. He'd retired it years ago, but couldn't resist. "I know it was bad, but you gave me the perfect setup."

Caryn thought of the conversation with her mother. "My mom mentioned that it's been years since my dad has had an exam. She's worried about him."

Will didn't like the sound of that. He and his partners had dealt with their share of patients who'd waited too late or who were seeking advice on how to get a loved one to come see him. Statistics show that men wait longer to have something checked out. "Does he have any symptoms?"

"He calls it getting old. Just some aches and pains."

Not wanting to worry her unnecessarily, he reached over and rubbed her thigh again. "That could be all it is—but I do think he should get seen. Bring him to the office. I'll take a look at him."

"Thanks, Will. I'm going to talk to him."

Gazing out the window, Caryn noticed the sign just as they turned off the main road. "Oh, no. I don't think so. I'm not doing that."

"Oh yes we are," he said, pulling into a parking space.

"Says who?"

"Says the tour guide."

"I don't know about this, Will."

"Have you ever done this before?"

"No; and I'm not sure I want to start now."

Will parked the car in the lot and unhooked his seat belt. Turning off the engine, he opened the door but didn't get out. "Come on, Caryn. If you can handle multimillion-dollar business deals, you can handle this."

When she didn't make a move to get out of the car, he reached across the seat and unhooked her belt. Leaning across her body, he felt the heat of their closeness and turned to face her, just inches from her lips. His eyes cut down to her lips before he raised them back to hers. "Do you want to be kissed?"

The response was nonverbal as she leaned up and

pressed her lips to his. At first, her touch was gentle, getting reacquainted with him again. But as the seconds ticked off, she gave in to her eagerness and slipped her tongue inside. Without regard for the awkwardness of the front seat, she turned and leaned her body forward until her chest pressed into his. As his hands rubbed her back, she caressed his neck, probing deeper and deeper. Giving herself freely to the passion that stirred inside her, she moaned from deep in her throat.

Will heard the sound and felt his manhood come alive. The sensual sound, coupled with the stroke of her hands on his neck, sent his body into overdrive. Reluctantly, he pulled back, leaving her with soft, butterfly kisses on her lips, cheeks and nose. "That's one serious diversion tactic."

"Did it work?" she said breathlessly.

"Almost," he said, wanting to head back to his place and pick up right where they'd left off. "But since we're here…"

Caryn glanced out the window again at the other people heading for the check-in area. Turning back to Will, it was plain to see her skepticism.

Will got out of the SUV and walked around to the passenger side. Opening her door, he held his hand out to her. "Trust me."

Chapter 15

Caryn strapped on her life jacket, mumbling under her breath. "I don't believe I agreed to this. This man must be out of his mind. He'd better know what he's doing."

"What did you say?" Will asked as if he were talking to a two-year-old. "You've been grumbling for the last half hour. Did you hear one word the guide told us?"

"I said I can't believe I'm risking my life for you." This time she said her words sharply, loud and clear. A few other people stopped what they were doing at her outburst. But Caryn didn't care. "Did you hear that?"

They'd gathered in the small prep building that looked like a log cabin, listening to safety instructions. The more she heard, the more skeptical she became.

"Let's see," Will said, counting on his fingers. "You are arrogant, confident and an overachiever. We found out earlier today that you were also jealous. Now I can add spoiled to that ever-growing list."

Caryn stopped fumbling with the hooks on her jacket and put her hands on her hips. When her eyes narrowed and her lips drew in tight, it was evident that she was ready for war. "What did you just call me?"

A few more people glanced in their direction at her second outburst, but she couldn't have cared less.

Will mimicked her by putting his hands on his hips and raising his voice to a high pitch. "Where are we going? When will we get there? That's not fair. He better know what he's doing. Whine. Whine. Whine. Whine."

"I'm going to knock that silly grin off your face if you don't stop mocking me," she said, making a fist and waving it at him.

"See," he said, dropping his hands to his sides. "That's exactly what I'm talking about. All the whining comes out when you're not in control. Face it. You can't stand not being in the driver's seat."

Unwilling to admit he had a point, Caryn stated the obvious. "Like I said, we're a lot alike and when we get going today, neither one of us will be in control. I can't wait to see how well you handle it."

"You make it sound like that's a bad thing," Will said, moving closer to her. "Losing control can also be quite freeing."

Shifting from one foot to the other, Caryn teetered between complete attraction and all-consuming discomfort. He had the amazing ability to make her feel special one moment, and in the next instance, he had her questioning every part of her life.

Taking hold of her hand, he pulled it up to his mouth

and brushed it with his lips. "When is the last time you've been completely free?"

Looking around the lobby, she noticed that other people had stopped paying attention to them, continuing their own preparations. But that didn't stop Caryn from feeling as if she had been put in the spotlight. The stroke of his lips against her skin had taken her by surprise and his nearness was overwhelming. For a moment she couldn't focus on anything but the sense of excitement he generated in her.

Numbers she knew. Handling high-powered business deals she understood. Asking for the bathroom in seven languages had become second nature. But Dr. William Proctor? He was turning out to be a little more than she'd bargained for. He was right. Being out of control didn't work for her and it seemed that ever since he'd walked into her life, he'd stripped her of it. Now she decided to take some of it back.

Pulling her hand away from him, she continued to work with her vest. "Can we just get this over with?"

Will watched her struggle with clasping the belts. "Come on, now, this is going to be fun."

Caryn looked past him at the deceivingly calm waters. "I think we need to clarify the definition of 'fun.'"

The guide called out for the group to make its way out of the building to begin. Caryn exhaled loudly and halfheartedly headed in that direction.

"Wait," Will said, blocking her walk. He adjusted her vest and double-checked the hooks on the jacket, making sure they were locked and secure. "I can't have anything happen to you. That wouldn't look good on a tour guide's record."

Motionless, Caryn let him finish his work without responding. As the belts tightened around her waist, the
unexpected gesture on his part conjured up unfamiliar
feelings. A new and surprising wave of apprehension,
mixed with a surge of affection, coursed through her. He
was taking care of her. Making sure she was safe. It was
something that no one had done for her since college.
It was something she didn't let anyone do for her.

The men that had come and gone in her life had complained about her travel, her commitment to her job and
her uncompromising attitude toward them. Her work
came first—always. When they got tired of playing
second fiddle, the relationship fizzled out. The plan that
she developed for her life didn't give her the luxury of
compromising. Settling. Finding the middle ground.
Making concessions. She refused to give up that control
she had in her life—and the power. But Will was changing
all that. He was taking care of her and she liked it.

She'd never taken to men who tried to do things for
her like volunteering to change her oil, repairing something in her home or going with her to purchase big-
ticket items. Did they think she couldn't handle it? She
resented their intrusion in her life and they resented the
distance she kept between her and them. Today, for the
first time in her life, she willingly allowed a man to do
for her. To take care of her. It was a small concession
to the outside world, but for her, it was huge.

"Looks like you're all set," he said, leaning back and
admiring his handiwork. "Come on, baby. It's show-
time."

The endearment threw her for a loop and temporarily stunned her. Baby? Sweetheart? Boo? Honey?

She cringed at hearing those words from men. Too personal. Too possessive. Pet names and nicknames were reserved for couples that had a foundation and a future. She and Will had neither. Yet she found herself strangely pleased that he'd used that word with her.

Ten minutes later she stood on the edge of the water, feeling the pressure of twelve eyes staring at her. The guide, two other couples and Will sat, somewhat impatiently as they waited for her to join them. The white-water rafting run was scheduled to begin three minutes ago. She'd never done anything close to this in her life. Adventurous outdoor activities weren't her thing. Twisting her fingers together, her wide eyes showed her uncertainty.

Will held out his hand to her. "Trust me."

Taking hold of his hand, she jumped into the raft and took her position. Picking up her oar, she nodded to the guide that she was ready to go.

Four hours later, Caryn had finished her first white-water rafting run and she could not stop talking about it. "Oh my God, did you feel the rush of that last drop."

They had been on the road for almost twenty minutes and Will hadn't gotten a word in. "I thought I was going to fall into the water at least three times."

"To hear you tell it," he said, "it sounds like you had fun."

"You and that *F* word are starting to get on my last nerve," she said, hating to admit how exhilarating the experience was.

"In other words, yes, you had fun."

When she remained silent, he filled in the space. "I

guess you could say that I'm batting a thousand with this tour-guide duty."

Caryn didn't want to cut him any slack. "You could say you were batting a thousand with that arrogant attitude."

The ring of the BlackBerry interrupted their banter. The sound made her jump. She hadn't thought about work all day and forgot that she'd brought it with her. She'd left it in the car and hadn't bothered to check to see if anyone had called. Looking at the name that popped up, she thought twice about answering but pushed the Talk button.

Will kept his eyes on the road and his ears on her conversation. Without her computer or files in front of her, she was winging most of her answers. The only part he could make out was that someone was meeting with a client and wasn't prepared. Twenty-five minutes later she ended the call.

"Sounds like trouble."

"Sounds like they can't live without me," she said, and for the first time that thought aggravated her. "We went over that information last week."

Caryn leaned her back against the headrest and rubbed her neck.

"You okay?"

"Yeah," she said. "I'm wondering if she's going to get it right."

The carefree attitude that existed between them before the call completely disappeared. Will watched as Caryn's mood deflated faster than a popped balloon. "I don't think you're okay."

"I'm fine—really. I'll follow up with her."

"I'm not talking about this call. I'm talking about your work in general."

"What about it?"

"Each time your job comes up, your entire demeanor changes. Your back stiffens, your face tightens and you roll your neck around, as if you're trying to loosen your muscles. The fun we shared earlier vanished when that phone rang."

Caryn didn't want to admit it, but taking that call had reminded her of a couple of things that needed to get done. If Stacy had those questions, there were probably a few other questions that Stacy hadn't anticipated looming out there. If she reviewed the data tonight, she could get that info to her in the morning. "I don't have to justify my actions to you."

When his hand reached for her thigh, she ignored it. "How is it that you go from footloose and fancy free to uptight and worried in a matter of seconds?"

"Stop doing that."

Her angry tone was ignored. "What?"

"Trying to break into that second layer. Let's remember what this is about."

"Remind me," he said. He didn't know if he could say the words and wanted to see if she could.

Caryn didn't look his way but continued, "A few weeks of rest, relaxation and the *F* word."

Will's philosophy about relationships told him that this is where he was supposed to get off. The lines were becoming blurred. It became less about the things they did together and more about the memories they were creating. The good food, the intelligent conversation and the latest social event were by-products of being with each other, sharing with each other and getting to know each other. This is where it was less about the physical and more about the spirit. This was about beginning to break his rules. "Do you still think that is what this is about—what we are about?"

Staring out the window, watching the trees go by, Caryn understood exactly what he was asking. The last couple of days had been the first time in a long time when work was not at the forefront of her mind. It was the first time she'd looked forward to seeing someone. Being with someone. And in a few weeks, she had the unsettling stir in her stomach that it would be the first time she dreaded leaving someone.

Pushing down those thoughts, she couldn't afford this confusion in her life right now. She had a plan and people were depending on her. "What else is there?"

Will couldn't believe that he was finally going to admit that something was happening between them and she was going to pretend that there wasn't. "There are the moments."

When Caryn remained quiet, he continued, "The moment I walked into the office and said 'hello.' The moment I pulled you into my arms at the party and our bodies melted together. The moment overlooking the White House when you leaned back into me as I rubbed your shoulders. The moment we started down that river and laughed, joked and had fun. This moment. Right here. When I hear the stress and see the anxiety that comes with your job and I want to make it all go away."

"Will," Caryn said, refusing to relive their time together, "don't do this."

"Do what?"

She faced him, but her confidence had declined and her eyes pleaded with him. "Change the rules."

Will didn't answer. Instead, he focused on the road.

Chapter 16

The Escalade turned onto Caryn's street, the remainder of the trip made with only a few comments here and there about trivial things neither cared about. Will, dropping the subject of them, gave Caryn a reprieve. Mainly because he was swimming in unfamiliar waters and he couldn't be sure how deep he wanted to go.

"Looks like someone's having a party."

Caryn saw all the cars parked along her street and recognized a few of them. "You've got to be kidding me."

Double-parking in front of her driveway, Will put his blinkers on and jumped out. Before he could get to her side, she'd already opened the door and got out.

"I would have helped you," he said.

Will had been a perfect gentleman since they met.

Holding doors for her. Helping her in and out of cars. Double-checking her life vest. A woman could get used to those courtesies. Caryn decided it would be best if she didn't get used to them. "I don't need your help."

The double meaning hung in the air and Will exhaled loudly, backing up. "Whatever you say."

"Caryn, honey, we're so glad you're back."

Both turned toward the house to see her mother coming down the walkway.

"Mom, what's going on?"

"Your aunt Betty called this afternoon asking about you. When I told her we were having dinner tonight, she insisted on coming. She hasn't seen you in years. Well, of course, she would bring your uncle Chester."

"Of course," Caryn said sarcastically. "But that doesn't explain the other ten cars."

"Betty spoke to Veronica, who spoke to your other cousin, Glenda."

"And who did Glenda talk to?" Caryn asked, already figuring out how this story was going to end.

"If Glenda and Veronica were coming over, I couldn't leave out your aunt Alice and uncle Elbert."

Caryn paused when she heard the names. "They live two hours away!"

Bonnie could see the panic rising in her daughter's voice. No doubt this was a little overwhelming for her. "I know it's unexpected. But they were all excited that you were home and wanted to see you. How could I say no?"

Caryn realized her agitation didn't stem from the impromptu gathering but rather from the phone call from work and the inquisition from Will. Things were happening too fast. How could someone come into her life for a short period of time and turn her world upside down? How could he waltz into her space and make her rethink everything that she was about? How could he make her angry one minute and calm her spirit the next?

Giving her mom an encouraging smile, she said, "It's okay, Mom. I want to see them, too."

"Good," she said. "Your father has fired up the grill and your aunt Betty brought over her world-famous potato salad."

"I'll go up and shower and change and meet you in the backyard," she said before turning to Will. It was obvious there was unfinished business between them but she was thankful that she wouldn't have to deal with it today. "Thanks for today, Will."

"You are more than welcome to join us, Will."

Both turned to Bonnie at the unexpected invitation.

The request was the one rule that Will had maintained vigorously over the years. Meeting families led to expectations, questions and indicated that a relationship was more than casual. The excuses could roll easily off his tongue. *Thanks, but maybe another time. Thanks, but I already have other plans. Thanks, but after a long day, I really need to get home. Thanks, but I don't want to impose on family time.*

Caryn saw the hesitation on Will's part and stepped in to save him. Evidently, all that talk about getting closer and wanting to be with her was just lip service. "Mom, I don't think Will—"

"Would rather do anything else but join you."

The agreement to stay caught them both off guard

and Caryn eyed him with a curious stare. His type would never do family events. No matter what they'd shared.

"Let me run home and change. I'll be back in about an hour or so."

"Great," Bonnie said, satisfied at the way the evening was shaping up. "We'll see you then."

Forty-five minutes later, Caryn walked into the kitchen dressed in a pair of blue jeans and a T-shirt. Feeling completely refreshed from her shower, she smelled the aromas of summertime food. The scent of hamburgers, hot dogs, chicken and ribs wafted from the backyard as the sliding glass door opened and closed as people moved in and out. Her mother stood at the island cutting up vegetables while her aunt Betty used the mixer to combine the ingredients for her chocolate cake.

Washing her hands at the sink, Caryn dried them with a paper towel and stood beside her mother. "What can I help with?"

Suddenly, the flurry of activity dwindled to nothing. Her mother stopped chopping and her aunt stopped mixing. Both women exchanged a knowing look before their lips creased into a small smile. At that moment, her cousin Veronica entered the kitchen and noticed the lack of commotion.

"What's the matter?" she said, glancing at all the women. "Did something happen?"

Veronica was dressed in a pair of black shorts and a baby-doll top, but her protruding stomach was the first thing Caryn noticed. About the same height and size, the two of them had been called the Bobbsy Twins as children. They'd done everything together. But things had definitely changed over the years. There was very little that was similar about them today. They chose very different paths in their adult life.

"Caryn just asked us what she could do to help with the food."

Veronica wasn't as polite as the others and broke into a laugh.

"Would someone like to tell me what's so funny?" Caryn said.

"You can't cook," Aunt Betty said, resuming her duties.

"Yeah, Caryn," Veronica said. "I've never known you to make toast. But then, I guess it's fine with you. Who would you cook for? You don't have a family. You're always on the road. Aunt Bonnie never mentions a boyfriend."

"Now, Veronica, on the other hand, has become quite the chef," Aunt Betty continued. "Christopher insisted that she take time off when they had Lauryn. He didn't want his wife working late, dropping off their child in day care or worrying about getting a boss that wouldn't understand that her family came first."

"Christopher was the best thing that ever happened to me," Veronica said. "I was so busy working my way up the corporate ladder that I almost let that brotha get away."

"But you came to your senses," Aunt Betty said. "You made the right choice. You can pick up your career anytime."

"I'd have to do a lot of catching up to come anywhere near Caryn's success."

"She has just as much catching up to do," Aunt Betty said, giving Caryn a look. "By the time she finds time to get married and have children, the baby in your belly will be old enough to babysit."

Caryn tuned the women out as they continued to talk about husbands, babies and unborn children. Veronica had been a star at the marketing firm she'd joined right out of college. Two years later, she met Christopher Miller, an executive with a clothing manufacturer that had been a client. Within a year, all the career plans Veronica had so carefully laid out went by the wayside. Instead of talks of promotions, corner offices and expense accounts, the conversations switched to bridesmaid dresses, honeymoons, new homes and decorating.

Before her marriage, Caryn and Veronica managed to squeeze in several phone calls a month. Comparing their jobs, bosses and next moves, they encouraged each other and cheered each other on. Now those calls no longer took place.

Once Veronica's honeymoon was over, their conversations were strained and uncomfortable. Caryn would be thrilled to share news about the latest developments with her boss or a client, and Veronica could only talk of fabrics for window treatments and furniture for the nursery. Over the years, those calls became more and more infrequent. Before today, it had been two and half years since the two of them had spoken.

"It's hard to believe that it will be five years of marriage in a few months," Veronica said, rubbing her belly. "Christopher was talking about celebrating in the Caribbean, but who wants to waddle on the beach seven months pregnant?"

Aunt Betty nodded in approval. "I agree with Christopher. You need to take it easy. No need worrying about going this place or that when you have a family at home."

The banter continued between the two women and Caryn suddenly lost her desire to stay in the kitchen. "On second thought, I think I'll go outside and talk to Daddy."

Bonnie stared after Caryn as she disappeared into the backyard. Firm in her conviction to build her career before making time for anything—or anyone—else, Caryn never let conversations like that get to her. But the exasperated look on Caryn's face when she left told a different story. Bonnie made a mental note to talk to her daughter about it.

"Hey, Daddy," Caryn said, giving him a kiss on the cheek as he flipped burgers on the grill.

"Hi, there, sweetie," he said, wiping a little sweat off his forehead with a paper towel. "I know it's supposed to be the three of us, but one thing led to another and…"

"And the whole family decided to come over."

"How was your rafting trip?"

The smile went unnoticed by Caryn as she relived her adventure from earlier today. The activity was enjoyable, but it was the man she'd shared it with that made it memorable. "After Will helped me get over my initial fear, it was amazing."

"He seems like a nice young man."

"Daddy," Caryn warned. "Don't start."

"Start what? Talking about grandbabies? Talking about walking my baby girl down the aisle. Talking about seeing you more than a couple of times a year?"

"You'll get all those things," Caryn promised. "After I finish—"

"Your plan." Lloyd had heard that sentence more times than he cared to remember. "There's probably a master document somewhere in your house where you have a checklist of career goals. Make a hundred thousand dollars—check. Make senior management—check. Log millions of miles in frequent-flier program—check."

"There's nothing wrong with wanting to be accomplished," Caryn said.

"I'll never disagree with you on that. But your drive to succeed can make anyone exhausted. I just want to make sure that you're doing it for the right reasons."

"I don't understand."

"Your mother and I are proud of you. You should be proud of what you've accomplished. There's no need to prove anything to anybody."

"How about you?"

"What about me?"

"What are you trying to prove by not going to the doctor?"

"I can tell you've been talking to your mother."

"Doesn't matter who I've been talking to."

"I'll tell you like I told her. I'm fine."

"Will is a doctor, Daddy."

"That boy is young enough to be my son. What does he know about medicine?"

"More than you."

Lloyd continued to work the grill, ignoring her.

"Hey, Lloyd, the troops are getting anxious. When are those burgers going to be ready?"

Uncle Chester pounded her father's back a few times, leaning over his shoulder to look at the grill.

"They'll be coming up in just a few minutes."

With Uncle Chester continuing to badger her dad about the food, Caryn headed back inside. Bypassing the kitchen, she headed for the living room. She wasn't in the mood for any more conversations about the choices she'd made in her life. However, peace and quiet would have to wait a little longer. Christopher was there with his daughter.

"Oh, Caryn," he said, getting up from the floor. "I'm so glad to see you. Can you watch Lauryn for a few minutes? I left some of her games in the car."

Before she could answer, he gave her a quick thank-you peck on the cheek and headed for the door.

Caryn stared down at the three-year-old and settled into a full-fledged panic. Caryn didn't do well with children. As an only child, she'd never been around them, and as an adult, she'd only had passing contact. The wide brown eyes of Lauryn stared expectantly up at her, waiting.

"Hello, Lauryn," Caryn said, taking a seat on the floor beside her.

The little girl reached for one of the large puzzle pieces she was playing with and handed them to Caryn.

"Thank you," she said, pulling the cardboard base of the puzzle closer to her. "You want me to help you with that?"

Nodding yes, she crawled to Caryn and climbed into her lap.

The move, so unexpected, froze Caryn temporarily. Had she ever held a child before? Her stiff body began to relax and the little girl made herself comfortable by snuggling between her legs. "Let's put your puzzle together."

Will stood quietly at the entrance of the living room. He'd arrived a few moments earlier and Christopher, after introducing himself, led him into the house. After being directed to Caryn, he stopped short when he saw the scene unfolding. Caryn sat in the middle of the floor holding a child, talking softly with her as they put a children's puzzle together. A surge of longing went through his body and he had to put his feelings in check.

Thoughts of fatherhood had been few and far between. Taking on that role would be the most work any person could do. It shouldn't be done if the parents aren't willing to give one hundred percent of their time and energy to raising a child. But watching Caryn smile at the little girl, talk sweetly to her and helping her, all the while stroking her hair as she sat in her lap, conjured up a family portrait that included a wife and a child.

"I'm sorry, Caryn."

Will stepped to the side as another woman entered the room.

"I can't believe Christopher left you here with her," she said, picking the small child up. "We all know you have limited patience for little ones."

Caryn stood and dusted off her jeans. "No, it was okay. We were putting our puzzle together."

"In any case, I'll take her."

When they left the room, Caryn stared after them before stooping down to pick up the pieces from the activity off the floor.

"Let me help you with that."

"Will?" she said. "Where did you come from?"

"Christopher let me in."

"Oh," she said, finding the puzzle box on an end

table. "You have good timing, the food should be ready in a few minutes."

Will watched her fumble with the box, never looking at him when she spoke. "Are you okay?"

Caryn nodded but turned her back to him, setting the box on the coffee table.

When she didn't make a move, Will reached out and touched her arm. "Caryn?"

Without warning, she turned and stepped to him, wrapping her arms around his waist.

Though taken aback by the unexpected gesture, that didn't stop the automatic response. Hugging her tight, he pressed his head against hers and whispered, "Hey, what's wrong?"

Throughout her adult life, she'd faced some of the most trying tests. Proving that she was good enough. Proving that she was strong enough. Proving that she could handle big responsibilities. All along, she had one rule that she held hard and fast to. No tears. The last image she wanted to convey was that of weakness. But these last couple of days had her on an emotional roller coaster and she felt as if she was reaching her breaking point.

Her boss and team continued to treat her as if she wasn't on vacation. Will had been pressing her to reexamine the choices she'd made about her career. Her mother had her questioning how much material success was enough and her father told her that he loved and was proud of her and proving herself over and over again wouldn't serve her in the long run. And now there was Veronica.

Listening to her rave about her husband, her

children, her life as a wife and mother started to grate on Caryn's nerves. It wasn't jealousy that reared its head, it was something inexplicable. It was as if Veronica, Aunt Betty and her mother were part of a special club and she was left out.

"Food is up," Bonnie said, interrupting their private moment.

Caryn tried to jump out of Will's arms, but he wouldn't let her. He held her tight.

Bonnie saw the intimate moment and watched Will's reaction to Caryn carefully. Caryn had been running from personal relationships her entire life, always meeting someone and pushing them aside for her career. From all that she could see, Will wasn't one to be pushed. She liked that.

"We'll be right out, Mom."

Bonnie focused her eyes on Will. "Take all the time you need."

When she left, Caryn went into damage control mode. "I don't know what came over me. I must be completely exhausted from such a full day. All of my muscles are starting to get sore from the rafting trip."

She wiped her eyes with the back of her hand and walked right past him. "Let's go outside. We don't want our food to get cold."

Will opened his mouth to stop her. She wasn't getting off the hook that easily. Then he changed his mind. This wasn't the time, or the place. That would come soon enough and he would find out exactly what was going on in that pretty little head of hers.

Chapter 17

Friday afternoon Will sat in his office flipping through his screen of appointments. A little before three, he wanted to make sure he could be out of the office by four. He had plans with Caryn and needed to do a few things before he picked her up at six. After the family gathering at her parents' house, they decided to put a moratorium on his questions and get back to hanging out.

He'd taken two days off during the week, spending them with Caryn. They'd packed their time with a ton of stuff, including paddle boating on the Potomac River, enjoying lunch on the pier in Old Town, seeing the dolphin show at the Baltimore Aquarium and taking a day trip to Williamsburg.

Seeing Derrick walk past his office, he called him in.

"Look who decided to come to work today," he said, dropping down in the seat in front of his desk.

"Very funny," he said.

"Hey, I just call them like I see them. I've spent more time with your patients this week than you have."

"And I need you to see my last two patients for today."

"Where are you off to?"

"Plans with Caryn."

"Tell me something I don't know. I don't think you've ever done a week of going out with one woman. What's going on with you?"

Will shut down his computer. "I wish I knew."

"What about your rules?" he asked. "I'm sure seeing her just about every day this week breaks at least one of them."

"That's just it," Will confessed, walking around to the front of his desk. Leaning against it, he toyed with how much he should share with Derrick. They were best friends and had been through a lot together. For that reason alone, Derrick could probably help him. "The truth is, I've been breaking rules from the moment she stepped into my life."

"Really?" Derrick said, remembering his behavior at the party. "I thought waiting for her at the door and being nervous was way out of the ordinary for you, but what else has been going on?"

"I met her parents."

"Oh."

"And her family."

"Wow."

"I questioned her focus on her career and not on her personal life."

"Will, you're treading on dangerous territory."

"Tell me about it."

"How can you go from dropping a woman for the slightest infraction of your rules to breaking just about all of them in a matter of a week?"

"You don't think I haven't been asking myself that same question over and over again?"

"What's the answer?"

"I don't know," he said, his frustration mounting. "The only thing I know is that I like her. I like spending time with her."

"Then this is good news. Sherisse was worried about you treating her friend like all the rest, when the two of you are moving in a more serious direction."

"Well, one of us is moving."

"You told me that you felt something different toward her. How can you still resist developing something stronger—something deeper?"

"I'm not the one resisting."

Several moments passed before the full meaning of his words registered with Derrick. After which his mouth curved upward and his laughter filled the air.

"I should have known better than to tell you any of this."

"What's going on?"

"Oh, Jeff," Derrick said, waving him into the office. "You are right on time."

"For?"

"You're gonna love this," Derrick said. "Go ahead, Will. Tell him."

"This is ridiculous," Will said, standing and putting his white jacket on. "We've got patients to see. We don't have time to stand around all day talking."

Derrick could see that Will was getting agitated, but he didn't care; he'd been through too much with Will's crazy personal life to let him slide with this one. Derrick moved back to D.C. from California almost two years ago. Going through a painful divorce, he couldn't believe his good fortune when he met Natalie. During their courtship, they'd had some challenging times and Will had been there for him. Not interested in anything that remotely resembled a monogamous relationship, he'd cheered Derrick on, helping him win over the woman he loved, while dating several women.

In the time that they'd been partners, Will had never apologized or wavered from his rules. Now it looked as if that was changing, but there was a snag in his plan. A very funny snag. "Will has been seeing Caryn."

"Cool," Jeff said. "So what's so funny about that?"

"Will has broken a few of his rules," Derrick explained.

Jeff pretended to clean out his ears. "Will never breaks the rules."

"Yeah, well," Will said.

"What's funny about that?" Jeff said.

"You misunderstood," Derrick said. "I said Will was breaking rules. I didn't say anything about Caryn."

"You mean…" Jeff started.

"Will wants something more out of this relationship and she's not interested."

"I always heard karma was a—"

"That's enough," Will said. "I should have never said anything."

"Okay," Derrick said. "I'm sorry. But you have to admit it's the most ironic thing I have ever heard. The king of emotionally detached relationships is starting to have feelings for a woman—and she's not interested."

"You guys should be able to help me out," Will said, glancing from one to the other. "Both of you have much more experience than me in trying to woo someone who doesn't want you."

"Hey!" Derrick said. "Low blow."

"But true," Will said. "This time last year you were singing the blues about Natalie. You must have proposed to her at least twenty times—and she said no nineteen times. I figured if anyone would know how to help me it would be you."

"He's got a point, Derrick," Jeff said. "You were moping around here for months trying to figure out what to do."

"And what about you?" Will said, turning his attention from Derrick to Jeff.

"What about me?"

"You and Yolanda have been on one day and off the next for a year. When are you going to make up your mind about her?"

"I think we should keep this conversation focused on the main topic—you and Caryn." Jeff didn't want any added attention on his relationship with Yolanda.

"What about Will and Caryn?"

Sherisse stood at the door waiting for someone to answer her question. She'd tried to do the mature thing and mind her own business ever since she'd passed on Caryn's information to Will. When they left together at the party, she wanted to warn Caryn not to get too involved with him but held her tongue.

Over the past week, Caryn told her she'd been spending quite a bit of time with Will, sharing some of their dating adventures. Sherisse had to admit that regardless of what she thought of Will, he had gotten Caryn to finally take her mind off of work

Hearing Caryn's name, she wondered what was going on.

Working in an office with three men, she'd heard her share of locker-room stories. Not so much from Derrick, but definitely from Will and Jeff. Stories about the latest woman that they were either starting to date or breaking up with. They were never disrespectful, but if they were talking about her friend, she was going to have to set them straight.

"Looks like you were wrong," Derrick said.

"About what?" she said.

"The last thing you should worry about is Will taking advantage of your friend or having her deal with his rules," Jeff said cryptically.

"Is that so?"

"Go ahead, tell her," Jeff prompted.

Will didn't mean for his personal life to be gossip for the entire office. He was hoping that by talking it out with Derrick he could figure what—if anything—he should do. Instead of bringing Sherisse up to speed, he decided to break camp. Opening his desk drawer, he pulled out his car keys. "I'm sure the fellas can fill you in."

Walking past all of them, he headed out the door. "Thanks for seeing my last few patients, Derrick. I'll see you guys tomorrow."

"What in the world is wrong with him?' Sherisse said, confused by his strange behavior.

"Have a seat, Sherisse. I'll tell you all about it," said Derrick.

Bonnie sat reading in the living room when Caryn came in. They had spent the better part of the day scouring antique shops in D.C. and northern Virginia. Finding a few pieces for her condo, she planned to have them shipped to her next month. Today, Caryn took only three calls from her office, but they each lasted at least a half hour. It was still too much for Bonnie, but it was less than in the past. "You look lovely, Caryn."

Choosing to dress up for dinner, Caryn had gone back to Danielle's and picked out a couple of summer dresses. This one had a halter top that tied around her neck, a tight waist area and a flared skirt that ended well below the knee. The magenta color set off her gold earrings and the long, slim chains she wore around her neck. Doing a twirl she ended with a pose that would make Tyra Banks proud. "I'm glad you like it."

"What time will he be here?"

Checking her watch, she could see it was almost six. "Any minute now."

Bonnie had always been aware of Caryn's approach to dating. The times that she was seeing someone, her conversations about the man would be completely blasé. Something told her Will was different. "Things are going well between the two of you?"

"Yes," Caryn said, having a strange feeling she knew where this conversation would lead.

"You don't like me getting in your business and I know you don't want to hear any lectures on paying more attention to your personal life. But I would like to offer some advice."

"I'm listening," she said, and this time she meant it. Will had her jumping between two worlds. The world of work and the world of him. At any given moment one had the edge over the other.

"Don't fight it so hard."

"What does that mean?"

"That means that if your feelings start to grow, let them. If you want to get to know him, do it. If there's a strong connection developing between the two of you, allow it."

The doorbell rang before she could answer.

"And Caryn?"

"Yes?"

"You are thirty years old—there are no curfews in this house."

"Mom," Caryn said, noticing the wicked look in her mother's eyes.

"Tell Will I said hello."

"So what's on the agenda for tonight, Mr. Tour Guide?"

Easing into traffic, Will headed into the city. "I would take a wild guess and say it's been a while since you've been pampered—taken care of. That's probably true, not just because of time constraints, but because you don't let people take care of you."

Caryn opened her mouth to speak, but he cut her off.

"Tonight—it's all about you."

"Well, at least it doesn't sound like I'll be racing down a river."

Laughing at the first of their many adventures, he turned onto a quiet street and turned into a parking garage.

"Where are we?"

"My loft."

Danger. Too close. Too intimate. Caryn's physical attraction to Will was a no-brainer. She'd wanted him from the moment she met him. In the last couple of days, he'd shown her that he was more than a sexy doctor. He was someone who challenged her, took care of her and showed her how to let loose. Their kisses had been filled with power and his touch had set her soul on fire. But all of those instances had been in places with other people around. It gave her a buffer. What would happen if she spent the evening with him without a one? "I'm not sure about this, Will."

Will watched the expression on her face and figured out exactly what she was thinking, because he had those same thoughts. Each time he held her in his arms, kissed her and touched her, his body demanded that there be more. But he held back. He wanted her, without a doubt, but he wanted her to want him. Not just his body, but all that came with it. He wasn't sure she was ready for that—and he had his doubts if he was ready.

Caryn not only awakened feelings in him he'd never known, she'd created them. The need to see someone. The need to be in her presence. The need to talk to her. Be with her. That was new territory for him. He didn't want to mess it up by having his hormones in overdrive.

All he wanted was to show her what it was like to surrender. To have someone take the weight off of her—if only for tonight. Cutting the engine, he turned to her. "Trust me."

Chapter 18

Will opened the door to his loft and stepped aside for her to enter. All of her senses came alive the moment she stepped over the threshold. The first thing she noticed was the soft sounds of jazz playing. Next, her nose picked up the spices and herbs that indicated good food was close by. Finally, she heard the pitter-patter of little feet—no, big feet. "Oh my God!"

Apollo came barreling down the short hallway to meet them at the door.

"He's harmless," Will said.

"To what—a lion?"

Still not convinced, Caryn was extra careful not to make any sudden moves. Then she realized the dog had something in his mouth. When Apollo got directly in front of them, Will gave the command to sit, and he did, pushing his face toward Caryn.

"Go ahead, Caryn. You can reach down. He won't bite."

Carefully, she reached her hand out. Apollo, sensing her fear, met her halfway, setting a bouquet of flowers in her hands. Will gave another command, and he trotted off, disappearing into another room.

Raising the flowers to her nose, she was glad to see they smelled floral and not like dog breath. "Nice touch."

"Not sure if you noticed, but the yellow flowers with the dark brown center are black-eyed Susans—the Maryland state flower."

"Always the tour guide," she teased, secretly pleased at his attention to detail.

"Follow me," he said, walking down the short hallway to a space that opened up to a wonderful great room. The tall ceilings, exposed brick and the exposed pipes gave the place an urban feel. With the large picture windows, she could see out over the D.C. streets.

The modern decor was elaborate yet functional. The furniture had sharp lines, but appeared inviting and comfortable. Warm chocolates and tans were strategically accented with burgundy, and the entire space could have been photographed for a design magazine.

"You like it?"

"Are you kidding me," she said, letting her arms travel down the back of his couch. "It makes me think of my condo in Boston."

"Yours in decorated much the same way?"

"It would be," she said.

His eyes told her he didn't understand. "The only room that has furniture in my condo is my bedroom. However, if I ever get around to using the decorator I retained, I have a strong feeling I would create something like this—warm, inviting and cozy."

Will went to her and spun her around in his arms. "Until you finish your place, you are always welcome here."

Caryn couldn't respond because his lips captured hers and devoured her mouth, causing her body temperature to rise a few degrees.

"Have a seat. Dinner will be ready in a few minutes," he said after pulling away.

"The polite thing for me to do would be to offer to help, but I have a confession to make," she said, still reeling from those kisses.

"What?"

"I can't cook."

For a moment, he stared at her, and she wondered if she had gravely disappointed him. Her mind ran through all the times her mother had tried to teach her the basics. All the times she'd patiently watched as Caryn destroyed one meal after another. She thought about all those times she was too busy to help in the kitchen. Remembering all of her mother's theories on what it took to get a man, an uneasiness settled in her stomach as she had a thought that he wanted someone who knew their way around a kitchen.

"Then I guess I'll have to do all the cooking," he said.

The statement hung in the air as he went into the kitchen. The inference was that they would be spending many meals together.

Caryn took a seat on the sofa and tried to put away all the powerful feelings she was developing for Will. Taking a look around, she occupied her time with a visual tour. While nicely decorated, the place still had the trappings of a bachelor pad. A large plasma television hung on the opposite wall. Stacks of sports magazines were in a crate beside the end table. And she would bet money that if she went into his kitchen, she would find more than a fair share of frozen dinners.

"I propose a toast," he said, returning with two glasses of red wine. "To being pampered."

They clinked their glasses and took a sip. Taking her hand in his, he gave her a mysterious smile. "Now, don't take this the wrong way, but I want you to go into my bedroom and take off your clothes."

"What way should I take it?" Appalled by his audacity, she actually entertained the idea of following his order.

"Remember the theme for tonight—pampering?"

The chimes of the doorbell sounded and Caryn eyed him suspiciously. "What's going on?"

"Stay right here."

He disappeared into the foyer and she heard voices but couldn't make out the words. Then he was back, along with a woman.

"Caryn, this is Anastasia. She's a licensed masseuse. She's going to set up in the spare bedroom. You can use my room to prepare."

Caryn couldn't help but smile at his originality with the massage she was about to receive. It had been years since she'd treated herself to a day at the spa and even longer that she fully enjoyed it.

"You said you were a little sore from the rafting, not to mention all the other activities we've done. I thought this would help."

Ever since Will came into her life, she'd had more

emotional outbursts that she'd had in the past ten years. What was it about him that made Caryn Stewart—the together businesswoman—turn to Caryn Stewart— emotional wreck?

"You ladies can follow me."

Once they got to the top of the steps, Anastasia was directed one way, while Caryn was escorted into the master bedroom. The first thing she noticed was the king-size bed and the king-size dog that lay on the floor beside it. A robe was on the bed. "I don't think I need an audience."

Will moved next to her and wrapped his arms around her waist. "Are you talking about me or Apollo?" he asked, playfully kissing her on the neck and ears.

"I'm talking about both of you."

"All right, we'll leave you alone, but hopefully, one day soon, one of us will be able to stick around when it's time to get undressed."

"Hope springs eternal!"

"Ouch! My ego!"

"I'm sure you and your overinflated ego will be just fine," she said, pushing him out the door. "And take this mini horse with you."

Almost an hour later, Caryn floated down the stairs without a care in the world. The massage was exactly what she'd needed to completely relax her body. She'd changed back into her dress, but kept the feeling of euphoria the magical hands of Anastasia had created. She'd heard voices before the front door opened and closed and she figured the masseuse had gone.

When she got to the bottom of the steps, Apollo was there, blocking her way. She started to yell out for Will when she noticed the note around his neck. Common sense told her the note was for her, but the size of that dog told her that the last thing she might want to do is stick her hand out toward him. She may end up with nubs. Then she remembered what Will had been telling her all week—trust him.

"Okay, Apollo."

At hearing his name, his ears perked up, but he still remained seated.

"Good doggie."

His tail started wagging and she took that as a good sign. At least he didn't growl.

"I'm just going to get this note from around your neck."

He continued to stare at her and Caryn had the strange feeling that he understood exactly what she was saying. She reached out her hand and was glad to see that he didn't move. She bent slightly and her hand came closer and closer to him. "Nice Apollo."

When she reached the string that held the piece of paper, she lifted it over his head and breathed a sigh of relief when he maintained his position. Opening the note, she smiled. *Meet me on the roof.*

Forgetting about her fear of Apollo, she walked past him and followed Will's instructions. Stepping through the access door, the cool breeze of the air met her, along with Will.

"How was your massage?" he asked, taking in the radiant glow that shone off her skin. He could look at her and see his answer. In the time that he had been with her, she teetered between all-consuming stress and total relaxation.

Over the years, women had tried to make Will care about them in a way that would make him want them to be a permanent part of their life. But he had never met anyone that touched him the way the woman standing before him did. Caryn had a toughness about her that had helped her climb her way up the corporate ladder, yet there was a tenderness that searched for a resting place. She was happy and proud of what she had accomplished in her life, but fulfillment seemed to escape her.

He could say that it had been the same for him. The work that he'd committed his life to gave a level of giving and a feeling of contribution to the greater good than he could have ever hoped. But there was something missing. Until Caryn came into his life, giving him what he had no idea he needed. A friend. A companion. Someone who he got and someone who got him.

Caryn searched for any word that would describe what was happening to her. On the outside, her body tingled from the masterful hands of Anastasia. Working from her neck, to her shoulders and arms, down her back and then her legs. With each stroke, she allowed all the pressure and questions that had been raised over the past week in her conversations with Will to float away.

As she released her physical stress, she let her internal struggle melt away, as well. The intellectual battle she'd had with Will from the moment they met had her bouncing between her plan for her career and what life could be like if she allowed room for something else. Someone else.

The longer she hung around Will, the easier he made it for her to do just that. He was forcing her to pull out a side of her that she had buried long ago. The side that could sleep in late. The side that could break away from the phone and computer. The side that was ready and willing to have fun.

Without thinking, she wrapped her arms around him and kissed him on the neck. "Ahh, it was perfect. I can't remember the last time I've felt so relaxed."

Will could have sworn his heart was going at over a hundred beats per minute. By now, they had kissed more than he could count. They had danced, held each other and shared late-night conversations, yet here he was, his heart opening up to her as if this was happening for the very first time. The exhilaration of the moment set him off balance and he wondered how he was going to handle it when she walked out of his life in a couple of weeks.

Unable to allow those thoughts to enter his mind, he inhaled the fresh scent of her hair. "I'm glad to hear that, because my job is to give you the best vacation possible."

Leaning back, she stared at him with appreciative eyes. "You've already given me more than I could have ever hoped for."

"There's more where that came from," he said, leading her to the other side of the pool. "I hope you're hungry."

The last thing she'd put in her mouth was a bagel with cream cheese when she and her mother had stopped for coffee around eleven o'clock. They'd spent the morning at a few home stores looking for just the right additions to her condo. Bonnie pointed out several pieces she thought would complement Caryn's style, but each time, Caryn decided to leave them in the store.

Unfortunately, the furnishings might not make it to Boston, but she would. Her vacation time was rapidly coming to an end. "Famished."

The rooftop recreation area was spectacular. The center of the activity was the pool. With its stone deck all around it, it was a great place to spend lazy summer days and romantic nights. The lounge chairs, tables and umbrellas had all been put away and the only thing that remained was a table for two, set with candles, flowers and steaming dishes.

Will pulled out a chair for her and took his seat.

"Last time we drank good wine and ate good food, we stared out over the White House. This time, I thought it would be nice to enjoy this night staring out over the capital."

Caryn hadn't noticed the surrounding views, as she was too busy taking in the view right in front of her. This man was taking romance to an entirely different level. Pampering her oozed out of him, and with each passing day the idea that this was temporary began to weigh heavy in her heart.

As a little girl, she could recall those conversations with her cousin Veronica and later on in life with Sherisse. They painted a picture of the perfect man. Handsome, successful, would do anything for her. Those childhood dreams had finally become a reality with the man sitting across from her. "You called me spoiled a couple of days ago," she said. "If you keep this up, you'll be considered an enabler."

"I'm finding that spoiling you is what I do best."

Fixing their plates, they feasted on Cornish hen stuffed with wild rice and fresh asparagus tips. The wine he'd chosen was perfect and Caryn couldn't recall a time when she'd had a better date.

Finished, they stood against the railing and looked out over the city. Neither spoke as they took in the sights of the capital and Union Station in the distance. As the gentle breeze floated through the air, Will wrapped his arm around her, but still remained quiet.

They remained that way for at least fifteen minutes, each in their own thoughts about what was happening between them. Caryn was the first to break the quietness. "You were right."

"About?"

She faced him and relented to the truth. "What I needed. I needed to have fun. To enjoy life without the constant threat of work looming over my head."

"You deserve this treatment on a daily basis," he said.

"From whom?" she said, thinking of her life back in Boston, "I don't think Jeremy is the type to offer massages and home-cooked meals. He's more of a get-it-done, bottom-line kind of person."

"Your boss?"

"And mentor," she added. Jeremy had gone to bat for her many times, and she was sure there were times that he supported her with other colleagues or clients and she never knew it. "He's taken me under his wing and showed me the ropes. I don't think I would have made it this far without him."

"Everyone needs a break."

"And this month has been mine," she said. "Once this time is up, it's back to my life. Back to Boston. Back to work. Back to world travels and business deals."

"I hear an underlying message in that."

"The message has been on the table since we started this."

"And what message is that?"

"Will, don't get me wrong, I find myself strongly attracted to you. You've awakened things in me that I had pushed deep away. You've made me laugh. You've made me try things I never would have done—and that includes taking a note from around the neck of a very mean-looking German shepherd. But we knew this when this started."

"Knew what?"

"Come on, Will. Your rules. My job. We shouldn't ask for something that neither one of us can give."

"So what can you give?"

"Will, I don't live here. Hell, most times I don't live in Boston. Anything beyond my vacation isn't possible."

"You don't believe in long-distance relationships?"

"At this point in my life, I don't believe in relationships."

"You're lying."

"I am not."

"At this point in your life, you want desperately to believe in relationships—a relationship with me."

"Your arrogant ways are showing again."

"It's not arrogance when it's the truth."

"You've had too much to drink."

"And you've lived in denial too long."

Before she could respond, he pulled her close and lowered his head to hers. The gentleness of the evening was a sharp contrast to the power of their touch. All of the feelings that he had been pushing down for the past week came rushing forward as if a dam had been broken. When she opened her mouth to receive all of him, he confirmed what he'd decided before this evening began. She was special. She was unique. She was extraordinary. She produced feelings in him that had never existed before she came into his life. She was passionate. She was amazing. The only thing she wasn't was his. And he wanted that to change tonight.

Caryn had never been challenged in the way that he was challenging her. Most men accepted that she wasn't ready for a serious relationship. Most men gave a halfhearted effort to change her mind. Some men gave a valiant effort to change her mind. But Will was unlike any of those men. His efforts weren't forced and his point of view was spoken with honesty.

She wouldn't deny that she had entertained the thought, but those thoughts were fleeting. Relationships where people were in the same house didn't always work out, that made it next to impossible for two people in different states, and sometimes different countries, to have half a chance. But it was moments like this, when his arms caressed her, when his lips tantalized her and his touch set her body on fire that she wished beyond all wishes that there was a way to make this work.

Caressing her bare back, his kiss deepened and he pushed her up against the railing. "You taste so sweet."

Caryn couldn't control the flames that were raging

inside of her. Every part of her cried out to connect to him in the most natural way. She knew that it wouldn't last. She knew that she would go back to Boston. But she wanted to have more of those moments that they'd shared together. More memories that could carry her through the long flights and the lonely nights. Without thought to the future, she wrapped her arms tightly around his neck, massaging the nape. When she heard moans of pleasure coming from deep in her throat, she made the suggestion to move their date inside.

"Not so quick," he said, breaking contact. He wanted her so bad that he thought he would burst. But this wasn't about him—it was all about her. There was a promise that was made when they started this thing. With sexual tension so thick it could be cut with a knife, he had a few more surprises for her. "Remember I promised you adventure, fun and total relaxation."

The gleam in his eyes made her take a step back. "Why do I feel like I should be afraid—very afraid?"

Instead of a verbal response, he tilted his head to the left several times.

"Uh-uh," she said, figuring he was pointing to the body of water that looked calm and innocent. "If your mind is contemplating anything that has to do with that pool, give it up right now."

"But it would be so much fun."

"Swimming?"

"Swimming is for the ordinary," he said, mystery hooded in his eyes.

"What else is there?"

"Ever been skinny-dipping?"

Chapter 19

"You have obviously been smoking something that could get you arrested if you think for one minute that I would take off my clothes and jump in that water naked."

"If you do," he said, looking down at her dress, "you wouldn't ruin that gorgeous outfit."

"Why would I do this?"

"Because it's fun and…"

"And what?" she said, wondering what he was holding back on.

"And I would bet money that you haven't done anything remotely this spontaneous, Miss Corporate America."

Caryn shook her head and gave him a scornful look. "Do you honestly think reverse psychology will work on me?"

"It's not psych 101 if it's the truth."

Holding her look, she didn't want to give anything away. But if she was honest, Caryn would admit that he was right. When she entered college she was focused on getting her education to set her up with a career that would shoot her straight to the top. That plan allowed for little time to hang out at frat parties, late nights in the student center, club hopping or crazy stunts like the one he was asking her to do tonight. "Call it what you want, but I'm not falling for it."

Playing with the tie on her wrap dress, he twirled it around in his hands without pulling it. "Come on, Caryn, you know you want to have one wild and crazy night in your life."

"Hey, I've had wild nights."

"Name one," he said, giving her tie a tug.

Caryn cut her eyes down to his hands but didn't stop him. His voice was challenging and playful at the same time and she racked her brain trying to come up with one time in her life when she completely went wild for one night—or at least one hour. "For the sake of the discussion, let's assume that you're right."

Giving a short laugh, he nodded slowly. "Of course—for the sake of argument."

"What makes you think I would get wild and crazy with you?"

Will gave her tie a harder tug and the bow disappeared. "Because the thought of getting naked in the pool excites you just as much as it excites me."

There was that arrogance, and Caryn hated to admit that he was absolutely right. "This pool is for your building. What if someone comes out here?"

Stepping closer, both his hands continued to untie her dress. "My thousand-dollar check the building has already cashed ensures that we have the entire roof to ourselves tonight."

Nervously glancing around, Caryn stared at the access door for a full minute, as if she was waiting for someone to show up and prove him wrong. Finally, she stepped back, out of the range of his hands and tied her dress. "I don't think I can."

Will didn't answer and Caryn almost caved under his intense stare. Without an explanation, he turned away from her and walked to the far end of the terrace. Picking up a small box, he returned to her. "It was worth a shot."

Taking the box, she tore off the wrapper and underneath the tissue paper was a black-and-white one-piece bathing suit.

Fifteen minutes later, Caryn came out of the changing room and noticed Will was already in the water. She breathed a sigh of relief when he swam toward her and she could see he was wearing trunks.

Caryn tried to remember the last time she had been in a pool. Just about every hotel she's stayed in the last ten years had had them, but she'd never managed to go for a swim.

Sticking her toe in the water, she quickly pulled back. "It's cold."

"It's heated," he said, leaning up against the edge.

Walking to the other end of the pool where the stairs were, she put her foot in and scrunched up her face. "Heated, huh?"

"Come on, Caryn. A smart businesswoman...I

would think you would know better than to ease into the water. When it comes to stuff like this, you gotta just jump in."

When she put her other foot in, she only felt slightly assured that she wouldn't go into shock from the temperature of the water.

"Here," he said, reaching for her hand. "Let me help you ease in."

Her eyes thanked him and she reached and slid her hand into his. Suddenly, he gave her a quick jerk and she went flying into the water.

"Oh, oh," she screamed, going completely under. Coming back up, she wiped her face, pushing the wet strands of hair out of her eyes. All she could hear was his laughing apology.

"I'm so sorry, honey."

"Sure you are," she said, determined to make him pay. Pretending to struggle to gain her footing, she began to flail her arms wildly.

"Caryn," he called out, moving quickly to get to her. "Are you okay?"

When he got within striking distance, Caryn dipped underwater and grabbed his legs, pulling them from under him. Immediately he went under.

When they both resurfaced, Caryn couldn't hold back a look of triumph as he shook water from his face and hair.

"So you want to play games," he said, coming after her.

"No, no," Caryn said, trying to swim away. Within seconds he was on her. Grabbing her at the waist, he picked her up and held her in the air.

"Don't do it, Will."

"Say you're sorry."

"Okay," she said before breaking into a playful smile. "You're sorry."

Under the water she went.

Instead of coming up right away, she swam around his legs and came up behind him. By the time he turned around, it was too late. She'd grabbed his legs again and they both hit the water. She came up for air first and waited for him. When his head popped up, he started toward her.

"You're going to get it now."

"No," she yelled between laughs. Trying to make a run for it, she frantically put one foot in front of the other, but she was going nowhere fast. In ten seconds, he was on her.

Turning her around to face him, she smashed into his chest and he held her, not letting her back away. Their breathing, heavy and labored from the frolicking, was the only sound that could be heard in the highly charged sexual atmosphere.

Without warning, his lips descended on hers and all signs of amusement evaporated. The connection of only that one body part wasn't enough. His hand began an exploration that covered every inch of her. Starting with her shoulders, he worked down her arms and around her waist.

Caryn felt his hand over her body and struggled to contain her excitement. Her nipples hardened as the sensations of the water, his kiss and his hands combined to raise her body temperature at least ten degrees. With their bodies meshed together and the water swirling around them, she felt the overwhelming surge of his member against her. Before she could think, or stop herself, she lowered her hand inside his trunks and began to stroke him.

"Oh, baby, you don't know what you're doing to me."

"I have a pretty good idea because you're doing it to me."

Will reached behind her neck and unhooked the clasp of her suit. The fabric quickly fell away, exposing beautiful, brown breasts that cried out for attention. Placing his hand over the left one, he squeezed and kneaded.

"That feels so good," she said.

He lowered his head, and Caryn raised out of the water to meet him as he took her other breast in his mouth, tasting her.

"Yes," she whispered into the night air.

He pushed her back against the side of the pool, and his mouth recaptured hers. He moaned as she continued to stroke him.

"We should stop," she managed to get out in between kisses.

Will heard the words and everything in him screamed out to ignore her. He didn't want to stop. He wanted to rip the rest of that suit off of her and take her right here and right now. Her touch had gotten him so hard he could barely contain his increasing desire. But while he was disappointed and horny, he never let that override a woman's desire to stop.

If she wasn't ready, he had no intention of forcing her. He'd learned a long time ago to control his needs.

When it came to the time and place for them to consummate their relationship, it would be her choice. Reluctantly, he dropped his hand and floated back in the water.

"We should stop doing this in the pool and take this back to your place."

The words were spoken clearly, but Will still couldn't believe she'd said them. "Are you sure?"

She swam toward him, not bothering to adjust her suit. "You told me I would have moments with you…memories to take with me. I want this to be one of those moments."

Kissing her tenderly on the forehead, he led her out of the water. Wrapping her in a thick terry-cloth robe before doing the same, he gathered up their belongings and headed back to the loft.

Apollo met them at the door, and after a quick command from Will, the dog headed to the dining area, curling up on his bed. "I'll put these dishes away if you want to shower and get the chlorine off."

Caryn took the basket out of his hand and set it on the floor. Locking hands with his, she guided him toward the stairs. "If I shower alone, who will wash my back?"

The multiple jet sprays had been set to the perfect temperature. Caryn stood in front of Will and untied his robe. She pushed the robe off his shoulders; it fell to the floor and she ran her fingers across his chest. The soft sighs of pleasure coming out of his mouth told Caryn that she was touching all the right spots.

Before she could get too far along with her own personal massage techniques, Will reciprocated by untying her robe. Moving his smooth hands over her breasts, they peaked once again. When the material fell away, he happily became reacquainted with her two beautiful breasts. His hand immediately cupped one and the nipple came alive as his lips covered hers in a passionate kiss full of promise.

The feel of his hands on her soft mound sent shivers of pure delight through her body and in return, she slid her hand down his shorts again, stroking and rubbing as it grew larger and larger.

Will moved his hands from her breasts to the bottom of her suit. Without breaking contact, he pushed the fabric over her small hips and Caryn wiggled out of them. Naked, Will stood back and studied the woman that physically excited him, mentally challenged him, and on some level, had made it to his soul. She may have been looking for memories and moments, but he was looking at a lifetime.

A moment of panic raced through him and he felt it touch every part of his body. His head. His arms. His legs. If finally settled in his heart where he could feel it pumping a hundred beats a minute again. This was not supposed to happen. This was supposed to be about stage one of a relationship. This was never to include mortgages, in-laws and family. But that's what Will had on his hands. For the first time in his life, he didn't want a relationship to end—ever. The revelation caused him to pause and second thoughts shot into his mind like darts.

Will had never backed away from a challenge. Throughout his life he dealt with people honestly. This time would be no different. He wasn't sure how Caryn would feel about breaking the rules, but he had to find out. He had to know if she loved him like he loved her. Putting his arm around her waist, he squeezed her affectionately. "At the pool, we talked about moments... memories."

"You're giving me all of those."

Without hesitation, he told her exactly what was on his mind. "I want more than moments, Caryn. More than memories."

The sincerity with which he spoke resonated with her and she had to acknowledge that her feelings for him had grown deeper than she ever could have imagined. But she forced herself to push them away. "How much more?"

"I want to keep seeing you after this vacation is over. I want to be a part of your life. I want to be your lover, your friend, your man."

Caryn closed her eyes and pictured what life would be like if she granted him that request. How could she give him that with her current lifestyle? "You're asking for more than I can give."

Will, crushed that she couldn't give him what he needed, accepted her words—for now. He still had time to work on her. "What can you give?"

"I can give you now. This moment. And believe me, it will mean more to me than any other moment in my life."

"What if I want more?"

"Let's start with tonight and worry about the rest later."

He would abide by her rules for now, but somehow, someway, they would be together. With that newfound inner proclamation, Will stepped back and out of his trunks.

Caryn's eyes widened in appreciation of the man that stood before her. His large, broad chest, his rock-hard stomach and his athletic legs together were the package of a Greek god. Opening the glass door to the shower, he held out his hand, and she gladly took it.

The sprays from the six showerheads pounded their bodies, and Will retrieved a washcloth and soap and proceeded to wash her. Lathering her up, his hand moved across her entire body, leaving not one part untouched. Caryn closed her eyes and enjoyed the second massage she'd had today. While Anastasia was good, Will was an expert, kneading and rubbing her from top to bottom.

When it was time to rinse off, he pressed her against the wall and let the water drench her from head to toe. With his body just inches from hers, he reached for shampoo and began to wash her hair. The tips of his fingers manipulated her scalp and she reveled in the pleasure. Who knew that a head massage could be such a turn-on?

Rinsing the shampoo out of her hair, he kissed her temples, followed by her cheeks and finally her lips. As their tongues danced, his hands stroked her back. When his lips pulled away, Caryn immediately felt the loss, but he quickly made up for it when his head went lower and he covered her breasts with it, licking and sucking her nipple.

"Ooh, that's it," she said, unable to control the reaction her body was having. Between the power of the water and the power of his tongue, she was in the midst of losing complete control.

When he backed away from her breasts, she took advantage of that time to try to regroup, to regain some composure. But just when she started to breathe normally, Will dropped to his knees and buried his head in her most sensitive spot.

"Yes!" she moaned, her words swallowed by the sounds of the water. She opened her legs wider, while his tongue assaulted her in the most intimate way and her knees began to buckle. With his hand cupping her behind, he pressed deeper and deeper into her until she gave in to the pleasure and allowed herself to fully go. As she reached the heights of pleasure, her body shook and shivered, giving her permission to completely let go.

For several minutes neither of them moved and the only sounds that could be heard was the water falling.

When he reached over and turned the water off, the only sound floating through their air was their heavy breathing. Without saying anything, Will stepped out of the stall and retrieved a towel. With gentle strokes, he dried her body from top to bottom.

She reached up and stroked his cheek with the back of her hand. "Make love to me, Will."

He promised he would pamper her. Treat her like a queen. He wanted to give her every desire. Including this. Leading her to his bed, he laid her on her back and admired her natural beauty. Her hair was wet and flat to her head. There were nothing but faint remnants of the makeup she wore, and their intimate exchange in the shower had left her vulnerable.

Joining her, he slid his hand across her stomach, circling her navel.

"What do you think, Doc?" she asked, enjoying the very thorough exam he was giving her.

"I think I need to run a few more tests." His other hand moved to her core and he slid his finger inside. She was ready for him.

Reaching over to the nightstand, he opened a condom.

"Allow me," she said, propelling him onto his back and straddling him. Covering him completely, she positioned herself above him and eased down.

When he entered her, what was left of Will's rules shattered. He'd been breaking one here and there when it came to Caryn, but he'd justified them all. She was only in town for a month. She wasn't looking for anything serious. He wasn't looking for anything serious. But as she rode him, he reached up and caressed her breasts, feeling everything that was her become a part of him. There wasn't a rule in play that could stop him from making this woman a permanent part of his life.

Caryn's body took all of him in and the power of the connection caused a slight panic in Caryn. This was what fairy tales were made of. The emotional connection she'd found with him was only matched by the physical bond between them. Her body began to give in to all the resistance she'd tried to put up. All of the excuses about her job, her plans and her life before him started to melt away with each stroke of her hips. Finally, there was nothing left but the raw, unchecked emotion that resembled nothing she'd ever experienced before.

"Yes, Caryn, that's it. Let it go," he encouraged, thrusting deeper and deeper.

Caryn obliged the requests and stopped thinking and only felt. Felt his passion. Felt his caring. Felt his love. The last word sent Caryn over the edge and she shattered into a thousand sexually satisfying pieces.

Will awoke the next morning feeling happier than ever. Turning over, he reached for Caryn and was surprised that she wasn't there. Sitting up, he looked around the room for any sign that she was still there. There was nothing. No dress. No shoes. Not even the robe she wore last night was anywhere to be found. If his body didn't ache from all the lovemaking they'd done last night, he would have sworn it was all a dream.

Pushing the covers back, he looked at the clock and saw the note on the nightstand. For some reason, he dreaded opening it. He knew in his soul it wasn't good news.

Hearing the stirrings of his master, Apollo came to him, looking for someone to take him out. Taking any excuse to leave that piece of paper alone, he grabbed the leash.

Twenty minutes later, Will was back in his room staring at it. With a deep breath, he opened it.

Thank you for the memories and the moments. It meant more to me than you will ever know. I didn't want to wake you... I'm going home. C.

He showered and dressed in less than a half hour. He turned on to her street twenty minutes later. Almost nine o'clock, he figured he wouldn't be waking up her parents. He rang the bell once, but the rapid beat of his heart wanted him to ring it continuously until she answered the door.

Finally, the door swung open.

"Good morning, Will."

Bonnie spoke to him as if she expected to see him. Unfortunately, her eyes gave him the answer she dreaded. When Caryn said she was going home, she wasn't talking about her parents' house.

"I'm sorry, Will. Her flight left a half hour ago. She went back to Boston."

Chapter 20

Will sat in his office staring at a stack of invoices. It was the same stack that Barbara had put on his desk a month ago. She'd stopped asking for them days ago because his response was always the same—he'd get to it when he could. Each time she poked her head in his office, she hesitated before leaving, seemingly wanting to say something. Instead, she remained silent. Will had been chopping off the heads of anyone who mentioned Caryn's name, and Barbara decided it was best to leave him alone.

Almost six o'clock, his last patient left hours ago, but he wasn't in the mood to go home. She'd only been in his place for a short time, but the memories were everywhere. His bed hadn't felt the same since she left. He couldn't take a shower without smelling her scent.

BC—his code for Before Caryn—he spent his summers swimming laps several times a week. Now he couldn't bring himself to go up on the roof and he definitely wouldn't be able to get in the water. That's why his office had become his second home.

Arriving early and staying late, his new daily routine was his only hope for working to exhaustion, therefore being able to get a somewhat good night's sleep. He'd become the person to make the first cup of coffee in the morning and had become quite friendly with the night cleaning crew. If it wasn't for Apollo, he wasn't sure if he would spend any time at home.

Turning around in his chair, he stared out into the small park area. The traffic was changing from people leaving work to couples heading out on a date. The idea of happy couples parading in front of him pierced his soul. Never in a million years would he have thought that he wanted to be one of them. But here he sat, wondering what the hell happened. He didn't bother to turn around when he heard a quick knock on his door, before someone walked in.

"Jeff and I are headed out for some dinner. Come with us."

"No."

Derrick stepped in and closed the door behind him. When Will remained with his back to him, he decided enough was enough. How long was this going to go on? "Is this how it's going to be from now on?"

No response.

"Why don't you call her?" Derrick said.

The casualness of the request annoyed Will, but he refused to turn around. After all that had happened between him and her, Derrick had the audacity to make such a suggestion? Not bothering to cover his agitation, a curt, one-word response was all he gave. "No."

Not backing down, Derrick made himself comfortable by taking a seat in one of the chairs. "It's been a month."

Instead of responding, Will spun around and stood. Derrick was pushing him to have a conversation he wasn't interested in. He couldn't care less if it had been a day, a week, a month or a year. Talking about her was not on his agenda. Picking up his keys, he headed for the door. "Bye."

Derrick watched Will do what he had been doing for the past four weeks. Running away and avoiding the situation—and driving everyone crazy in the process. "You're letting her go—just like that?"

The question stopped Will dead in his tracks. The question plucked at his nerves, and the internal battle raged as to whether he should dignify it with a response. Then he remembered waking up. The sinking feeling in his stomach. The note. The frantic ride to her parents' house. The moment her mother confirmed what his heart already knew. "Let her go?"

"Yes," Derrick said, hoping to get his friend talking. When Will returned to work after she left, he was a completely different person. Grumpy, cantankerous and irritable, he managed to pull together a halfway decent bedside manner with his patients, but with everyone else, he was taking no prisoners.

The details are still sketchy, but what everyone had figured out was that she was gone. Not just gone from D.C., but gone from his life. The first day back in the office, Will practically ripped everyone's head off that dared to even say "good morning." With no details, Derrick's attempt at asking questions rendered nothing.

This was new territory for Derrick. Not once in their friendship had he ever been in a position to deal with Will when he was having serious problems with his girlfriend. Actually, it was the first time Derrick could recall Will having a bona fide girlfriend. Caryn swooped into town and gave Will everything he didn't know he needed. Will had adjusted his days for her, and the sparkle in his eyes when he spoke of her told everyone that she was something special. And he never mentioned the rules after their first date.

Will let go of the doorknob and faced Derrick. He had every intention of avoiding discussing her with anyone—ever. But the idea that Derrick thought he should be the one to take action—to do something— to contact her, grated on every nerve in his body. Anyone who had an inkling about what that woman had done to him would never make such a suggestion. In only two full strides, Will stood less than a few inches from Derrick, seething with anger. With piercing eyes, his face tightened and wrinkles formed around his nose and mouth. "Let me clarify something for you, Derrick. I can't let her go because she was never mine."

"The two of you…" Derrick started.

"Had a deal," Will said, completing his sentence. He couldn't bear to hear whatever words Derrick was going to use to finish that sentence. *The two of you had something special. The two of you were so happy. The two of you could work it out. The two of you should find a way to be together.*

"I'm just trying to help, Will. Be there for you." Derrick's voice softened as he tried to get his friend to open up. To talk about what happened. He'd kept it bottled up inside and that wasn't healthy for anyone. If Will wasn't careful, he was liable to explode.

"Actually," Will continued, releasing the tension in his neck and shoulders and taking a deep breath, "I'm getting exactly what I deserve."

The flippant comment didn't fool Derrick for one moment. Maybe it was a statement that served as a coping mechanism. Maybe it was a way to bury his true feelings. But Derrick didn't believe him. Derrick was there the days Will came to work, beaming with excitement at having spent the previous evening with Caryn. Derrick was there when he meticulously planned every outing to show Caryn a good time. Derrick was there when Will confessed that he was starting to truly care about her. There was no way that Will was getting what he deserved. "I don't understand."

"Simple…" He shrugged, as if the outward motion of nonchalance would seep into his soul. "We had an agreement. Our time was restricted to her vacation. No more and no less. Those were the rules we agreed to."

"And your point?" Derrick said, knowing that that may have been how they'd started out, but it was in no way indicative of where they'd ended up. The two of them had become people that had grown to care deeply for each other.

Will had thought about his next words many times ever since she left. It was a hard truth to swallow. Saying it out loud would add the validity that he had been avoiding. But the truth was the truth. The sooner he faced it, the better off he would be. "I was the one that tried to make it something it wasn't. I was the one that crossed the line. I was the one that said I could handle the arrangement and couldn't. I was the one that fell in."

Will stopped short of making the declaration to Derrick. The night they had dinner by the pool, Will knew. He knew that she was someone that he wanted to give his heart to. He knew that she was the one that he could spend the rest of life with. He knew that she had become the one person in his life to show him what love was all about.

So in awe of the revelation, he kept it to himself, adjusting to the feeling of wanting and needing someone to be in his life. Making love to her had been an experience beyond any that he'd had before. There was a hunger mixed with tenderness sprinkled with need that drove him to join with her in every possible way—not just in the physical sense, but in his spirit and his soul. The morning Caryn left, he intended for her to hear those words. Now he swallowed them. What would it accomplish to say them now? Will wasn't sure what made him sadder—the fact that she'd left him or the fact that she'd left without knowing how she'd changed him.

Derrick didn't need to be psychic to fill in the rest of his sentence. It was obvious to anyone that paid a little attention to Will the past month that he was changing—for the better. He'd found someone to drive away those stupid rules and old relationship philosophies and make room for true love.

When Derrick was having challenges with Natalie

before they married, the last thing he wanted was advice or interference from anyone. But Will had refused to let him idly sit by and watch his relationship go down the drain. Will had helped Derrick fight for Natalie and their love and in the end it paid off big-time. Derrick wanted to return the favor.

So far, all of his attempts had come up empty: Dinner invitations were turned down, grabbing a drink didn't interest him and a pick-up game of basketball didn't appeal to him at all. Derrick was running out of ideas, but he refused to give up. "Look, man, I know…"

"No," Will said, refusing to believe that anyone could know what it feels like to have a knife stuck in your heart, continually twisting and turning. Because that's what he had felt like since that fateful day. He'd tried to numb the pain by overworking, overexercising and by refusing to think about her. But nothing helped. The pain was severe and constant.

Derrick and Will stared at one another, each challenging the other. Will dared Derrick to say anything related to that woman, and Derrick dared Will to do the one thing that he had been dreading for weeks. The time continued to tick away, but neither cared. Both were determined to get what they wanted—now. Will wanted Derrick to leave him alone and Derrick wanted Will to deal with the painful situation. Finally, one of them caved.

"You have no idea what I'm going through," Will said, taking a seat and unloading some of the pain that had wreaked havoc with him. The life that he'd known BC no longer existed. How could he go back to that after having tasted the power of attraction, joy and love? He couldn't. But he didn't know how to move forward.

Derrick sat in the other chair but kept his mouth shut. If Will was ready to talk, he didn't want to interrupt or discourage him.

Running his hands over his face, Will leaned forward and rested his head in them. For several minutes he didn't say anything. Not given to outward expressions of emotion, Will allowed all the pain, confusion and anger to bubble to the surface. No longer trying to suppress it, he gave them free rein. Tears over a woman had never been an idea to him, but Caryn had changed everything about him, including this. The welling in the corner of his eyes represented the hurt that had consumed him. While the drops didn't fall, it was the closest he'd ever been.

"Being with her revealed a need in me that never existed," he said quietly, barely recognizing his own voice. Raw and vulnerable, he continued, "She was everything I didn't know I wanted. How can someone completely infiltrate your being in such a short period of time? How can I go from thinking about the future to imagining a life without her in it?"

Derrick sat quietly.

"I didn't think that this would be easy," Will said, giving himself some credit. "She lived in Boston and work was her number-one priority. But I thought we would figure it out because I didn't believe I was in this alone. I thought we wanted the same things—to be together. Therefore, we would find a way to work it out."

Will stopped speaking but didn't raise his head.

After all of the women. All of the rules. All of the dates. Will had finally discovered what a real breakup felt like. "Now there's nothing and I'm supposed to just go back to my life as if she was never here."

Derrick could offer words of encouragement or advice. He could tell Will things like "everything happens for a reason" or "somehow things will work out." But he wasn't the type to offer comfort words that had no real meaning or impact. So he didn't open his mouth at all. Instead, he walked to the desk and picked up the phone, holding the receiver out to Will.

Raising his head at hearing the dial tone, Will's look of despair and desperation quickly turned to agitation. "Forget it. There's no way in hell I'm calling her."

"Fine. Tell me the number and I'll call her."

The week after she left, Will had been in no mood to be around anyone. His staff witnessed him breathe fire at anyone who got in his way. His patients saw the other side of his normally congenial manner. Derrick and Jeff gave him space and Sherisse only said "hello" and "goodbye."

By the second week, there were rumors of an uprising if someone didn't do something about him. Derrick was chosen. Derrick considered it his personal mission to make Will do something about his situation.

"She made a choice. End of story."

"Don't you have a say in this? How come she gets to be in the driver's seat? You were a part of this, too. This is the time to have your say."

"Spare me the pop psychology," Will said, annoyed that Derrick might have a point.

"You need to talk to her."

Standing, Will took the phone out of his hand.

Relief flooded Derrick and he smiled. "Good choice."

Instead of dialing, he slammed the receiver back into the cradle. Grabbing his keys off his desk, he decided he'd had enough of this discussion.

"You're making a mistake," Derrick said.

"I don't care."

"Yes, you do," Derrick said.

Derrick was right. He did care. But that didn't mean he had to act on it. "Have a good night."

Chapter 21

Caryn sat in the meeting on autopilot as she worked with Jeremy to close a deal involving two pharmaceutical companies. This was the third closing she'd been involved in since returning from D.C. Taking on each new deal with a vengeance, she worked nonstop at a level that surpassed Jeremy's expectations. So impressed, he began to talk about expanding her role. Thinking of his age, Jeremy hinted that as he looked to cutting back or retirement, he could see her stepping in and filling his role.

The words were exactly what she had been waiting to hear for years. It was what she had sacrificed just about everything for. Now she was so close she could taste it. Her work had always been the one constant in her life and she'd counted on it many times to squash the feeling of loneliness or that she was missing out on something. It was the one thing that never failed her and she counted on it to do that for her again.

Unstoppable, she was pulling twelve-hour days and crashing into bed from exhaustion. But sleep rarely came easy. She would be driven awake by the images and dreams that had taken up residence in her head. Dreams of him. Dreams of them. Dreams of the moments that gave her more than she ever thought possible.

Her last night with Will culminated times of unimaginable feelings of fun, excitement and love. *Love.* That one word changed everything for her. She met him and thought him cute. She talked to him and thought him flirty. She spent time with him and thought him fun. She opened up to him and found him compassionate. She allowed him to infiltrate her hard exterior and found love.

Finding the one person that inspires you to be better is what little girls dream of. It's what every person needs in their life. Spending time with Will made her realize why she had been able to put her career above everything and everyone—because she had no idea what it meant to be in love. Her perceptions and understanding about being committed to someone were completely off base.

She'd never factored in the smiles, the laughs and the desire to share the little things. How could she have known that when you meet that one person—it would become a priority—not because it had to, but because she wanted to. That was what happened to her that night and it completely freaked her out.

She'd woken up just after 5:00 a.m. Will peacefully slept beside her, his mouth in an easy, slight smile of contentment. Gently, she placed her finger on his lips, remembering all the naughty and nice things he'd done with them throughout the night. Time after time they connected with each other, their bodies unable to stand the separation. The concept of a perfect night had never been a thought to her. But the experience of being with him showed her a glimpse of what her future life could be like if she gave up the life she had.

Pushing up against the pillows, she watched the rise and fall of his chest and felt the stiffness in her body. Remembering their swim, their rendezvous in the shower and their marathon in his bed, she realized that Dr. William Proctor was the complete package. Sweet, kind, gentle and powerful at the same time.

For several minutes, she watched him sleep and her thoughts of contentment and satisfaction began to give way to questions, confusion and, ultimately, sadness. What would this lead to? What would happen when she went back to Boston? She had to go back to her life. Her goals. Jeremy had dropped hints that the closer he got to retirement, the more he would look to her. The last ten years of her life had been spent preparing for that role. Could she give all that up?

Quietly, she'd extracted herself from the bed and searched out her clothes. Her heart told her to stay, talk to him and figure it out. But that part of her was drowned out by the other part that was screaming to be heard. *Stick to the plan. There'll be time for this after you reach your goals. You can't stop now…you're so close.*

Gathering her belongings, she went into the bathroom to dress. When she reemerged, she didn't feel the relief she'd expected upon seeing that Will was still sleeping. A part of her wanted him to wake up and stop her. To tell her that it would be all right. But his deep breathing indicated that whatever decision she made, it would be one hundred percent owned by her.

Her motions did wake someone, however, and Apollo came into the room. The dog seemed to move his head from her to him as if he'd figured out exactly what was going on. When his eyes finally rested on her, she could have sworn she saw shame and disappointment in them.

"Don't look at me like that," she whispered before walking past him and creeping down the steps. The closer she got to the door, the more she convinced herself that she was doing the right thing. In business, there were times when you had to make the tough decisions and move forward; there was no time for second-guessing. That's the way she looked at this, even though she didn't believe she was right for doing it.

When she got to the door, she realized she wasn't alone. Apollo had followed her and now sat at her feet, his eyes telling her to think about what she was doing. "Stop looking at me like that," she whispered, but he didn't cut her any slack. He continued to stare at her until she shut the door in his face.

The moment she walked into her parents' house, she had a one-track mind. Pack her bags and get out. Calling the airport as she opened up her carry-on bag, she made a reservation and had a little less than an hour to make her flight. The flurry of activity didn't go unnoticed and her mother came to her room just as she hung up with the airline.

Bonnie stood in the doorway and watched her throw clothes and jewelry haphazardly into her suitcase. She didn't expect her back last night, so Bonnie wasn't surprised when she and Lloyd had breakfast alone. What did surprise her was that Caryn burst through the front door like a bat out of hell, barely speaking to anyone. "I'm not sure what's going on, but my instincts tell me that you're making a big mistake."

"I'm going back to Boston."

Stepping into the room, Bonnie stood in front of Caryn to stop her from packing. "Today?"

"In less than an hour, to be exact," she said, stepping around her and dropping a couple of tops into her bag.

"Why?"

Caryn finally stopped moving and held her emotions in check, giving no indication that her insides were swirling like a tornado. Holding her voice steady, she spoke with her mouth but begged with her eyes. "No questions, please."

Bonnie had born witness to the transformation in Caryn the past couple of weeks. She'd learned how to relax. How to have fun. How to let something other than work consume her. That credit could only be given to one person—Will. Had he done something to hurt her? Holding her daughter's hand, she said, "Did he harm you?"

Caryn's body stance completely changed from defensive to resigned and she shook her head in the negative. The last thing Will had done was harm her. The only thing he was guilty of was giving her a glimpse of what loving a man and being loved felt like. "Can you take me to the airport?"

The tone in her voice gave Bonnie a strong indication that Caryn was running away, and that wasn't like her daughter at all. "Why don't you take a minute and sit down…talk about it?"

Again, Caryn shook her head in the negative. "I can call a cab."

Over the years, Bonnie had learned that her daughter could be headstrong and stubborn to the extent that no one could talk to her. Her passion for her work outweighed any opinions her parents had about how it affected her personal life, and she wouldn't budge. That's how this situation was shaping up. Whatever transpired between her and Will that had forced her to make this decision caused that same reaction. Her mind was made up.

"I'll get my keys."

Caryn stood still for several seconds after her mother left, and for a split second Will's smile flashed in her head. She forced it out as quickly as it came. Zipping her bags, she grabbed her purse and headed for the door.

The first five minutes of the ride was done in complete silence. Caryn not wanting to talk and Bonnie not knowing what to say. "This is how you're going to end your vacation?"

Caryn stared out the window at the passing trees. "I don't want to talk about it."

"Fine," Bonnie said. "Don't talk. Listen."

Caryn shifted uncomfortably in her seat, but Bonnie didn't care. She was determined to have her say. "Your entire adult life has been spent spinning your wheels for material success. When are you going to stop and live?"

"My life is fine, thank you."

"That's your problem Caryn," Bonnie said, wondering how someone who was fleeing town could make that claim. "You want to always be in control. Adamant about what you're going to do, how you're going to do it and who you're going to do it with. Well, that song and dance gets real old when you start to hurt the people who love you."

Caryn turned to her mother and fear gripped her eyes. "How am I hurting you and Dad?"

"You hurt us because we can't stand to see you hurt. And for the record, I wasn't talking about us."

With those words, Caryn turned away from her mother again. "I don't want to talk about him."

"So that's it?" she said, not hiding her frustration at the conversation. It was as if they were talking in circles. "You finally open yourself up and this is how you react?"

"There's nothing wrong with my reaction."

"That man did more for you in this short amount of time that anyone I've ever known. You laughed. You had a glow. You were happy. Do you want to give all that up?"

Caryn couldn't deal with her mother or Will. All she knew was that she had to get away. Things were moving too fast and people were asking more of her than she was prepared to give. A part of her was back in that loft. Back in that bed. Back with Will. But what did that mean? Was she supposed to chuck everything she'd worked for just like that?

That was about a month ago and the confusion that she felt that day had never quite gone away. Now she sat in Paris, with Jeremy to her left, putting together one of the biggest deals of her career. Eleven people sat around a huge conference table, with several assistants sitting behind them against the wall. Three companies merging into one had taken up her days and nights since she'd arrived back in Boston. This was the culmination of several hundred hours of work by several people, and once the papers were signed, there was nothing stopping Jeremy from making good on his promise of promotion.

Two hours later, the deal was complete. The papers were signed. Press releases were written and distributed. Internal communications to staff and employees had been drafted. Monies had been transferred and Caryn's company had made a handsome profit.

"Good work," Jeremy said, sitting in a taxi as they headed back to the hotel.

"Thanks," she said, unable to muster up the same enthusiasm as her boss.

"How about dinner tonight with our clients?" he said, scrolling through his BlackBerry. "They want to thank us for all our hard work."

The last thing Caryn wanted to do was spend any more time with her boss or their clients. They had been together for the last four days, working almost nonstop. Wasn't he tired? Didn't he want to take a break? Didn't he want some downtime? It was their last night in Paris, did he really want to spend it talking shop?

That's when she stared at her boss and took a good look at him. It was as if her eyes were opened for the very first time and she saw her future. A future that she'd wanted at all costs. Now she wasn't so sure.

The one thing she was sure of was that she didn't want to spend her last night with him or their clients. "Thanks, Jeremy, but I'm going to have a light dinner in my room and get some sleep."

Jeremy stopped sending an e-mail and faced her, obviously thrown off by her answer. "Since when have you not been up for a celebration? Are you coming down with something? Do you need a doctor?"

The innocent question stirred a bevy of emotions inside Caryn and she was glad that the taxi was pulling up to the hotel entrance. *Do you need a doctor?* That question conjured up all sorts of answers. She did need a doctor—for fun, for laughs, for late nights and early morning.

Gathering up their briefcases and laptop gave her some time to get herself under control. The welling in her eyes was unexpected and she refused to have Jeremy witness a breakdown. She'd managed to hold it together for the past month, and she forced herself to keep it together for another ten minutes until she got to her room.

She jumped out of the car before it could come to a complete stop. Jeremy followed her out, and they went into the hotel. Before he could ask again, Caryn pushed the button on the elevator and prayed that it came quickly. Stepping in, she pushed the executive level.

"Caryn, are you sure you're all right? You seem a little preoccupied."

"Really, it's nothing, Jeremy," she said, waving off his concern. "I'm just looking forward to a quiet evening."

Relief flooded her when the elevator doors opened. Walking ahead of him, she slipped the key into her suite door and stepped inside. "I'll see you in the morning."

Dropping her stuff on the couch in the living room area, she started to strip off her clothes before making it to the bedroom. Changing into a pair of cotton pajamas, she curled up on the bed and closed her eyes, not bothering with lights or television. As with every other night since she'd left him, memories of their time together crept into her mind. Initially, she fought to keep those memories at bay. It was too painful to relive his touch, his kiss, his ability to make her feel special and loved. But that battle had long been lost, and now she spent her nights remembering.

The idea that she'd walked away from him without a word shocked everyone around her. When her mother finally pulled the whole story out of her a couple of weeks ago, she was appalled at the callousness of her actions. After arriving back in Boston, she called Sherisse and relayed all the events. Sherisse couldn't fathom the idea of sneaking out and told Caryn she at least owed Will a call.

Calling Will wasn't something that Caryn disagreed with, it was just something she couldn't do. There were so many times she picked up the phone, but that was as far she got. When she'd made the choice to leave, she didn't want to talk to him because she wasn't sure she wouldn't change her mind, but now, how could she call? What would she say? After all this time, would he even take her call?

She recalled who he was when she first met him. A

player. A flirt. Someone who liked to have a good time. A part of her feared making the call because after what she did, he might have moved on. Being apart from him challenged her in every way, but finding out he'd moved on would crush her. She wasn't ready to find out.

Caryn had made a choice long ago to live without regrets, but this was the most challenging situation she'd ever faced. As she drifted off to sleep, she recalled the old but true statement: *You made your bed, now you have to lie in it.*

Chapter 22

"Will, your next patient is waiting in room number two."

"Thanks, Barbara."

Will didn't bother to look up until he realized that she was still standing there. "Was there something else?"

"Yes," she said, walking in and taking a seat. "I need you to stop acting a fool."

She was dressed in her uniform of white pants and a multicolored top; her graying hair and the slight wrinkles around the eyes and mouth gave her a motherly look that indicated she was kind and gentle. But that wasn't the case when it came to talking with Will. Her stern voice caught him off guard. "Excuse me?"

"I'm talking about Caryn."

Will reined in his anger and took a deep breath. "I don't care to—"

"I don't give a hoot what you care about," she said, pointing at him. "Now, I'm old enough to be your mother, so I'm going to assume that you would listen to me out of respect for your elders."

Every time she wanted to get her way, she would pull the "mother" card. That was probably because each time she used it, it worked. Will would never disrespect her. "I guess you have something you want to say?"

Sitting forward, she leaned her elbows on his desk and launched into a speech she'd most likely put together weeks ago. "I've watched you date half this city. Your relationships were like a merry-go-round. Every time someone got off, someone else got back on. I never understood how you could go through life without putting down some roots. Walking around here as if you couldn't care less about things people build their entire lives around—family, children, marriage and love."

Will had to admit that she was right about one thing—he had too much respect for her to interrupt, but he wasn't sure he wanted to hear the rest of what she had to say.

"Caryn was the best thing that ever happened to you. Not because you ate at fancy restaurants. Not because you bought her beautiful flowers or expensive chocolates. It was because she was the one person that got you thinking about something other than your business and yourself."

"I've never been selfish," Will said in defense of his past lifestyle.

"No," Barbara said, giving credit where credit was due. "But you've been one-dimensional. She opened up your world and your heart. Now you can sit around here and bark orders at people while you try to convince yourself that you can get over her. Or you can take action."

She sounded like Derrick. Asking him to do something. Telling him to make the first move. Well, he wasn't going to be pushed by anyone. Caryn left him. He'd be damned if he was going to contact her. "Are you finished?"

Barbara stood and opened the door. "I've said my piece. I hope you find yours."

Will stood to follow, wondering about peace. BC, he thought he was content with his life. Thought he had peace. But from the moment she entered his life, she gave him more peace than he ever thought possible. Now his insides were in a complete uproar. In disarray. He hadn't quite figured out how to fix it, but he did know one thing. However he got past this, it would not include calling her.

Standing outside room two, Will gave himself a quick pep talk. Since she left, some of the passion that he held for his work had faded. His easy demeanor with his patients had not been so easy the last several weeks and he performed his duties out of pure knowledge, with very little from the heart.

"Are you okay?"

Will turned to the voice and gave a half smile. "No, but you already know that."

Sherisse had been standing at the end of the hall for almost five minutes watching Will. Avoiding him for the past several weeks, she couldn't put off talking with him any longer. When Caryn and Will started dating, the only thing she could think about was being there for her friend when things fell apart. She always thought that Caryn would be the one moping around. That Caryn would be the one unable to focus on work. Her friend would be the one that barked orders at co-workers. Things had a funny way of turning out.

Sherisse was on point in that the relationship did fall apart. The shock was that it was Caryn who did the dirty work. When Sherisse spoke to her, she practically begged her to contact him. But Caryn wouldn't budge. Since then, each time they talked, Caryn would find a way to ask about him and Sherisse's answer was always the same. *If you want to know something about Will, you'll have to ask him yourself.*

Over the years, Sherisse had watched Will go through women like water, running his relationships on the basis of stupid rules and blaming the women when they broke up. Subconsciously, Sherisse thought she would rejoice on the day that Will met his match. Payback could be brutal and after watching him with other women, she thought she would be ready to pounce on him with words of "serves your right" and "now you know how it feels."

Taking pleasure in someone else's pain had never been her style, but she thought for Will, she would make an exception. It was easy to picture him in pain, suffering, feeling abandoned, alone and unwanted when the tables finally turned on him. But standing here today, rubbing his face in this was the last thing she wanted to do. "I wanted to talk to you—about Caryn. I'm sorry about what happened."

Those words were the last ones Will wanted to hear. They had pity written all over them and he couldn't stand the idea of people feeling that way toward him. "I don't have time for this, Sherisse. I have a patient."

The anger in his tone told her the pain was still fresh and raw. It's funny that they'd been worried about a strained partnership because of his actions, when it was Caryn who'd ended up causing all the tension. "Can we talk later?"

"I don't think so." Without waiting for a response, he grabbed the file off the bin on the side of the door. Without looking at it, he opened the door and stepped inside the exam room.

Shutting the door, Will started to greet his patient, when he swallowed his words.

"I guess you're surprised?"

BC, Will usually arrived early in the morning and checked his schedule for the day. He hadn't done that lately and found himself perusing the file right before he went into the exam room. This time, distracted by Sherisse, he walked in without so much as looking at the name. It was probably a good thing, because if he had, he might not have ever opened the door. Pulling on every fiber of professionalism he could muster, he gave a quick smile and held out his hand. "Mr. Stewart."

"I told you to call me Lloyd."

Will recalled the day the request was made. The day they went rafting. The day he caught his first glimpse of the real Caryn. The Caryn she hid from the world because of her career goals. The Caryn he met that day was lively, fun and open to new adventures. It was the first day he began to see her as someone he wasn't sure he wanted to live without.

Each time he came to pick her up, her parents were always around. He and Lloyd had talked sports, the best way to barbecue and how much they both cared about Caryn. Standing in front of him today, Will could see that those carefree days of conversations with Lloyd were long gone. In its place was awkwardness and discomfort. Neither of which he wanted to deal with.

Not wanting to appear rude or affected by the demise of the relationship with his daughter, Will opened the chart and honored his request. "Lloyd."

Caryn's father sat on the exam table, wondering what was going through Will's mind. It was apparent by the look on his face that he had no idea who he was coming to see and he could tell the situation made him uncomfortable, but Lloyd had to find out what took place between this man and his daughter.

He'd tried to get information out of Bonnie but she didn't have many answers that made sense. Why would Caryn leave a man that she cared about? Refusing to address his questions in e-mails and keeping her phone calls short and simple, Caryn wasn't a good source of information. If he had a chance of finding out any information about what happened, it would have to come from Will.

Bonnie and Caryn had been bugging him about getting a checkup. They didn't buy into the fact that he knew his body and would know if something was seriously wrong. So each time they tried to coax him into making an appointment, he outright refused. The aches and pains he dealt with had to do with spending a lifetime doing physical labor. His health challenges were normal for anyone his age.

Bonnie had become a nag and his daughter had given him several lectures before she left, but the only thing that could get him in this room was the strange situation between his daughter and this man. "Everybody in my family has been after me to get an exam for years. So here I am."

The explanation sounded weak to Will, and his gut told him that this long-overdue visit to this office had nothing to do with his wife's pleas. It probably had more to do with Caryn, and Will refused to open that can of worms. Instead, the doctor in him kicked in and he began his examination.

Going through the normal routine of asking questions about his family history, Will let all of his nervousness, mixed with aggravation, slip away as the professional in him took over. "Now that we've gotten the talking out of the way, let's check a few things."

Lloyd nodded.

With his stethoscope on his patient's back, he asked him to breathe.

"I've never seen her more happy than when she was with you," Lloyd said, looking for a way to start the conversation. He figured it would garner more information if he started on a positive note.

"I need you to breathe deeply," Will said, refusing to acknowledge the comment. "No talking."

When that part of the exam was done, Will reached for the instrument on the wall to take a look in his ears.

"I think you scared her."

Will continued with his work, as if Lloyd hadn't

said a word. Will couldn't care less what she was—did that give her the right to walk out on him? He'd opened up to her in ways he had never done and this is what she did to him?

"Caryn had never experienced love."

The word froze Will's actions, but he recovered a few seconds later. That word had never been uttered from her lips, yet their last night together demonstrated it. "I need you to lie back."

"She didn't know how to handle it."

"I'm going to press around your abdomen area, let me know if you feel any discomfort or pain."

Lloyd didn't blame him for avoiding this conversation. He'd had his share of bumpy relationships—before Bonnie and with her. He'd had breakups and heartbreaks, so he understood what Will was going through—and why Caryn did what she did. "Running back to what was familiar to her was likely the only way she could deal."

Will motioned for him to sit up.

"I usually don't interfere, but I think if you would just call her, she would…"

The idea of another person requesting that he contact her almost pushed him over the edge, but he managed to maintain control. "Are you still taking pain medication?"

Lloyd's frustration level rose slightly. With one hardheaded daughter who wouldn't listen to reason and a doctor that was more intent on poking and prodding than going after Caryn, Lloyd decided to change tactics. "Yes, I am. Do you love her?"

The only indication that he'd heard the question was

a slight flinch in his jaw. "I'm going to run some blood tests and check all your levels."

Lloyd was determined not to let him off the hook. "Are you going to ignore my question?"

Will finally looked up from his chart and stared at the man who was forcing him to deal. It was the first time he noticed that she had his eyes. "Angela, the nurse, will be in here shortly to make your appointment for your blood work. After which you can get dressed and meet me in my office."

He left the room without another word.

Pacing had never been Will's style. Nervous behavior had only become part of his repertoire since she walked into his life. BC, he had everything completely under control. His career, his personal life, his social life and his future plans. Now all of that was royally screwed up. What he'd come to realize was that it didn't happen because she left; it occurred the moment he laid eyes on her. How could he have known that someone so special, so authentic, so beautiful could come with such power that he would do almost anything to have her in his life? Almost.

Derrick and Lloyd obviously thought that he should be the one to do something about this jacked-up situation. Somehow, people viewed him to be the catalyst for solving this problem. But they didn't understand. Rejection was not a new experience for him. As with anyone, he had had his fair share over his lifetime. But never this hard—and never this deep. Caryn had created a wound that was still too raw and too exposed to begin to think about the possibility of talking with her. He wasn't sure he'd be able to recover if she turned her back on him again.

"Dr. Proctor?"

"Come in."

Lloyd took a seat and Will started with his regular doctor talk.

"I couldn't care less about what's in that chart," Lloyd said, completely shutting him down. "I want to know why you won't go after her. Why you're letting her run away from the best thing that's ever happened to her."

"She made a choice," Will said, finally giving in and having the conversation that he was pushing him to. "She packed her bags. She got on a plane. She hasn't made contact since. Obviously, only one of us is suffering because of it."

"I know her, Will," Lloyd said, recognizing the pain in his eyes. "You messed with her plan. You came into her life and put a monkey wrench in the perfect little world she created for herself. You were supposed to come later. You were supposed to come after the presidency of her division. You were supposed to come after the condo and the beach house. You were supposed to show up when the bank account had more zeros than she could ever spend. But you didn't cooperate. You showed up too soon and swept her off her feet."

The memories of their time together came flooding back to Will. Refusing to let them in after she left, he thought it too painful to remember the view of the White House, the rafting trip, the special dinners, their late-night swim and the amazing sex. Surprisingly, as he allowed just a few flashes of those times to pass through the self-imposed barrier, the pain wasn't as deep as he suspected it would be. In fact, the memories brought a pleasant smile to his face.

"I know that look. It's the same one I had when I realized I didn't want Bonnie out of my life—not even for a day."

"That sounds sweet," Will said, "but obviously she can live plenty of days, weeks and now months without me."

"Trust me," Lloyd said, with the wisdom of a father, "she's not living. She's just surviving."

Chapter 23

Almost nine o'clock at night, Caryn sat alone in the living room of her suite in a pair of cotton underwear sipping tea and staring at the television. The show, in French, barely held her attention. With only a vague idea of what they were saying, she gave up following the storyline.

Jeremy remained eerily silent when she said she was going to stay a few extra days. She had never been the type to take mini vacations and he'd questioned her again about whether everything was all right. Assuring him that she could work just as easily from Paris over the next couple of days with her phone, computer and e-mail, he left her to her own devices.

Once alone, she realized she had no interest in working. She'd been going nonstop for the last month, and now that she'd made the decision to take a break, it was easier than she'd ever imagined. Having been to Paris three times, Caryn had never taken the time to see the city. This trip, she planned to do things differently. She decided to have some fun.

She'd called down the concierge earlier in the day, who'd sent up brochures and information on tours and excursions. The Eiffel Tower, a trip to the Louvre and shopping on the Champs-Élysées had all been placed on her agenda. She also toyed with the idea of a few side trips to other cities, getting the full flavor for this part of Europe.

Clicking off the television, she thought it best to go to bed to get a good night's sleep for her busy day tomorrow. She turned out the light, checked the bolt on the door, walked down the hallway to the bedroom, kicked off her slippers and got under the covers. In the silence of the darkness, thoughts of him crept into her mind.

During the day, she kept busy enough where pushing him out of her mind came somewhat easily. But at times like this, it was impossible. There he was—smiling, laughing, opening doors for her, kissing her, making love to her. With him, everything was brighter and elements of fun followed them. Turning over, she fluffed her pillow and closed her eyes. Would her days in Paris be fun without him?

As the warm water formed in the corner of her eyes, she fought to keep them at bay. Her bouts of crying were rare, but that didn't mean the pain was any less. Some would say that a good hard cry was exactly what she needed—to release her pain. But Caryn wouldn't allow it. Others would say to just call him. But what would she say? It had been weeks without a word from her. Chances were, he didn't want to talk to her.

The ring of her BlackBerry sitting on her nightstand charging pulled her out of her trance, and she debated whether or not to look at it. She didn't bother to look at the number—she knew it wasn't him. In her warped way of thinking, she'd hoped he'd call when she got back to Boston. Not because he should have, but because she wanted confirmation that she'd made the right decision.

If she could talk to him, she would hear him declare that their agreement, and their lifestyles, made what she did the only choice. She waited for him to call and say he understood. He understood that she was scared and confused. He understood that what had happened between them was a whirlwind and she needed time to regroup. She wanted to hear him say that he understood that she needed some time, and while she could have gone about it a little differently, he didn't begrudge her. The call never came.

Going back to work with a vengeance, she focused on her career like never before. Jeremy had commented on the fact that her vacation must have done her a world of good because her commitment level was the highest he'd seen. What he didn't realize was that the majority of her energy came from a need to put Will out of her mind. If she focused completely on her job, there was no time to consider what could have been.

When the days turned into weeks, and the weeks turned into a month and she heard nothing from him, she toyed with the phone more times than she could count. His cell was on speed dial, the line to his office was direct, and she could instant message him anytime. Yet she did none of those things.

When Sherisse found out what happened, she let Caryn have it with both barrels. How could she do this to him? How could she leave in the middle of the night? What was she thinking? Why didn't she say something—anything—to him?

The questions came at her like bullets—one after the other. Caryn held the phone to her ear, saying nothing. What could she say? All of the questions, all of the blame, all of the guilt that Sherisse was putting on her were well deserved.

Confused. That's the word that Sherisse kept using over and over again. She didn't need to explain to Caryn what she meant by that. From the moment Caryn and Will had their first date, Caryn kept Sherisse in the loop, giving her a blow by blow of their blossoming relationship.

Initially, Sherisse remained skeptical that her business partner had turned over a new leaf and could be in a relationship that ran deeper than a few dates. But Caryn made a believer out of her and Sherisse didn't hesitate to offer an apology for all the negative things she said early in the relationship.

The cell phone stopped ringing and her curiosity got the better of her. Reaching over to the table, she looked at the missed call. The number belonged to her parents. After she left D.C., talking to her parents was like talking to Sherisse. They couldn't understand what she was feeling. Couldn't understand how she could treat Will in that manner. Finally, realizing they weren't going to get the answers they sought, they let the subject drop.

Trying to appease them, she'd done a better job of keeping in touch with them. She sent her itineraries through e-mails, and kept them abreast of where she was going and where she was staying. Talking with her mother over her vacation made her realize how much she had unintentionally cut them out of her life. She didn't want her parents to worry or wonder about her.

The next afternoon, Caryn put the last of her items in the carry-on. She'd only done half the things on her agenda before returning to her hotel. Roaming the city had not been as much fun as she'd hoped and it didn't take long for her to figure out why. Everything about Paris screamed romance and as she suffered through her morning of tourist activities alone, she finally decided to stop fighting and admit that the reason it wasn't fun was not just because she was alone—it was because he wasn't here.

Contacting the commercial airline, she had no problem changing her flight to leave today. As the agent confirmed her new itinerary, Caryn realized that she didn't like the idea of going back to Boston any more than she liked the idea of staying in Paris alone. She had the agent make one more change. Her final destination would be Washington, D.C.

Once the decision was made, Caryn had no second guesses. She'd run away because she was afraid of the unknown. But she was more in the dark than she had ever been. Where was the thrill of her work? Where was the drive that would keep her going ten, twelve hours a day? Where was the enthusiasm that came with kudos from her clients and boss?

There was no automatic smile that had become a

staple when she was with Will. There was no laughter
that surrounded her spirit when she was on vacation.
Where was the joy of experiencing life with someone?
Where was the excitement in trying something new?
Where was the fun?

The answer to those questions didn't lie in her work.
They didn't lie in her taking time to see the world.
They didn't lie in the reason she'd left Washington,
D.C. The answers were with Will. Caryn wasn't sure
how Will felt about her now, or what the future held for
them, but she couldn't pretend any longer that she
didn't want to find out. It was time to face the music.

The knock at the door signaled the beginning of the
decision she'd made. The minute her plane landed, she
only had one destination in mind. Her parents would
have to wait. Sherisse would have to wait. The only
person that mattered was him. If she had to, she would
sit outside his house until they spoke.

Checking around the room one last time, she pulled
her largest bag to the door. She opened the door, then
turned to go back to her bedroom and get her smaller
bag. "I've got a smaller bag inside and you—"

"I'm not here for your bag."

Caryn's feet froze in midwalk at that voice. How was
this possible? Was she going crazy? Not wanting to
appear foolish if she was wrong, she turned slowly,
allowing her eyes to confirm what her ears already
knew. "Will?"

He stepped inside and allowed the internal fight
between anger and love to rage inside him. Lloyd had
left a copy of her itinerary in his office just in case he
needed it for any reason. Will had taken the informa-

tion and tossed it in the trash. He refused to be the one to make the first move. But as he sat in his office after everyone had gone home, he thought about what Lloyd said and it touched a nerve. While Will couldn't stand what she'd done to him, he also couldn't deal with the idea that she was suffering because of it. Without thinking too hard about it, he booked a flight and headed to Paris to get the answers to all the questions he'd had since she left.

Now that he stood in front of her, all he could see was her beauty. How could someone look so amazing? Everything seemed different yet the same to him. Still beautiful in a pair of capri pants and a light cardigan sweater, her hair hanging loosely around her face. The curves of her body filled out those clothes perfectly and he recalled how she molded perfectly with him. However, her eyes told a different story.

When he first met her, they were filled with confidence, assurance and sass. Their first date, they were overrun with sadness, questions and curiosity when he questioned her about her career choices. When they made love, they were overflowing with passion, excitement and love. Now they darkened in shock, astonishment and surprise. "Why did you leave me?"

Shock coursed through every cell in her body as the question was spoken with a calmness that contradicted the storm that was raging in his eyes. Opening her mouth to answer, no sounds came out. Closing her mouth, she swallowed deliberately and tried again. Still, nothing.

"Why did you leave me?" This time, the internal battle between anger and love showed signs that anger was the winner. The voice was low but the words were strong.

Caryn took a few steps back as he entered the room. His eyes bore into her, searching for answers. His purposeful stride said he would not be satisfied until he got exactly what he flew all night for. "Will…I… You… We…"

"What, Caryn?" he said, giving no sympathy for her look of surprise mixed with confusion. He ignored those lips that called out for his. He kept his eyes off her chest that rose each time she took a deep breath.

Hearing the door shut behind them, Caryn stopped in the living room of her suite. "Will, what are you doing here?"

There would be plenty of time to talk about all kinds of things—including that. But not before he got what he needed. "Nothing gets discussed until you tell me why you walked out of my life in the middle of the night."

Suddenly, all of the emotions that had swirled about in Caryn since she left came crashing forward. The decision to leave, the feeling of loneliness, the dissatisfaction from work, her broken heart. From the inside out, her body began to cave to all that she'd emotionally been through.

Her heart rate increased, her hands started to shake and her breathing became labored. From the moment she arrived back in Boston, she'd only allowed one or two teardrops to fall. Tough choices had been a part of her life and she'd survived them. In her mind, she would survive this too. But that wasn't the case.

In the past month, her world had slowly begun to

crumble around her, but she'd carried on her day-to-day activities as if it wasn't. With his body less than three feet away and his eyes moving past the outer layer and peering into her soul, there was no more hiding. No more pretending. No more hoping that her inner pain would go away. With a deep heave and a sound that crossed between a scream and a moan, all of the pent-up frustrations came crashing down and the tears flowed freely for the first time.

Will observed her body crumble as she sat in a chair near the desk. Sobbing uncontrollably, she covered her face with her hands and her shoulders shook. Outward expressions of emotion rarely moved Will and he'd borne witness to many women using this very tactic to get their way. But there was nothing in Will's mind that made him think that this was an act.

When he boarded the plane, he made a decision that he wouldn't allow his emotions to get the best of him. He came to Paris to get an explanation for what she had done to him. When he walked into the room, the battle between love and anger was easily won, but now that he was watching her fall apart, he wanted to go to her, hold her and tell her he loved her.

"Damn," he mumbled, moving toward her and kneeling. He wanted to hurt her, wanted to hate, wanted to show her what she'd given up. Instead, he just wanted to show her that everything would be okay.

Caryn had no idea how long he held her, nor did she care. For the past four weeks, she told herself that it was best that she'd left. It was best that she didn't make contact. For four weeks, she'd proclaimed that it was easier this way. Her job, her plans, where she lived and how she lived could not possibly be conducive to having a serious relationship. But on this day, in this suite, in Paris, she finally admitted that she had been fooling herself. The reality was that it was almost impossible to function without him.

Will's arms held her at the waist as her head stayed buried in her chest. Not sure what he expected when he arrived, he let her have her release. The only reason he was here was because of Lloyd. Before he left his office, he'd convinced Will that if he would talk to Caryn, he would open the door for resolution. Will couldn't argue with the fact that he needed that very thing. Whether they ended up together or apart, he needed to be able to close this chapter in his life. A phone call wouldn't do justice to what needed to be done. Whatever she had to say, he wanted her to say it so he could see her eyes.

When her sobs turned to sniffles, she lifted her head and he reached up and wiped her tears away. The gesture was done with such tenderness that he realized that his feelings could get out of control quickly. Standing, he put some distance between them and turned his back. The tension in the room swelled and neither spoke.

Finally, she stood and walked to him, putting her hand on his back. "I'm sorry, Will."

Will closed his eyes at the words he'd waited to hear from her, but that didn't answer his question. "Sorry that you left, or sorry because this isn't going to work?"

Moving around him, she stood in front of him and stared into the eyes that gave her comfort, peace and joy. "I was a fool—a scared fool. You awakened emotions that I'd never had to deal with. You forced me out of my box and I couldn't handle it. I panicked."

The explanation eased a little of Will's pain, but it didn't fix everything. That might explain why she left, but it did nothing to indicate where they would go from here. "What are you now?"

That was the easiest thing Caryn had to answer in the last month. Without hesitation, she said, "I'm miserable."

Neither spoke, each battling their own emotions. Caryn wanted to say so much but didn't know where to start and Will had so many emotions but had no idea how to put them into words. As if they were in complete harmony, they both decided at the same time that no words were necessary and reached for each other simultaneously.

The moment their lips locked, every question Caryn had ever had about her life was answered. She belonged with him. The details didn't matter. They would find a way to work it out.

With his tongue reacquainted with hers, every part of her body came alive. How did she think she could survive without him? His hand caressed her back and she pressed closer, not wanting a beam of light to be able to pass between them. The sweetest thing she'd ever tasted was his lips and she wondered what she was thinking when she'd walked away from this man.

Breaking away, she couldn't go any further without saying what she had been afraid of when she left. "Will, I love you."

Those were the three words that Will had worked to avoid his entire life. It signified something that equaled suffocation, a loss of freedom, demands on his life and time that he couldn't imagine giving in to. Each time a woman said it—or something similar to that—he'd pulled no punches in letting the woman know exactly where he stood. Replying in kind was never an option because he never felt for them what they felt for him.

But when he heard those words come from her lips and saw the emotion reflected in her brown eyes, he realized that he'd been waiting his whole life to hear that, not just from anyone, but from her. "I love you, too, Caryn."

Slowly, Caryn pulled his shirt out of his pants and lifted it over his head. Without losing eye contact, she reached for his belt buckle, unhooking it before opening the button on his pants and pulling down his zipper. "I have missed your smile. Your ability to make me laugh. Your thought-provoking questions and your infusion of fun in my life. But do you have any idea what I've really missed?"

The wicked grin on her face told Will all he needed to know to answer that question, and he didn't want to disappoint. He began to work the buttons on her blouse, ready to reveal those beautiful breasts he'd come to know. "I've missed your smart mouth, your quick wit and your fear of adventure. But I can also think of a few other things I've really missed."

Bending down, he unhooked the clasp in the front of her bra and took one mound in his mouth, licking and sucking on her nipple as it jumped to full attention. Working his way to her pants, he opened the front and slid them down over her hips where she stepped out of them.

"The bedroom is through that door," she said between kisses, feeling as if her body would go up in flames.

"The floor is right here," he countered, kneeling and taking her with him. Removing her bra, he laid her on the floor and rested on his right elbow beside her, staring at her perfect body. With only her lacy panties on, he took the time to take in the full view of what belonged completely to him. With the tip of his finger, he traced the outline of her body, starting with her neck, moving to her shoulders, and then down her arms. Coming across her stomach, he circled her belly button several times, before lowering his hand down the front of her underwear.

When his fingers reached that sensitive spot, her sharp intake of breath and the arch in her back gave every indication of the pleasure she was receiving. Leaning over her, he nipped at her lips before capturing them completely in a full kiss.

"Oh, yes," she whispered, moving her hips as he gently massaged her.

"You like that?"

"Mmm," she said, her eyes closed.

"Then you're gonna love this."

Will pulled away and Caryn immediately felt the loss. "No, come back."

"Don't worry, sweetheart," he said, taking a condom out of his pocket. Once he protected them, he lay on top of her but stopped short of entering her. "I want you so much because I love you so much. I came to Paris because I had to know if there was a chance for us to make this work. You not only broke my heart, you broke my spirit.

I need to know that you won't do that again. Because if you leave me again, I promise, I won't follow you."

"Will, I'm supposed to be on my way to the airport to board a plane to D.C. I was coming back to you. I didn't know if you had moved on or if you would have me back, but I intended to find out. What I did was stupid, but I'm smart enough to learn from my mistakes. I'll never leave you again. I love you."

Will believed every word she spoke and confirmed it by entering her. The moment he made contact with her, all of the hurt, frustrations and confusion of the past month evaporated into thin air. As her hips began to move in harmony with his, the overwhelming sensation of passion and pleasure consumed him from head to toe.

Caryn screamed his name in pleasure as he moved in and out of her. All of the questions that had consumed her over the last several weeks were answered. Her body, her spirit and her soul were in synch with what her heart had just declared. This was where she belonged. This was what her life should be about. What they shared had now become her number-one priority.

"That's it, baby," Will said as she dug her hands deeper into his back. "Let go."

As her hips rose to meet his thrusts, there were no more thoughts of mergers, clients or Jeremy. Her focus completely shifted. Jeremy was right. She did need a doctor. Thank God Will had the cure for everything that ailed her. Giving her hips a final thrust, her body took in all of him and shuddered and trembled at the over-whelming sensation. It wasn't long before Will followed with his own release.

Neither spoke as they both got a handle on all that had transpired in the past hour. Finally, Will moved off her and pulled her into his arms.

"I don't know what your schedule is like, but can you stay a couple of days?" Caryn asked.

"Sure," he said. "What did you have in mind?"

Caryn nuzzled in his chest, content and satisfied. "F-U-N."

Chapter 24

The limo pulled up to Caryn's condo and the driver popped the trunk. Getting out of the car, she pulled her sweater tight as the cool September air indicated the season had begun to change. The driver placed the bags on the curb and Caryn thanked him with a big tip. As he drove off, Caryn saw Will coming out of her building.

Picking up her bags, he gave her a quick peck on the lips. "Welcome back, baby. Glad you're back from L.A., and that your deal came together without a hitch. Have I got a meal for you."

Caryn followed him into her place and the scent of herbs and spices tickled her nose the moment she walked through the door. "Something smells delicious."

"Go take a bath and get comfy. Dinner will be ready by the time you're done."

Caryn headed to her room, stripping off her clothes in the process. By the time she got to her bathroom, all she had on was her bra and panties. She didn't bother to turn on the lights because the soft glow from burning candles illuminated the space. Her house still didn't have much furniture or decor, but it was filled with something better. Love.

This had been her amazing routine since they got back from Paris. Just the thought of Paris caused her body to tingle with delight. They'd stayed an additional three days and did all the things she had on her list. This time, sharing them with Will made all the difference in the world. They'd stared out over the city on top of the Eiffel Tower. Waited in line to see the *Mona Lisa* through the protective glass and toured the castle at Versailles. Each moment—each memory—was colored with kisses, laughter and love.

The flight back was when they got down to business. Surprisingly, it wasn't as hard as she thought it would be. Will easily shifted seeing patients Tuesday to Thursday and flew to Boston on the weekends to be with her. They agreed that with her travel schedule already hectic, he would come to her. So far, it was working like a charm.

Easing into the water, she thought how Will had spared no expense in spoiling her. He'd been doing all the flying, the cooking and he hadn't slacked off one bit in the bedroom. Nothing about her working lifestyle had changed. After dinner, she'd have to handle some calls or do work. Her travel schedule hadn't changed much and Jeremy was just as demanding as ever, but Will didn't complain. As a matter of fact, he hadn't asked her to change one thing.

He promised her that they could make it work without her compromising her career goals and he'd made good on that. Not once did he make her feel guilty about a business trip or complain about nighttime conference calls she had to take because of time zones. And she wasn't the only one who was benefiting from this arrangement.

Bonnie and Lloyd were ecstatic that Caryn and Will were able to work things out. Lloyd finally believed his little girl had found her Prince Charming, and Bonnie couldn't help but say, "I told you so." Bonnie had always believed that Caryn could make room in her life for both her career and a man, and couldn't contain her joy at seeing it play out. But Caryn had her own "I told you so." Bonnie had to finally admit that a woman could snag a man without having any clue to using the many utensils she had in her kitchen.

"You look too sexy."

Caryn opened her eyes and stared at the man that had changed her life. Holding a bottle of wine and two glasses, he had nothing else, including clothes. She still had not gotten used to such a perfect physique. Looking at his broad chest, toned abs and muscular legs made her wet and ready for him. "Don't just stand there, join me."

Will slid in behind her and wrapped his legs around her. "Wait until you taste what I've prepared for you."

"One day, I'm going to learn how to cook something other than popcorn," she said, wrapping his arms around hers so they could cup her breasts. When he tweaked each one, she couldn't help but reach her hand back to stroke his manhood. It didn't take long for it to grow hard.

Will inhaled deeply at the impromptu massage. "The last room I'm concerned about you spending time in is the kitchen."

"Oh, yeah," she said, maneuvering herself to face him.

"That's right," he said, helping her straddle him in the confined space. "I think your skills are much better used in other rooms."

Easing down on him, Caryn's response was swallowed by her moans of ecstasy. After a day of meetings, hours on a plane and reviewing reports, this was exactly what she needed to unwind. "You like this?"

Will couldn't think straight every time he slid into her. The amazing connection was new each time. He never tired of being with her, talking with her, making love to her. Caressing her breasts, he leaned up to meet her descending lips. The power of the kiss, the feel of her body and the motion of her hips sent him into overdrive. As he prepared to explode, he felt her body shiver and she screamed out in pleasure. Seconds later, their labored breathing settled and they kissed, declaring their undying love.

Two weeks later, Will sat around his dining table staring down at his plate. Caryn had finally had business in Washington and had been staying with him all week. To thank him for all that he'd done for her, she'd decided that she would do the cooking tonight.

Since it was Friday and the start of a weekend, she'd made it a dinner party, inviting her parents, Sherisse, Jeff, Natalie and Derrick. But judging by the expression on the face of her guests, something didn't taste quite right.

Bonnie was the first brave soul to speak up. "You said this is chicken?"

"No," Caryn said, not sure if her mom was being facetious. "It's duck."

"Duck?" Derrick said, turning to his wife. "I thought it tasted like chicken."

"Very funny," Caryn said, watching the others stare curiously at the meat on their plate. "You guys can at least try the mashed sweet potatoes."

"Is that what this is?" Lloyd said, pushing the food around with his fork. "I thought you had chopped up carrots and then mashed them with water."

"I'm almost afraid to ask what this is," Sherisse said, picking up a long green stalk. "Is it broccoli, asparagus or green beans?"

"That's it," Caryn said, standing and starting to clear the dishes. "I slaved all day—well, half a day."

At the skeptical look on Will's face, she relented. "Okay, I spent at least two hours cooking and this is the appreciation I get?"

"We'll give you all the appreciation you want if you don't make us eat this stuff," Natalie said, looking her up and down. "Plus, it looks like you're wearing more food than what made it to the table."

Normally dressed to the nines, there was nothing sophisticated about her Ann Taylor slacks and blouse with a few grease stains and other unidentifiable spots.

"I actually had a late lunch, so I'm going to pass," Derrick said, passing his plate to Caryn.

Caryn narrowed her eyes and started to give him a piece of her mind, until she broke into laughter. "Is it really that bad?"

"I've been trying to give food to Apollo for the last ten minutes and even he won't eat it," Will said.

"Fine," Caryn said, continuing to clear the dishes. "You figure out what we're going to eat."

Without a second thought, Will pulled out his cell phone and dialed 411, requesting the information for the local pizza place. After ordering two pepperonis, one vegetable and a cheese pizza, all the guests around the table broke out in applause.

When the food arrived, they all sat around the living room listening to Bonnie and Lloyd share tales of their courtship. The idea that they were in the presence of a couple that had been married for over thirty years became surreal to each of them.

"We're definitely taking notes," Natalie said, looking at her husband lovingly. "It hasn't been a year, but it's been the happiest time of my life."

"Mine, too, sweetie," Derrick said, kissing his wife on the cheek.

"Oh, brother," Sherisse said. "I think I'm going to throw up."

"Don't be so hard on them," Will said. "Obviously, marriage isn't all that bad."

"Now I know it's time to go," Jeff said, standing and fishing in his pockets for his keys. "The day Dr. William Proctor starts singing the praises of marriage is the day the world just might come to an end. No offense, Caryn."

"None taken," Caryn said. "You're looking at a changed man."

"And a changed woman," Will said.

For several seconds they stared openly at each other, sharing their love for each other by silent communication.

Noticing the dreamy look in their eyes, Derrick stood. "I guess we better get going."

All agreed and started gathering their belongings. In the midst of their goodbyes, Caryn's cell phone rang. Because it was on the table in front of her, she glanced at the number. Jeremy.

Will saw the name pop up. "Take it. I'll say goodbye to the guests."

With a quick wave to everyone, she answered the call and headed upstairs to talk.

Twenty minutes later, Will sat in the living room reading the paper when she came back down the stairs, Apollo hot on her trail. Every time she stayed with him, it was obvious with whom the dog's loyalty now lay. But Will didn't mind. He understood anything male would want to be around her. "So where are you off to now?"

"This call wasn't about an upcoming client merger."

Her slow walk and talk told him that something out of the ordinary was going on. "What did he say?"

She took a seat beside him, Apollo lying down at her feet. "We're merging."

"Really—with whom?"

"Another financial institution."

"And?"

Caryn finally looked at him as if she was digesting

the words at the same time as she was speaking. "Jeremy wants me to head up the merger and…"

"What?"

"After which the company will have two major offices—he told me he wanted me to run the entire organization, that it was time for him to ease his way out and enjoy some of the money he's made."

In terms of her career, it didn't get any better than this. "That's incredible news, babe. Aren't you excited?"

Caryn decided to give out the rest of the information. "He wants me to work out of the new office."

"Sounds reasonable."

"In San Francisco."

"Are you sure you're okay with this?"

Will sat at the bar drinking a beer. It had been a month since Caryn's job offer and two weeks since she'd left for the West Coast. She'd been working nonstop and the only contact they'd had were brief conversations. Between the time zone and the work hours, finding any time to talk was becoming challenging by the day. "I don't have a choice."

"You always have a choice," Derrick said.

"I can't ask her to give up her career for me. It's what she's been working for her entire life."

"But you want to?" Derrick said, reading his mind.

"What I want is not important."

"Because?"

Will had this conversation with himself almost daily and the answer was always the same. "I can't ask her to choose."

"Move to California."

The simplicity made in his request was almost comical. Derrick spoke as if Will hadn't thought about that very thing on a daily basis. "My practice is here. My professional ties are here. My life is here."

"No," Derrick corrected. "Your life is working her tail off on the other side of the country."

Will thought about his words but realized it wasn't that black and white. "Moving to San Francisco wouldn't solve anything."

"How can you say that?" Derrick said, signaling the bartender for another round. "The two of you would be together and you wouldn't walk around looking like a lost puppy."

"That's just it," Will said, explaining to him what he'd already figured out. Caryn was in the process of merging staff, reorganizing her senior team and still working to close deals. "It's not the miles that keep us from being together. It's her job. I could pack my bags today and get on the next plane out of here, but when I got there…? I'd be sitting around her leased corporate apartment staring at the door waiting for her to come home."

"But when she did, you'd be there," he reminded Will. "That's more than you're getting now."

Will eyed him suspiciously before playfully asking, "Are you trying to get rid of me?"

"We could only be so lucky," he joked.

After their laughter died down, Will thought about his options. None of them were appealing. He couldn't ask her to give up her dream. She wouldn't have time for him if he went to California.

"How long do you think a relationship structured like this can last?"

That was the one question Will had been trying to avoid from the moment she got the call. Things moved so fast once she accepted that they barely had time to talk about it. The few times when the door opened to have the conversation about their future, they both avoided it. The reality was, this was going to be their life for the foreseeable future. His practice was here and her job was there. It would be years—maybe decades—before either of those situations would change. "Don't worry, man. It'll work out."

Derrick thought his words were spoken with more hope than confidence.

Things were not working out. Will hung up the phone and leaned back in his chair. Almost five o'clock, he tried to catch Caryn before heading out for a fund-raiser for Children's Hospital, but she was headed into a meeting before flying to Dallas for three days. It had been almost two months since she left and they barely had time to say hello and goodbye. He'd been out there once and might as well have stayed in D.C.

He wanted to talk to her today because their conversation last night didn't go so well. They spent the majority of their time talking—no, arguing—about how little time they had for each other. She claimed it couldn't be helped and that things would settle down in the next several months and he said that he didn't see anything changing anytime soon. The conversation ended in a standoff.

"You okay?"

"Huh?" Will said, looking up at the door.

"I've been calling your name for almost five minutes."

"Sorry, Sherisse. I guess my mind is elsewhere."

"California?"

The last conversation Will wanted to have was about California. He'd had it with Derrick, Jeff and even Lloyd. The subject was getting tired and he didn't have the energy for it. Reaching into his desk drawer, he pulled out two tickets for tonight's event. "Here you go. I won't be using these."

Sherisse picked up the tickets and stared at them. "This is your favorite charity. You go every year."

Standing, Will put on his jacket and grabbed his keys. "Not this year. I'm going home."

"She loves you, Will," Sherisse said, feeling as if she needed to justify the actions of her friend. "I know it's been tough on you, because it's been hell for her. She's just trying to figure out how to make it all work."

"Good night, Sherisse."

"You think this is easy for her?"

"I think this is not a discussion for you and me to have."

"Then I'll just say this," she said, thinking of the brief conversations she's had with Caryn over the past month. "She's taking on the world out there. People are rooting for her to succeed and some are waiting for her to fail. The only thing that keeps her balanced is you."

"I know what she's going through and I want to be there for her, Sherisse, I really do," he said. "But this can't be a one-way thing."

"She's giving all she can."

Will knew that statement was true. Caryn was giving him all she was capable of. What Will didn't know was whether that was enough. And if it wasn't, what was he going to do?

Chapter 25

Wintertime was in full swing and Thanksgiving was just a few short weeks away. Caryn sat in her office with her head in her hands. It had been a stressful week and things were only going to get worse. The merger was complete on paper, but the implementation was the biggest challenge of all. Combining staff, corporate cultures and leadership had been her challenge and she was performing to the task, yet she couldn't shake the feeling that it was in vain.

She didn't know a soul in San Francisco. She was working round the clock, and she came home to no one. The calls to her friends and family had dwindled and her times with Will were almost nonexistent. People would kill to be in her position, to make her money, to have her status. But the joy that she thought she would get from moving up had been eluding her. Not sure what to do about it, she just kept plugging away.

Unfortunately, she would have to change her plans for this weekend because of a report that was due to the board on Monday. She picked up the phone and started to dial but suddenly changed her mind. Until she had time to talk, she wouldn't call. She was due in a meeting in five minutes. Opening her e-mail, she pulled up his address and typed her message before pushing send.

Will sat in his office going through e-mails when one popped up from her. Things had been going from bad to worse and neither of them knew how to stop it. The visits were few and far between, the calls were diminishing and the e-mail that stared him in the face was the first one he'd gotten from her all week.

Friday, she planned to fly to D.C. for the weekend, the first time since she'd left. Looking forward to seeing and being with her, a sudden wave of dread encompassed him as he stared at the unopened e-mail. Pushing his silly fears aside, he opened it and read the contents in less than five seconds. Deleting the message, he moved on to the next one.

An hour later, he shut down his laptop.

"Heading for the airport?" Derrick said.

"Home."

"I thought…"

"Her plans changed." Will didn't want to talk about or explain it. Besides, it was the same old story. She had to work over the weekend and Thanksgiving was around the corner and she would come home at that time, when she would have more than the weekend.

The sentence was said so nonchalantly, but Derrick knew it was anything but. Will typically managed his emotions well, but everyone in the office could tell that he was looking forward to this weekend. Caryn was coming home for the first time in months and he'd planned a few special surprises for her. Now it appeared that all the work he'd done was in vain. She wasn't coming. "Will…"

"Listen, Derrick, I'm really not in the mood for a lecture on how she's in a new and demanding job," he said, his anger growing by the second. He'd been put off by her for months. No time to visit. Barely time for phone calls. And now she was canceling their plans altogether.

"No lectures, just wanted to know if you wanted to grab some dinner."

"No, thanks."

"What are you going to do?"

That was the million-dollar question that Will had no answer for. Could he demand that she give up her job? Could he give up his practice? Should he move to San Francsico? "I'm going home."

Will's routine had pretty much been the same since she left. Go home. Walk the dog. Eat dinner. Watch a game. Go to bed. This was nothing like his life before she entered it. He enjoyed going out. Attending parties, dinners and events. His friends and colleagues could count on him to make an appearance. But those days were long gone.

He'd gone to several events without her and it wasn't the same. She wasn't with him and he wasn't interested in meeting anyone. Staying for a short period of time, he was usually one of the first to leave. Was this going to be his life from now on? Making a quick decision, he ran upstairs to get dressed. The invitation to a birthday party sat on his dresser, from a woman he used to date. He'd immediately discounted going when he opened it, but he still had it. He could dress and be out the door in less than a half hour.

Standing near the bar at the country club, Will bided his time until he could leave. He'd arrived only twenty minutes ago, and had already concluded that he was ready to go. The birthday girl had introduced him to one of her friends, who was more than willing to deal with his rules of dating. It had been so long since he'd thought about them—or used them, it was hard to remember what they all were.

At five foot eleven, short, curly hair, green eyes, skin the color of honey and a body that would make a supermodel jealous, she made her intentions clear to Will with her flirty nature and roaming hands. First, they touched his arm, and then she playfully moved them across his chest before giving him a quick pat on the butt.

Caryn flashed in his mind and he quickly extracted himself from the situation. His status with Caryn was shaky, but he wasn't interested in someone else. Giving her a polite smile, he removed himself from her touch, before making his exit from the party, not stopping to say goodbye to the host.

Sitting in his car, he leaned his head against the steering wheel trying to figure out how this relationship was going to work, when the vibration of his phone went off. Pulling it off his hip, he saw it was his answering service. Within a minute, he was on the road heading for the hospital.

"Thank God, you're here."

Will gave Bonnie a big hug and told her to calm down.

"He was fine one minute, and the next he's doubled over in pain. I drove a hundred miles an hour to get him here. They took him in the back, but they won't tell me anything."

"You sit tight. I'll see what I can find out."

"Thanks, Will. I called Caryn. She said she was going to be on the red-eye. She should be here by morning."

The mention of her name used to bring automatic joy. Now it signaled stress and anxiety. Of all the circumstances to bring her home, this was the worst. "I'll check on Lloyd."

Bonnie reached out for his arm. "She loves you."

Will nodded but didn't say a word as he flashed his ID card and walked through the automatic doors. Everyone insisted on telling him how much Caryn loved him, but what no one could tell them was how she was going to show it.

Stopping at the nurses' station, he found out the name of the attending doctor and went in search of him. His first priority was Lloyd. He'd worry about the rest later.

* * *

Almost 7:00 a.m., Bonnie sat in the waiting room. Lloyd had been checked into a room a couple of hours ago and had been sleeping off and on. They were running a battery of tests and were awaiting results but had given him something for the pain. "Thank you for staying, Will."

"Don't thank me," he said, giving her a reassuring squeeze on the hand. "I'll leave when we find out what's going on."

"Mom?"

He heard her voice and stood along with Bonnie. He hadn't seen her in months and this is not what he'd had in mind when he did see her.

"I got here as fast as I could. How is he? Can I see him?" She came in like a whirlwind dressed in a pair of sweatpants, a T-shirt and tennis shoes. Her hair was in a messy, loose ponytail.

"He's resting. We're hoping to have some test results soon," Bonnie said. "Will has been keeping the doctors on their toes. I couldn't have made it through the night without him."

Caryn turned from her mother and saw Will. Her entire face lit up with relief and love. "Oh my God, Will. I've missed you so much."

She flew into his arms and held him tight. Raising her head, she reached up to kiss him. Just as her lips were about to touch his, she froze. Something was wrong. His arms were still at his sides and his head hadn't moved toward hers.

Bonnie noticed the exchange and excused herself. "I'm going to check on Lloyd."

Alone in the room, Caryn continued with her kiss, only to have her assumptions confirmed. His lack of response gave a strong indication that things were not well between them.

Deciding this wasn't the time or place, she asked about her father.

"He complained of abdominal pain and severe pain in some of his joints. They've given him something for the pain." He spoke professionally and anyone who overheard would never know that they shared an intimate relationship.

"Can I see him?" she said,

"Sure," he said, stepping aside. "Room 793."

Caryn hesitated before leaving. "Are you going to be here when I get back?"

The question was loaded with double meanings, and he knew what she was asking. The distance had put a strain between them and neither knew how to fix it—or if it could be fixed if nothing about their situation changed.

Will didn't answer right away because he honestly didn't know. Instead, he looked into her eyes. They were red and puffy; she'd obviously had a rough time sleeping on the plane. Then he saw tiredness. Not for lack of sleep, but from sheer weariness. "I have patients."

"Can't Derrick cover?" The question was more of a plea, and desperation could be heard in her voice. "We—I—need you."

"Do you?" He didn't mean to start the conversation, but the words just came out.

"Of course I do," she said, walking to him and reaching for his hand.

Will stared at their intertwined fingers. "This isn't the time or the place."

"For?"

"Discussing us."

"I know things are crazy right now, but—"

"But what, Caryn?" he said, frustration rising in him. "They'll get better? We'll talk more? We'll spend more time together? We'll find a way to make this work?"

Harsher than he'd intended, he took a deep breath to control his emotions. The idea of loving someone and not being with that person was tearing him apart. She'd asked if she should take the job and he'd said yes. Did he really have the right to complain about it?

"You're not being fair, Will," she said softly.

"I'm not the one taking the easy way out and sending e-mails to cancel plans that have been in the works for weeks," he said, keeping his voice even. He promised himself this would never be a fight.

"I have a board meeting on Monday" she said, trying to explain her position.

"Dr. Proctor?"

"Yes," he said, grateful for the interruption from the nurse.

"Dr. Goodwin is looking for you."

Turning back to Caryn, he said, "I'll see what the news is. You go see your father."

Before she could answer, he was gone.

* * *

Sunday evening Will sat in his living room flipping channels. The good news was that Lloyd had been diagnosed with hemochromatosis, a disorder that increases the level of iron to such an extent that it affects joints and organs, which explained his pain pill routine. With several treatments over the next couple of months, drawing the iron out of his blood, he should be as good as new. The bad news was that he hadn't spoken to Caryn since he'd left the hospital.

She mentioned taking a flight back sometime this afternoon for her meeting tomorrow, but he didn't want to deal with it. It would be too painful to watch her leave again.

The front door opened and Apollo started barking. Will jumped up and followed the dog. Who would be coming in his house this time of night?

"Caryn?"

She stood in the entryway, still dressed in the same sweats and still sporting the messy hair.

"What are you doing here?" he said, looking at his watch. She wasn't going to have any flight options if she didn't get to the airport.

"Is that all you have to say?" she said, not sure what she wanted but hoping for so much more.

The trembling in her voice didn't match up to the tough girl he met and fell in love with. This relationship was turning both of them into people they didn't recognize. Arguing wouldn't solve anything, so he didn't want to start one. "Do you need a ride to the airport?"

Caryn walked past him and patted Apollo on the head. Without stopping, she headed to the living room and took a seat on the couch. For several seconds she sat there, until finally the tears came. "I sat in the gate area as they started boarding. They called first-class and I didn't move. When they gave the final boarding call, I stood up and headed out the terminal. I couldn't get on that plane with things so strained between us."

"What about your meeting?" Will said in a panic. Missing a board meeting was a definite no-no. "Let me call the airline. Better yet, we'll charter a jet. You can still get there in time."

Caryn was disappointed that all he could think about was her job. She had herself to blame for that.

As she sat at the airport, all she could think about was his reaction to her at the hospital. This was the most important person in her life and he didn't want to be around her. Was a board meeting more important than that. "What about us?"

He appreciated her effort to talk things out, but there wasn't any time. "'Us' can't be fixed before your next flight."

"When did we get broken?" she said, realizing their troubles went much deeper than short phone calls and scattered visits. They were losing their connection.

Moving to sit beside her, he raised her head with his right hand and wiped her tears away. His heart ached when she cried and his frustration grew that there were no easy answers. "It would be easy to blame this on your job, but that wouldn't be fair. Neither one of us is in a position to compromise right now."

"That's where you're wrong," Caryn said. "On the cab ride over here, all I could think about were the compromises you've made. You came to Paris. You changed your work schedule. You flew to Boston. You said nothing when I took this job. All you've done is compromise."

"This isn't a contest, Caryn," he said, not wanting her to feel guilty. "All of those things I did willingly. I have no regrets and I wouldn't change a thing."

"So what do we do?"

"We don't want the same things right now," he said honestly. "We'll have to find a way to work around that."

"What do you want?" she said.

"I want us—together."

"That's what I want, too."

Will thought about his life and what he had in D.C. That's when Derrick's words rang in his ears. *Your life is in California.* He made a decision and immediately found peace. "I'll move."

Tears welled up in the corners of her eyes as she realized how much she loved him—and how much he loved her. Standing, she walked away from him to look out the window onto the quiet streets of D.C. "When I got the call that my father had taken ill, my heart stopped. I hated being three thousand miles away. I hated that they could need me and I wouldn't be there. But more than anything, I hated that I had to worry about my father alone. I should have been able to lean on you, and I couldn't."

"Caryn, your dad's going to be fine," he reassured her. "The illness, while rare, is treatable. He's getting the best care."

"He is…but I'm not."

"I don't understand."

Caryn turned to face him and her confidence was suddenly restored. She'd been torn between two worlds ever since she met him and it was time to make a choice. "I don't want you to move to California."

Will walked to her and held her hand. "Caryn, it's okay. I'll sell my part of the practice and I'll be able to set up in San Francisco fairly quickly."

Caryn raised his hands to her mouth and kissed them gently. "You once asked my why I do what I do. I couldn't answer it then and I can't answer it now. My job has given me money and status, but it's taken away the one thing that means the most to me—you."

"I'm right here, Caryn," he said, reassuring her that he would support her. "I'm not going anywhere."

"You're right. You're not going anywhere," she said, taking a deep breath. "I'm moving here."

The thought of her giving up her dream didn't sit well with him. "Caryn, I'd never make you choose between your job and me."

"You don't have to, because it's suddenly become an easy choice." And it was. Quitting her job had never been an option for her, but now that she'd made the decision to do it, years of stress seemed to evaporate from her shoulders. "That is, if you don't mind having an unemployed girlfriend who doesn't know what she wants to do with the rest of her life."

"Uh-uh," Will said. "That's not good enough."

"I promise, I'll get a job," she said. "I have more than enough money to tide me over until I find something."

"I'm not talking about the unemployed part," he said. "I'm talking about the girlfriend part."

"You don't want me to be your girlfriend anymore," she said slowly.

"No," he said, reaching for her hand and getting down on one knee. "I want you to be my wife."

Caryn covered her mouth in shock and nodded in the affirmative.

"Yes?"

"Yes!"

Dear Readers,

I love bringing stories of love and romance to life. I hope you enjoyed reading the story of Will and Caryn. Please feel free to drop me a note at doreen@doreenraineybooks.com or visit me online at www.doreenraineybooks.com

Until next time...

Doreen

To realize true love, sometimes you have to
weather the storm.

Bestselling author

Melanie
Schuster

Before the Storm

When Maya Simpson married Julian Deveraux,
the eldest son of the powerful Deveraux clan,
she thought they would be together forever.
But when overwhelming social pressures convinced
her of her husband's infidelity, she filed for divorce
and left—unaware that she was pregnant.

Now, four years later, they meet once again. Will their
reunion bring the family together or tear them apart?

"Schuster's superb storytelling ability is
exhibited in fine fashion."
—*Romantic Times BOOKreviews* on
UNTIL THE END OF TIME

BEFORE THE STORM will be available the first week
of January wherever books are sold.

KIMANI PRESS™
www.kimanipress.com

An emotional story about experiencing love
the second time around…

Sweet Memphis Crush

BRIDGET ANDERSON

Desperate to save her fourteen-year-old brother
from addiction, Jodie Dickerson moves back to
Memphis, Tennessee—just a stone's throw from her
dysfunctional family. She soon runs into sports-show
host William Duncan—the same gorgeous guy she
fell for years ago, right before he crashed a car that
killed Jodie's older brother. Can Jodie ever find
forgiveness so she and Will can realize their love?

"Anderson's wonderfully written romance is one
that readers are certain to appreciate and enjoy."
—*Booklist*

**Available the first week of January
wherever books are sold.**

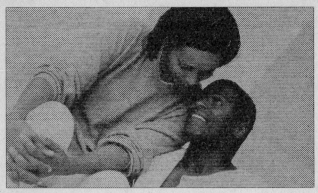

Essence **bestselling author**

DONNA HILL

If I Were Your *Woman*

The second story in the Pause for Men *miniseries*.

A messy affair left Stephanie Moore determined
to never again mix business with pleasure. But her
powerful attraction to Tony Washington has her
reconsidering—even though she suspects Tony may be
married. She'll need the advice of her Pause for Men
partners to help her sort out her dilemma.

**Pause for Men—four fabulously fortysomething divas
rewrite the book on romance.**

*Available the first week of February,
wherever books are sold.*

**KIMANI™
ROMANCE**